Corrupted Heir

Enemies to Lovers Arranged Marriage Mafia Romance

Kiana Hettinger

This book is an original production of Hardmoon Press.

This is a work of fiction. Names, characters, places, and incidents either are the product of the author's imagination or are used fictitiously. Any resemblance to actual persons, living or dead, is strictly coincidental. The publisher does not assume responsibility for third-party websites or their content.

Copyright © 2022 Hardmoon Press

All rights reserved.

No part of this novel may be reproduced, scanned, or distributed in any format without express written permission from Hardmoon Press.

BY KIANA HETTINGER

Corrupted Heir is the first book in the Mafia Kings: Corrupted Series.

Mafia Kings: Corrupted Series
#0 Cruel Inception
#1 Corrupted Heir
#2 Corrupted Temptation
#3 Corrupted Protector

Your Exclusive Access

Thanks a million for being here. Your support means so much to me.

The best way to keep in touch with me is by signing up for my newsletter - sendfox.com/authorkianah (I promise I won't spam you!) and by joining my readers' group on Facebook, Kiana's Kittens.

You'll receive bonus chapters, inside scoop, discounts, first access to cover reveals and rough drafts, exclusive material, and so much more!

See you on the inside,
Kiana Hettinger

Author's Note

I started writing Dominic and Fallon's story in a fit of inspiration, and it took me on this one hell of a ride. Of all the books I've written, this is probably the most memorable journey I've been on. I hope you enjoy this little world I've created.

I hope you find your limone

K

Table of Contents

Chapter One 8
Chapter Two 19
Chapter Three 31
Chapter Four 45
Chapter Five 50
Chapter Six 60
Chapter Seven 75
Chapter Eight 90
Chapter Nine 101
Chapter Ten 110
Chapter Eleven 116
Chapter Twelve 126
Chapter Thirteen 135
Chapter Fourteen 144
Chapter Fifteen 155
Chapter Sixteen 161
Chapter Seventeen 169
Chapter Eighteen 179
Chapter Nineteen 188
Chapter Twenty 199
Chapter Twenty-One 206
Chapter Twenty-Two 214

Chapter Twenty-Three 224
Chapter Twenty-Four 232
Chapter Twenty-Five 244
Chapter Twenty-Six 253
Chapter Twenty-Seven 256
Chapter Twenty-Eight 263
Chapter Twenty-Nine 269
Chapter Thirty 278
Chapter Thirty-One 282
Chapter Thirty-Two 290
Chapter Thirty-Three 295
Chapter Thirty-Four 300
Chapter Thirty-Five 304
Chapter Thirty-Six 308
Chapter Thirty-Seven 310
Chapter Thirty-Eight 313
Chapter Thirty-Nine 315
Chapter Forty 318
Epilogue 322
What's Next? 332

Chapter One

Dominic

Two trucks pulled into the lot and disappeared inside the last old rickety warehouse behind me. Our trucks, of course—though you wouldn't know it by the ridiculous cartoon fish scrawled across the sides. A smile on its face while it dangled on a hook. Grotesque, really, but why not? It was as good a logo as any, and it looked right at home here on the docks. No one would ever guess there wasn't an ounce of seafood in the back of those big white trucks.

Not that there was anyone around to notice. All the dock workers were long gone for the day. It was just me and Leo, waiting for a bunch of lawless, savage brutes. An ordinary Thursday evening in my world—the underworld of vipers and wolves. But Leo and I were Lucas, the top of the underground food chain.

Bullet whimpered behind me. Fucking mutt—my father's fucking mutt, to be precise. "You want to do something about that?" I barked at Leo.

"What the hell do you want me to do?" he barked back—one of the few men in the world who could do that and not lose his tongue for it.

"Pet it or muzzle it. I don't give a fuck which, just shut it up."

What the hell my father saw in the pint-sized ball of fur, I had no idea, but when Vincent Luca told you to watch the dog, you watched the dog.

Leo leaned over and grabbed the Chihuahua from the back seat, plopping it down unceremoniously onto his lap. The mutt panted happily and licked Leo's hand while Leo smiled down at the thing.

"You two need a room?"

"No, but you'll be needing a hospital room if you don't take better care of Bullet."

He was probably right. Dad loved that thing, maybe more than he loved the rest of us. Pretty soon, he was going to start parading the mutt around as the Luca family mascot. Wouldn't that be a sight to see?

"When you two are finished, you want to get to some business?" I asked, nodding toward the three vehicles that had just turned into the lot.

Big, black Cadillacs, of course. Was there a bigger sign to say "cartel approaching" than that? The Free Bird Cartel, stupid-ass name, if you asked me. Those motherfuckers were anything but free. They were forced into working for the "big boss" to pay off debts. A backstabbing recipe for disaster. No respect. No loyalty. Not like the Lucas, who would fight for every one of our brothers and sisters—even if it meant dying in the process.

I patted my slate gray jacket as the cars crawled forward, feeling for the familiar outline of the Sig Sauer P226 that waited in its holster beneath. The gun had gotten me out of countless bad situations in the past ten years and killed more men than I could count with all my fingers and toes. The Free Bird Cartel might be backstabbing motherfuckers, but they'd never get the chance to stab me in the back.

I swung open the door of my McLaren 570S—no black Cadillac for me, thank you very much. Their pathetic engines didn't have anything on my baby.

The moment I stepped out of the car, Bullet lunged across the driver's seat and out of the car onto the cracked pavement. Fucking wonderful.

"What the hell, Leo?"

Leo flashed a glance toward the oncoming cars then back down at the stupid mutt running laps around my legs. He shrugged his shoulders and laughed.

"Just get out here and try to look like you're not the proud owner of a pathetic fur ball."

"Gotcha." Leo nodded a little too happily then opened his door and got out. "Don't worry, big brother. No one's going to fuck with the almighty Dominic Luca no matter what mutt he's got trailing along behind him."

"I'm not worried, I'm pissed. Next time, you can stay home and babysit the damn dog."

"And miss listening to you bitch about it? I wouldn't miss this for the world." Leo smiled a goofy grin, checked his reflection in the blacked-out passenger window, then turned, straight-faced, toward the first of the three cars that had pulled to a stop twenty yards in front of us. They'd fanned out in a V formation, and while the front-runner had shut off his engine, I could hear the quiet purr coming from the other two cars. They were ready to move, but to flee or to attack? With the Free Bird Cartel, you never could tell.

"Game time," I muttered under my breath.

Ignoring the dog who had yet to sit still for a split second since loping out of the front seat, I walked toward the lead car. Leo fell into stride beside me, his shoulders back and chin high; all remnants of my goofy younger brother gone for the time being. It was difficult to tell he hadn't been making trades like this all his life. Difficult, but not impossible. I could see it there in the way his teeth dug into his lower lip and the way he clenched and unclenched his fists like he wasn't quite sure what to do with his hands. It wasn't his first time out by any means, but he was still wet behind the ears. Make no mistake though; Leo was just as lethal as the rest of us Lucas.

Three doors swung open on the lead Cadillac, and three men stepped out. Three men I'd never seen before. The tallest of them—younger than the other two by far—took the lead with a briefcase in hand, walking toward us in a navy blue suit that was stretched across his unnaturally large shoulders. Steroids, for sure. He would have been better off putting his money toward a better suit. Even from this distance, it was clear the thing was a department store find that had seen better days. If he was self-conscious about his cheap façade, he tried not to show it. He walked with his nose a little too high in the air, his wide shoulders pushed back a bit too far.

The lackeys that flanked him were dressed no better and equally as broad-shouldered. Maybe there'd been a three-for-one sale on steroids.

The three men moved closer. The back of my neck prickled. A sixth sense borne from years of experience, it had never steered me wrong.

"Keep your guard up, Leo," I said under my breath.

"No shit, Sherlock," he grunted, but he stiffened his spine and looked poised to reach for the gun concealed beneath his jacket.

"Easy, *fratellino*. Keep your head clear." It sounded like a simple enough instruction, but keeping one's mind sharp under pressure was no easy task.

Leo breathed out in one slow huff, but his eyes widened just a little as they settled on the lead guy.

"An old friend of yours?" I asked quietly enough to keep the conversation between the two of us.

"Yeah, a real piece of work. Don't trust him, Dom." Leo clenched his jaw.

"No shit, Sherlock." I scoffed. "Just stay focused."

Leo nodded just as the trio came to a stop two yards away.

The prickle at the back of my neck felt like needles poking into my skin. Something definitely wasn't right. It was all I could do to keep from shooting all three of the motherfuckers and calling it a day.

The lead guy nodded to me then turned to Leo.

"Cute mutt, Leo," he joked with an ugly, toothy grin. His teeth were yellowed, and it looked like his incisors had been filed down into wicked points. "Got yourself a new girlfriend?"

My hands clenched tight, and I could feel blood throbbing in my temples. Nobody spoke to a Luca that way. Ever.

Don't kill him. Don't kill him. I repeated the silent mantra over and over again, resisting the urge to put a bullet right between the fucker's eyes. No goddamned respect—that was the problem with this cartel. Someone needed to teach them some fucking manners.

But since Vincent's orders had been to make the trade, no mention of teaching these lowlifes a lesson, I unclenched my fists.

I committed every feature of the guy's face to memory. Every pockmark, every bristle of his goatee. Maybe today wasn't his day, but no one disrespected a Luca and lived to tell the story.

"Where's Alejandro?" I asked between gritted teeth while Leo took another breath. Alejandro was a piece of shit—he'd sell a man out for a quick buck—but the devil I knew was better than the devil I didn't.

The guy smiled. Damn, what fun it would have been to yank those ridiculous incisors right out of his mouth.

"Alejandro's been… retired," he said, crossing his meaty arms over his chest and dangling the beat-up briefcase from one finger. "I'm the new point man for the Free Birds now. Just think of me as the new team mascot."

I'd take Bullet as a mascot over this guy any day. "And does the Free Birds' new mascot have a name?"

"You can call me Jimmy."

"All right, Jimmy. As soon as I have the cash in hand, the two trucks in the warehouse are all yours. But you tell Harry, the next time he changes his point man, he better tell me about it first."

The two lackeys stood up straighter, their beefy hands hovering in front of their open jackets.

Jimmy just smiled, creasing the skin around his dark, beady eyes. "A bit arrogant of you, don't you think, Dom?"

The guy was just asking to die. "My family and my friends call me Dom. You're neither."

"My apologies, Mister Luca." An insincere apology if ever I'd heard one. No fucking respect.

"The money, Jimmy. Now."

"Of course." He tossed the briefcase, and it landed just inches from my shoes, forcing Bullet to scamper out of its way.

Leo leaned down to pick it up.

"Don't bother, Leo," I told him, keeping my eyes on Jimmy.

"What's the problem, Mister Luca?" the guy cajoled.

The problem was that a briefcase holding twenty-five thousand $100 bills—the exact price of the merchandise in the two trucks in the warehouse—weighed about fifty pounds. By the light thud this briefcase made when it hit the ground, no way it weighed more than fifteen pounds.

"You're a little light, Jimmy," I said, kicking the shitty leather case back at him.

"Am I?" He smirked, stopping the case with his worn black loafer.

"I'd say about one-point-five million light."

His beady eyes widened in surprise, but he recovered quickly. "I've got a message for you from Mr. Belemonte himself. Word around town is you've been planning to encroach on our territory." Jimmy swung his arms out, gesturing around the docks. "Did you think he wouldn't notice?"

"You heard wrong." The Luca empire was vast; what reason would we have to go sniffing around the Free Birds' pathetic back alleys? The properties we had our eyes on had nothing to do with the Free Birds. "Harry was well aware of what we were up to, and he knows it. Completely aboveboard. He knows we would have given him a good deal, but you fucked that up big-time," I said, nodding toward the briefcase.

"A bit ballsy, don't you think? Passing up my fine offer when you've got a gun aimed at your head?"

"You don't scare me, Jimmy. All you needed to do was give us our money so we could be on our way. Now we're going to have to punish you and everyone you work with for something they weren't even involved in, you piece of shit."

The men behind Jimmy drew their guns.

Although danger was imminent, I remained still, calm. It was the only way we would survive this. Leo seemed a lot calmer now, too. He'd get used to situations like these in no time. Though the muscles in my neck were tight, I breathed slowly and carefully.

"You should teach your lackey how to hold a gun properly." I gestured toward the crony on his left. His form was awful, and he would lose his balance if he fired his weapon.

The guy looked down at his gun and flushed. Good. Mind games would help in our situation. There was no way we would get out of this if we didn't employ a bit of wit.

Two men stepped out from one of the cars behind Jimmy's, each of them with an assault rifle in their meaty hands. Just fucking great. I needed to think this through carefully.

Jimmy let out a loud laugh. "You're gone, Dominic. And who the fuck are you to be preaching about honor? You're a criminal too, and we're not all that different. The Lucas aren't all that different from the Free Birds. You assholes just wear suits and act like you own the place, like you have some kind of kingdom. It's laughable, really. We're not in the Middle Ages, asshole."

I shook my head. "Not smart, Jimmy. Betraying a Luca is a big mistake. No doubt, you've heard what happened to all the others who tried?"

"Doesn't matter. You'll be dead before you can run to Daddy and tell him the news. Easy as pie," Jimmy said.

"What the hell happened to you, Jimmy?" Leo suddenly said, with a look in my direction and a slight nod. It was time. Leo was just stalling with his little speech. "You'll pay for this, man, you know that, don't you? You can't fuck with the Lucas and keep breathing air. We just can't let that happen. Walk away now, Jimmy. Tell your boss to hand over what he promised, and this doesn't have to happen."

I'd underestimated my little brother. He might be newer to fieldwork, but he was a good talker, and even I could barely see the way he was moving into position while he spoke. Well done.

"I ain't got no beef with you, Leo, but things are the way they are. No one standing in front of me five seconds from now is walking away today."

A bullet zipped through the air from behind Jimmy, narrowly missing their mascot, and ricocheting harmlessly off the ground five feet from me.

"You fucking moron," Jimmy roared without turning around. "You nearly shot me." And then Jimmy did turn around. In one fluid motion, he grabbed his gun from inside his jacket and shot the guy who'd accidentally almost shot him. The guy was fast—I'd give him that.

No one blinked as the assault rifle fell from the lackey's hand and he followed it down to the ground. Dead.

"Fucking amateurs," he cursed under his breath as he turned around with his gun still in hand. He didn't say another word. The glint in his eyes told me all I needed to know.

"Now!" I barked at Leo. He drew his gun in tandem with mine. We fired two shots before Jimmy could even pull the trigger—one in each of Jimmy's kneecaps because no one who fucked with the Lucas died nicely.

Jimmy screamed as he lost his grip on his gun and his legs collapsed out from under him.

"Call off your goons, Jimmy," I said as the rest of his men took aim.

"Kill the motherfuckers!" Jimmy shouted instead.

But he wasn't fast enough. I fired at the lackeys, making them duck for cover as Leo did what he was supposed to do—hightailed it behind the car.

Two seconds later, he laid down cover fire, and I sped back to join him. Bullets zipped past me, but I'd been right—these guys couldn't shoot worth shit.

A yelp sounded above the staccato beat just as I slid behind the car.

Bullet had been shot.

"Leo, cover me," I ordered as I crept along the side of the car toward the mound of fur and blood by the front left tire. I was risking my life for a goddamn dog. My father had better have a harem of gorgeous women waiting for me after this—if I made it out of here in one piece.

I took in the scene in front of me. Half the lackeys were laid out on the ground—well done, Leo. He kept up the cover fire as I darted out, grabbed the dog with one hand, and shot back beside the car. A bullet shot by too close. I didn't have time to dodge it, and it ripped through my side. I found the asshole who'd shot it, took aim, and put him down with a bullet through his throat.

The dog whined as I moved behind the car. Good, the thing was still alive, but the way its blood was soaking my hand meant it wasn't going to stay that way for long.

"I'm taking Bullet to the vet. Get to the warehouse, Leo," I said. "The Porsche is inside. Take it, and get back to the house. Let them know what happened."

Leo nodded as I turned to lay down cover fire. He didn't look any more ruffled than he had when we'd first arrived. He was more ready for this than I'd thought.

"Drive fast, and don't look back, *fratellino*," I called as his footsteps sounded at a steady thud toward the building's side door.

"You know I drive fast no matter the occasion," he called back. "*Vivere*, brother."

Only two men were left standing amid the Cadillacs, and one was spending an awful lot of time eyeing his driver's side door. The second I heard the warehouse door slam shut behind Leo, I headed for the driver's side of the McLaren, ignoring for the moment the holes and dents in the car because if I focused on what they'd done to my baby, I might have just torn them apart limb from limb.

With Bullet tucked beneath my arm, I slid into the driver's seat and revved the engine. A smooth purr despite the damage. The dog whimpered and whined while his small body trembled against me. I kept him on my lap as I shoved the car in reverse and sped out of the parking lot. Outside of a flesh wound, I'd made it out unscathed, but if the dog died, my father was going to skin me and Leo alive.

Chapter Two

Fallon

The pint-size Pomeranian stared up at me with tired eyes, tilting his head from one side to the other.

"You're gaining your strength again, aren't you?" I cooed, stroking the fur between his eyes over and over again.

He pressed his tiny head harder against my fingers and closed his eyes. It could have been the comforting stroke of my fingers that helped him settle and drift off, but I liked to believe it was something deeper. Like the animals I tended knew they were in good hands. Or maybe it was so similar to the way my mother used to stroke my brow after a nightmare, the animals couldn't help but feel the warm comfort that radiated from my memories.

"Pretty soon, you're going to be good as new. You'll be as strong as Maggie," I whispered to him, nodding to the two-year-old Rottweiler two cages over.

With the Pomeranian fully on his way to dreamland, I closed the cage door quietly and massaged the back of my neck. It had been a long day. Two broken bones, two surgeries, and four routine checkups; it had definitely been a long day. But all of my patients made it through, so I counted it as a good day. One more check through the rest of my patients, and I'd be on my way home.

"Don't you ever sleep?" Corinne teased as she grabbed the broom from behind the door and got to work sweeping up the floor. Corinne was a godsend. Not an angel, exactly—not with an arm covered in witchy tattoos and a glint in her eye that said she was always ready for a little mischief. But she'd been my own personal savior on more than one occasion.

"I slept last week, remember?" I teased back while I dried and put away the tools I'd sterilized. "Call it a night, Corinne. If I don't sleep tonight, I might need you at your best tomorrow."

She finished sweeping the floor, returned the broom behind the door, then leaned against it, eyeing me. "If I go home, you're not going to stay here all night, are you?"

It would save some time. If I could curl up on one of the exam tables, I'd be able to skip the travel time and sneak in an extra hour's sleep. But no, I wasn't quite ready to sink that low. "I'll go home, I promise. I'm just going to finish tidying up, and I'll be out of here."

Corinne nodded. "All right, but if I find you here in the morning, I'm going to kick your ass."

"Got it."

She nodded and left the room, but she hadn't made it two steps when she swung around. "By the way, what happened to that hunky guy with the black Lab?"

Ugh, not this again. "Nothing happened."

"You can't be serious, Fallon," she said, swinging her arms out in exasperation. "That guy was giving you major bedroom eyes, and you just let him walk out of here?"

"Goodnight, Corinne." I sighed and turned to focus on something… anything else.

"You do know you need the company of humans too, right?" She cocked an eyebrow at me.

I huffed and crossed my arms over my chest. I'd heard this lecture a million times before. "I have you, and I have Dad, I guess. What more do I need?"

"Unless you've got some funky relationship going on with your dad that I don't want to know about, what you need is some… human connection. A little human touch," she said, waggling her eyebrows at me as she unclasped her hair, setting her auburn locks free. They bounced into place just below her shoulders.

"Goodnight, Corinne," I replied, rolling my eyes. "Don't you have a date waiting for you?"

"All right, all right," she conceded. "I'll go. And I'll share all the juicy details with you tomorrow. Maybe that'll give you something to keep you company on those long, lonely nights."

"What would I do without you, Corinne?"

She just laughed and skipped toward the front of the building "Go home, Fallon," she called as the tinkling of the bell over the front door sounded. "Love you lots."

"I love you too, honey," I called back.

I looked over the room filled with my patients one last time then turned off the light and headed to the reception area. I could catch up on some paperwork. Or take a look at my schedule for tomorrow. Maybe do a quick inventory check.

Okay, even I could see it now—I was stalling. On the surface, I had my hands full with my practice, but behind the scenes, at home at the end of the day, there was nothing but four walls to keep me company. Here, surrounded by sleeping animals, at least I wasn't alone.

"You're hitting a new low, Moore," I mumbled under my breath while I grabbed my purse, turned the lights off, and entered the reception area. I left the building and had just turned the key when someone from behind me spoke.

"You need to help him. Now," the voice said, deep and clear but with a haggard edge in his tone.

I spun around, keeping my keys between my fingers like claws, but I gasped when I saw him. He was tall, perhaps the tallest man I'd ever been this close to, and though his dark hair was tousled, and a deep furrow was drawn between his brows, he looked like a freaking male model.

When my brief perusal reached his torso, my jaw dropped. There was blood, so much blood. There was a small pup in his arms, a long-haired Chihuahua, but so much blood saturated his brown fur, he appeared more russet and crimson than brown. The animal trembled, but otherwise laid lifeless in the man's arms.

"Oh my God, what happened to him?" I gasped. "Um, we just closed, but, of course, I'll treat him. Come with me and put him on the table."

The tall Italian nodded then followed me through the building to the steel table inside my operating room. He stood still while I prepared the table for the pup. Too still, aside from his eyes that seemed to be following my every movement. Most clients who came in with injured animals paced back and forth the room or fidgeted nervously. Their worry was written all over their faces, but this man didn't move, didn't flinch.

When the table was ready, I nodded toward it, and the man moved to put the Chihuahua down on it, leaving the dog's head hanging limply at an awkward angle.

I quickly stepped forward and took the dog from his hands.

"You have to be careful, sir. You don't want to hurt him further," I scolded mildly.

He glared at me, and a cold shiver ghosted down my spine.

I forced my gaze away and turned my attention to the injured animal, prodding gently through the long fur matted with blood.

"Do you know how he was injured?" I asked, figuring so much blood was likely the result of a car accident.

"He was shot," the man said plainly.

My hands froze. "Shot?"

Who the hell would shoot a dog?

Carefully, I turned the dog over, searching for the telltale blood that would signify an exit wound. There wasn't any. The bullet was lodged inside him.

"Poor baby," I crooned, stroking his small head. "We'll get that nasty bullet out of you, little guy."

The man laughed, though there was no humor in it.

"The dog's name is Bullet," he said when I cast a glance up at him.

A knot formed at the back of my throat. Bullet was in great distress—and had his very own namesake stuck in his side. If I didn't operate soon, I feared he would bleed out on my table. I wouldn't let that happen.

I grabbed the trimmer and went to work shaving the fur around the wound for easier access. The man came closer, practically leaning over my shoulder to watch what I was doing. He smelled of cedarwood and tobacco, like an heirloom trunk, or a box of expensive cigars, sprinkled with a bit of citrus. I would have liked the smell if the room wasn't filled with the metallic scent of blood.

Having him so close, watching me so intently, made me nervous.

"You need to take a seat in the waiting area. I'll come get you as soon as I'm finished," I told him in my best no-nonsense voice.

"I don't think so, Miss Moore," he said, completely unaffected. "I'll be staying right here."

I heaved a sigh. Bullet didn't have time for this man's stubbornness. "What's your name?" I asked, putting the trimmer down on the small, metal table beside me as I turned to face him. The sharp gaze in his gray eyes startled me.

"Dominic, though I don't see how that's relevant to the task at hand," he said, cocking a brow.

"Dominic, I need to be able to concentrate, and I can't do that with you hovering over my shoulder."

He took one step back, but that seemed to be the end of his concession.

"Get to work, Miss Moore," he said in a no-nonsense tone that put my own to shame.

Who was he to boss me around in my own freaking clinic?

It was only then I noticed the fresh blood that plastered his shirt to his side, just above his hip. It was too much, and too fresh to belong to Bullet.

"You've been shot," I blurted out.

"Yes, Miss Moore. I did notice that," he said with an upward quirk of his lips.

I shook my head and turned back around to get to work. Animals were my patients, not humans. I needed to get the bullet out of Bullet fast if I were to stop the bleeding before he lost too much blood. I injected him with an anesthetic near the wound, doing my damnedest to ignore the man hovering one step behind me. Male model or not, he seemed to have the personality of a rattlesnake.

I inserted the tweezers into the wound, hoping the bullet was intact and hadn't shattered upon impact. I felt the tips of the tweezer hit metal about two inches deep. I maneuvered them to get a grip on the bullet, but my hand shook, just the slightest tremble, but it was enough to foil my attempt. Shit. Shit. Shit.

I withdrew the tweezers, grabbed a handful of sterile cloths, and tossed them to the man behind me.

"Leave, Dominic. Go sit down and press these against your wound. I need you out of here so I can save this dog's life," I said, mimicking his chilling tone as best as I could and glaring at him for good measure.

He stared at me for one long moment, then nodded, turning on his heels and striding out of the room. I exhaled the breath I hadn't realized I'd been holding and turned my attention back to Bullet.

"Almost done here, little guy. You're going to be good as new soon," I crooned.

Without the man's unnerving gaze on me, my hands were steady, and it only took me a moment to insert the tweezers, grab onto the bullet, and remove it in one smooth movement.

"Now we're getting somewhere, aren't we, Bullet?" I said, smiling into the dog's eyes. I always wondered what they were thinking while I worked. Could Bullet tell instinctively that I was trying to help him? I hoped so.

I dropped the bullet in a small metal bowl. After sterilizing the wound, I pulled out a small machine. It allowed me to cauterize the wound to stop the bleeding quickly and help prevent infections. Because of the anesthetic, Bullet didn't even whimper when I applied it to his flesh. I breathed through my mouth as I worked. The smell of burning flesh was—to say the least—absolutely dreadful.

***

After applying a bandage and finding Bullet a free kennel, I laid him in a comfortable bed. He looked up at me before I closed the door.

"You're going to be okay, little guy," I cooed softly. "Fallon's going to take care of you. You look like a strong little man. You'll feel better than ever in no time."

Despite his pain, his eyes were so expressive. Bullet seemed to frown, and I stroked his head, giving him a moment to relax beneath my fingers before I closed the kennel door. I turned off the light and made my way to the reception area where Dominic stood, rather than sat, but at least he was pressing the cloths I'd given him to his wound. He stared at me with eyes so gray they were like storm clouds right before they let loose their fury.

"What happened to that dog?" I barked with my arms crossed over my chest. It seemed unlikely he'd shot Bullet himself and then brought him in for surgery, but it was also difficult to believe this man had played no role in whatever had happened. So, it didn't matter that he towered over me or that his shoulders were twice as broad as mine or that he could probably squish me like a bug. At least, I stiffened my spine and pretended none of that mattered.

"He was shot. I thought we'd established that, Miss Moore."

I huffed. "A dog doesn't just magically appear with a bullet lodged in his side."

"It would be best if you just accepted that he did," he said as lightning bolts seemed to shoot through the storm clouds in his eyes. "Now, tell me, is Bullet going to be all right?" He lifted his chin to look behind me, so I stood on my toes to block his view.

"The bullet didn't hit any bone or organs, thank God, and I was able to remove it in one piece. He's resting comfortably now. I think it's safe to say he's going to be okay." I didn't like to give that kind of assurance so early on, but Bullet had come through the surgery well. I was confident he would recover.

He nodded. "I'd like to take him home then."

"You still haven't explained how he was shot," I said, fisting my hands on my hips.

He grinned like I was somehow amusing. If I hadn't been angry as hell, I would have been weak in the knees.

"A stray bullet hit him while I was taking him for a walk," he said—a lie if ever I'd heard one.

"One stray bullet?" I cocked an eyebrow. Only an idiot would buy his bullshit story. "And that would mean you dove to protect him, the bullet went right through you, and managed to get lodged in that poor dog?"

He shrugged. "Something like that."

I rolled my eyes. This man was unbelievable! "Look, if you can't give me a straight answer, I'm going to have to call Animal Services."

More lightning flashed in his eyes as he strode toward me. Every step he took forward, I took a step back until I was pressed up against the wall and could go no further.

"I don't like to be threatened, Miss Moore," he said as his hands slapped against the wall on either side of my head, and he pressed himself up against me.

I swallowed back a scream while my heart pounded hard against my chest.

His gray eyes met mine, and like a viper's, they held me, mesmerized and terrified at the same time. I couldn't move. I barely blinked. It disgusted me that even as I shook with terror, my body couldn't help but take note of the hard, unyielding form of his body pressed against mine and the way the muscles of his throat worked as he swallowed.

"You'll tell no one about my late-night visit here. Do you understand me?" he said, enunciating each word clearly. My stupid traitorous eyes stared at his full lips as they moved.

When I didn't answer, he removed one of his hands from the wall and tilted my chin up to meet his gaze.

"Do you understand, Miss Moore?" he asked again.

I opened my mouth to reply, but my lips trembled too much to speak, so I nodded my head instead.

He took a step back, and my lungs gasped for air like he'd been using up all the oxygen. But now that I could breathe again, anger surged through my veins. I planted my palms on his chest and shoved him as hard as I could.

He didn't move, not even an inch. There was a gleam in his pupils accompanied by a slight wrinkle in the fine lines around his eyes, as if he was amused with me. I huffed, the anger in the pit of my stomach churning wildly.

"You don't come into my clinic and threaten me," I roared. "I don't know who you think you are, but—"

His eyes narrowed and the muscles of his jaw twitched, and I slammed my mouth closed.

"You don't know who I am, do you, Miss Moore?" He cocked an eyebrow at me. Oh God. Eye roll. He was one of those guys.

"Let me guess, you're some guy with enough money to think you own the whole freaking world?" I crossed my arms as I eyed him, my attempt to level with him.

"Something like that." His lips tugged upward, ever so slightly to the left.

Nothing seemed to humble this arrogant prick, and I was too tired to keep fighting. "Look, Bullet needs to stay here for the night. If something goes wrong, you might not be able to get him back to me in time to help him. So, go to a hospital or go home. I'll stay here to keep an eye on him, and you can come check on him tomorrow."

He was silent for a moment, staring at me. It was unnerving, the way he seemed to be peeling back my skin with his eyes to look beneath it. Eventually, he found whatever he'd been looking for and nodded.

"I'm only willing to leave him here because I believe you, Miss Moore. Don't make me regret that. I promise you won't like the consequences."

He turned on his heel and left the clinic without another word. I locked the front door right away, checking twice, thrice if the dead bolt was in place. I remained where I was as I listened to the click of a car door open.

The cushioned slamming of the door close.

The start of the ignition.

The rhythmic ticktock of the blinker.

The revving of the engine.

Kiana Hettinger

I waited until the only thing I could hear was my own heart pumping blood to the tips of my fingers.

If I never saw that man again in my life, it would be too soon.

Chapter Three

Dominic

My phone buzzed like a swarm of killer bees. Over and over again.

I swung my legs over the edge of the bed. I groaned. I'd forgotten about the bullet wound. Thank Christ it had only been a flesh wound.

I grabbed my phone, glancing at the time before sliding my thumb across the screen to stop the incessant buzzing.

"What?" I growled at whoever was stupid enough to call me at six in the morning.

"Good morning, sunshine," Leo joked from the other end of the line. Lucky for him there was no way to rip his vocal cords out from here.

"What can I do for you, Leo?" I ground out between gritted teeth.

"It's not what you can do for me, *fratello*. It's what you can do for the whole family," he said jovially despite the raised voices in the background.

"What?"

Cryptic messages first thing in the morning after the night I had? Leo should be getting on his knees to thank his fucking lucky stars.

"Would you please get your ass over here and explain to our father that his dog is going to be just fine… preferably before he goes homicidal on us."

Well, anyone could have seen that one coming.

"I'll be over ASAP," I said then hung up the phone and dropped it on the bed.

I managed to shower and shove a cup of coffee down my throat in seven minutes flat and then hauled my ass out the door. In some ways, it would have been more convenient if I'd stayed living in the Luca family home. It was tradition—as my father had reminded me at least a hundred times. But I needed peace and quiet, not a constant barrage of noise and activity. So, this was me; a spacious—and quiet—apartment in the city, already furnished in the oddest mixture of industrial and modern style furniture. And the best part about it: nobody but the closest members of my family knew the place existed. Information was power, and in this business, the less information our rivals had, the better.

In the parking garage, I slipped into the driver's seat, revved the engine, and closed my eyes, savoring the purr for just a moment. The next several hours were going to be anything but peaceful. I was going to latch on to every moment of quiet I could get.

As I pulled out of the garage, my thoughts turned to the events that had transpired yesterday. The goddamned Free Birds. Belemonte was going to pay for his betrayal, and there was no way in hell we'd be working with them ever again. In fact, maybe it was time to cut out the middleman altogether. Take the docks for ourselves and deal with the Russians directly; it would mean ruffling feathers left, right, and center, but how else did one get ahead in life?

It was time to move the Luca family into the 21st century. Casinos—that's what we were missing. I'd proposed the idea a half dozen times, but my father had been resistant. After Belemonte though, he was going to be looking for ways to minimize our dependency on others. And this was it. This was the way forward.

The twenty-minute drive to the Luca estate flew by too fast. I slowed the car as I approached the guard shack. I waved to Guido, and he opened the gate. The long path to the top of the driveway was lined with perfectly sculpted cedars, like a runway that led to a gaudy-looking fountain at the top. Ugly little gargoyles perched around a curvy, naked maiden in the center. Don't get me wrong; nothing wrong with the naked maiden, but those gargoyles were the ugliest things I'd ever seen.

I parked in front of the house and stepped out, but before I could even climb the front steps, Dante poked his head out the door with a finger over his lips.

"Keep it down, and get in here," he whispered, motioning for me to follow him inside.

Without another word, he led me through the foyer and down the hall to our war room. The place where all battles, major deals, and heists were planned. A large mahogany table occupied the center of the room with twenty chairs arranged around it. Mounted on the walls and in the cabinets around the room were various trinkets my father had either inherited or accumulated over the years. Antique weapons, a few Fabergé eggs, and other stolen items from some high-profile people. There was at least a million dollars' worth of items in here. More than some people made in a lifetime. Behind all of my father's knickknacks and trophies, the walls were soundproofed—a bit of paranoia on my grandfather's part given no man my family didn't trust set foot in this house.

Dante closed the door and scrubbed his fingers through his short, dark hair.

"All right, lay it out for me," I said, leaning against an empty space on the wall.

He shook his head and pursed his lips. "It's bad, Dom. Really fucking bad. He's going nuts—just as much over the damn dog as what Leo told him about Belemonte."

I chuckled. "Well, Bullet's going to be fine. And I bet as soon as he hears that, the beast will be pacified."

"Then, how about you go and tell him that?" Dante nodded at the closed door just as it swung open.

"He broke another glass," Leo said with his usual lopsided grin. "I thought I'd get out of there before I breathed the wrong way, and he chucked a glass at me." He chuckled.

"All right," I said, pushing off the wall. "Since none of you assholes seem to be able to placate the beast, I suppose it's Dom to the rescue."

Dante scoffed, and Leo moved away from the door, bowing and then motioning to it in an overexaggerated gesture. I had to hand it to Leo; nothing ruffled his feathers. The guy would go marching through the gates of hell one day with a goofy grin on his face.

"Dumbass," I muttered under my breath with a small smile as I crossed the threshold and headed back through the house to my father's office at the other end.

I knocked once then entered the room. Sitting behind his big, old cherrywood desk with his head in his hands was Vincent Luca.

The room was a mess. Broken glass on the opposite side of the room, papers on the ground next to an overturned chair. He was pissed about the betrayal, of course, but this outburst had nothing to do with Belemonte. This was about Bullet. And while I tried to pretend I couldn't see what he saw in the mutt, I knew. I knew the reason my father went crazy over the dog. Bullet wasn't originally my father's dog. The mutt had been a gift for Sofia. She'd bugged him for one of those little runts for months, and finally, she'd worn him down. He'd come home a week before her birthday with three-month-old Bullet in a miniature carrier with a big-ass red bow tied around it.

Two months later, my sister was gone, but Bullet was still here, mewling and whining for the kind of attention Sofia had heaped on it.

"Bullet's going to be fine," I said without preamble.

My father's head shot up. He looked at me with his dark eyes narrowed.

"I took him to the Moore girl downtown and stayed until she was certain he was going to make a full recovery. He'll be back in two days."

His suspicious gaze lingered for a moment longer, like he was trying to determine whether I was feeding him a line. I might have been a cocky son of a bitch, but I wasn't stupid.

Eventually, he nodded, and his features smoothed into a mask of indifference. "Then the next order of business is Belemonte," he said, settling back in his wingback chair.

I nodded. "I have a plan that will send a message—both to Belemonte and any other cartel stupid enough to try to pull that shit."

"I don't want to send a message, son. I want to wipe them all off the face of the earth."

I stared at my father and tried not to laugh at the 180-degree shift. One minute, he'd been going batshit crazy over a puppy, and the next, he was planning to rain down hell on an entire cartel.

"We can't wipe them all out," I said plainly.

"And why not?"

"Because the Free Birds take everyone they can get. They've got sixteen-year-old kids running for them."

He sighed heavily. "I suppose you're right."

Damn right I was. It was what kept the line clearly drawn between us and them—between us and the other pathetic hell-bound cartels out there. The Lucas had morals, if that's what they could be called. At the very least, we had standards by which we lived our lives. And one of those standards: We never murdered children—innocent or not.

"Fine, I'll trust you to take care of it," my father said. Not that long ago, Vincent Luca would never have left something so important in another man's hands, but times had changed. He'd groomed me for this for as long as I could remember, and I'd proven myself over and over again.

"You mentioned the Moore girl," he said just as I was about to turn around and leave.

"Yes, the veterinarian," I said, then under my breath, I muttered to myself, "Insufferable witch."

He laughed. "It's funny you should say that."

"Funny, how?" A prickle at the back of my neck started poking in overdrive.

"The Novas are encroaching on our territory. After everything that's happened in the past twenty-four hours, we need a little extra security. Tighter bonds with people that can help us when we need them. If things go south, Dominic, we're going to have a big fight on our hands, and we need the police force neatly tucked inside our pockets."

"We already have Douglas Moore on our payroll. He keeps his mouth shut when we tell him to, and he hides evidence when we need it." I held my father's gaze, willing him to agree as I balled my hands into fists.

"Like I said, we need tighter bonds," he said as he poured himself two fingers of bourbon and swirled it around in his glass. He took a hearty swallow then looked at me. "It's time you marry Fallon Moore, Dominic. We've put this off long enough."

Fuck me. I kept my face arranged in an unreadable mask, but inside, I was ready to take my own ride into batshit crazy town. That woman was mouthy, and defiant, and uppity, and everything else I sure as hell didn't want in a wife—not that I wanted a wife at all. So what if she was hot as hell and the image of those pouty lips wrapped around my cock might just star in every fantasy I had for the next six months? Those kinds of qualifications made her an excellent candidate for a night of dirty, sweaty sex. Not the kind of qualifications that made me want to be stuck with her for life.

"There has got to be another way," I argued, though I knew it was futile.

"This is no surprise, Dominic. You've known it was a possibility for years. The only way to secure absolute loyalty from Douglas Moore is to marry his only daughter and ensure her protection. If we do this, the chief of police will be stuck in our pockets for life."

He was right—not that it made the prospect any more palatable.

"Besides, if not this woman, then what woman, Dominic? You're thirty-four years old, and your longest relationship has been, what—four hours long?" He raised his eyebrow at me, clicking his tongue.

"There was that girl I took to Fiji last year," I rejoined, not that it was much of a rejoinder.

"And what was her name?"

I wasn't sure if her name had ever come up, to be honest. Words weren't really what had been on the agenda that weekend.

"I'm not talking about a girl you can fuck. There are plenty of them out there, Dominic, and I'm sure you've sampled plenty of them. But I'm talking about a woman to lead by your side when the time comes for you to rule my kingdom."

I nodded stiffly. It was my duty as eldest son of the Luca family, and I was loyal to this family no matter the cost.

"Go speak to her father so we can begin preparations. The sooner we get this done, the better."

And with that, I was off—to see the chief of police, of all people. Not how I wanted to start my day, but the Moore girl was in for one hell of a surprise too. Something told me she wasn't exactly prepared for a life steeped in crime and all the murder and corruption that went with it. The idea of seeing that uppity woman squirm brought me a modicum of comfort. At least I wouldn't be the only one stuck in marital hell.

***

The greasy smell of frying burgers wafted out the open front door of the Main Street Diner. I stood outside, trying to breathe shallowly while I looked inside in search of Police Chief Douglas Moore. He wasn't a difficult man to spot given he was rather large and round for a member of the police force. I spotted him at a table far in the back, shoveling one of those revolting burgers in his mouth. Thick sauce dripped from his fingers, but he didn't seem to mind. I could almost hear the whooshing bruit of his clogged arteries.

I entered the establishment—if the dirty checkered floors and the crude collection of rickety tables and metal chairs could be counted as an establishment—and made my way toward the poster boy for heart disease at the back. The four stars embedded on his collar twinkled beneath the fluorescent lighting, like a neon sign driving attention to some badge of honor pinned beneath them. I sniggered. The man didn't have an honorable bone in his body.

"I'm on lunch until one o'clock, so buzz off," he mumbled between bites without looking up when I stopped directly in front of him.

I resisted the urge to wrinkle my nose at the pathetic heap of a man and waited for him to look up and realize his mistake.

He swallowed an oversized mouthful of food and glanced up irritably, but the moment his eyes met mine, his widened in surprise and he coughed and spluttered. Disgusting.

"Dominic, I'm so sorry. If I knew… well, of course… I mean…" He swallowed again, giving himself a moment to collect his composure. "There are no lunch breaks when it comes to helping my good friends. Please, sit down." He motioned to the empty seat across from him.

"I'll stand, thank you. This won't take long."

"Oh?" he said, glancing around like he might be able to find reinforcements amid the riffraff here. If I was here to kill him, did he really think anything could have stopped me?

The thought of letting him squirm, wondering what was coming his way, was tempting, but I just wanted this over with. "The Lucas have decided it's time for our families to be joined… permanently."

His eyes shifted back and forth like he was still looking for a lifeline. "You… you mean the marriage?" he stuttered. "Oh, no." He cringed, running his greasy fingers through the graying tufts of hair around his head.

"Oh, yes, Mr. Moore. I will be marrying your daughter, have no doubt about it. Be grateful I'm an honorable man, and decided to give you fair warning first."

Arranged marriages were a long-standing tradition in my family, as was the tradition to speak with the bride's father first. Of course, Police Chief Moore really had no say in the matter. In this case, it was more of a courtesy.

"I… I thought that it wouldn't happen considering how long it's been since the betrothal," he said, eyes darting around.

"Ain't that just the way?" I smirked.

"Please, she doesn't know about any of this, Dominic. Nothing of the mafia life. Fallon doesn't know I'm involved at all. She's a normal girl."

"And?" I tilted my head at him. "It's not my problem you chose to keep the truth from her. You've known about the engagement for decades."

"But you can't do this. You just can't. Fallon won't be able to handle it."

Yeah, I'd met the woman. Agreeable was not how I'd describe her. But no one who'd met me would describe me as the marrying type, and it wasn't like I got a say in the matter. So, she could damn well just suck it up. "If you don't hand her over, you know we'll just take her."

I turned to leave, but he threw out his grease-covered hand.

"Wait. Please, Dominic. She's a good woman, a kind person."

Were we talking about the same woman here?

"She'd never hurt a fly, so just… just…" He floundered, but then a light sparked up in his eyes. "Just take her on a date. Yeah," he said, nodding to himself. "Yeah, if you take her on just a few dates, you could, you know…"

"You want me to seduce your daughter, Douglas?" I didn't bother trying to hide my amusement.

"Yes… I mean, no…" He looked away, flustered. "What I mean is… you could get her to have feelings for you… Sweep her off her feet, you know? And then you could propose, and she'd never have to know…"

"She'd never have to know that her father is a slimy piece of shit?" Douglas Moore had a long history of doing favors for very bad people. People far worse than the Luca family. "What was that gaming commissioner's name?" I asked, hitting a nerve and making his eyes bulge out of his fat face.

"I don't know who you're talking about," he said, pulling at the collar of his shirt.

"Come now, Douglas," I said, placing my hands on the table and leaning down until his eyes shot up to meet mine. "You're not going to play dumb with me, are you?"

He shook his head. "It's just... I don't know what that has to do with anything."

"An innocent man is in jail because of you. Don't you remember?"

"Keep... keep your voice down. Please..." he whispered while his eyes darted left and right.

He was pathetic, but it sure as hell was fun to make him squirm. "The gaming commissioner had a drinking problem, didn't he? Everyone knew it. He had a few too many before he decided to go on a little joyride."

Douglas nodded, though his hands were clenched in front of him.

"It was late afternoon. Hell, the guy couldn't even make it to happy hour."

"Look, I don't know what any of this has to do with Fallon. Please, Dominic, I'm begging you. I know you're not a father, but I know you Lucas. Family is important to you. You can't do this to my daughter. We don't need a marriage to keep things good between us. There has to be something else."

No, the guy was too slimy. He'd keep handing out favors to the wrong people if we didn't put a leash on him. Once his family was tied to mine in matrimony, well, he couldn't afford for bad press to get out about the Lucas. It would cast too many shadows over his own name.

"Your gaming commissioner friend took his little joyride through a quiet residential area, didn't he?" I pressed.

Douglas looked away just as tears welled in his eyes.

"He wasn't paying attention," I continued. "He slammed right into a woman and her child walking across the street. And when neither of them made it, what did he do? He went crying to you, didn't he? Begging you to cover up his mess. But you couldn't hide two bodies… or the car… or the blood…"

"Stop," Douglas whispered, staring at the half-eaten burger on his plate. "I know what I did, Dominic. Why are you doing this?"

"Because you can't fool me, Douglas. I know what kind of man you are. You're the kind of man who would pin two murders on an innocent nineteen-year-old who had his whole life ahead of him… until you ripped it away."

"I know what I did, damn it," he confessed miserably. Or maybe he was just one hell of an actor. Either way, I was bored.

I opened my mouth to tell the piece of shit I was coming for his daughter, but an image of Fallon's sapphire eyes, wide with fear, flashed through my mind. I closed my mouth, but before I could wonder what was wrong with me, it hit me: The perfect solution. "If you want me to try this your way, you're going to do something for me, Douglas. You're going to have to call in the favor that murdering scumbag commissioner owes you, as well as a few others."

Douglas pressed his lips together, and I could see the gears turning in his head. He might feel remorse for what he'd done, but he wouldn't relish giving up his leverage over the commissioner—even to protect his only daughter. Motherfucker.

"Fine," he said after a beat too long. "I'll do it. I'll do whatever you want."

"Damn right you will." That was just a given. "One favor buys you one date, got it?"

He nodded slowly, the misery in his eyes clear as day.

"All right then." I nodded and stood up straight. "Set it up, and I'll take your precious princess on a date." Fuck, entire evenings with that haughty woman. Douglas Moore was going to be doing me some damn big favors for this. "Now, for your first task, Douglas…"

Chapter Four

Fallon

Dad showed up out of the blue—not that I minded. I already had dinner cooking on the stove, and I always cooked enough to feed a small army. Sure, it was sad to see a pot of uneaten food afterward, but it also meant I had ready-made lunches on particularly hard days. All I needed to do was pop some leftovers in the microwave, and voilà, hunger gone.

I swirled the cooked pasta around in a large saucepan coated with olive oil, garlic, parsley, and parmesan. It wasn't the most complex meal—aglio e olio—but it was good. And better yet, it was easy. I'd learned it back in college when I'd gotten sick of living on ramen noodles and frozen vegetables.

I plated up two servings and carried them out to the small red Formica table in the dining room. My father sat there with his legs stretched out in front of him and his hands clenched together in front of his gut. It was typical Dad except for the far-off look in his eyes and the way his teeth worried at his bottom lip.

"So, what's up?" I asked, not bothering to ease into it. If he had something on his mind, it never took much to make him spill. In fact, my father was very good at spilling, I thought bitterly, then tamped it down. It wasn't much of a problem now, but it had been difficult when I was a kid, dealing with my own problems and all the ones he'd dumped on my shoulders. He didn't do it on purpose; that was just Dad. He didn't have normal coping mechanisms, nor did he understand that a kid wasn't capable of dealing with the world's troubles.

"Can't a father just want to have dinner with his little girl?" he asked.

Sure, he could, but like I said, that wasn't really my father's style. For the most part, I'd made peace with it. And the little bit of bitterness that crept up now and then—well, what could I say? It didn't make me the most maladjusted young woman out there, did it?

"Okay, so spill it, Dad," I pressed, taking a seat and pushing my fork around my pasta.

He looked down at his plate, picked up his fork, and shoveled a forkful into his mouth.

This was new. "So, did I tell you about the dog that came in the other day just after closing?" I said. Sure, that brute of a man said I wasn't supposed to talk about it, but that was the great thing about Dad; he didn't really take anything I said in.

"No," he mumbled around his mouthful of food.

"An adorable Chihuahua, the poor thing had been shot. I got him patched up, though."

His gaze slowly moved from his plate up to meet my eyes. Maybe he really was paying attention.

But instead of responding, he stared at me with a look on his face I couldn't quite read. Sadness, maybe? Anger? Remorse? I wasn't sure. I shifted in my chair. My father was usually pretty easy to read.

"I need you to do something for me," he blurted out.

Of course, he did. Damn it. Just when I was starting to think it had been something… more. "What is it you need me to do, Dad?" I asked, stabbing my fork at my food.

"It's simple, really. No big deal," he said, but there was a strain in his voice that didn't lend much conviction to his downplaying.

I continued stabbing, my appetite long gone, while I waited for the shoe to drop.

"It's just a date, really. A date with a… young gentleman."

I laughed. This was a joke. It had to be. But my father wasn't laughing.

"This isn't a joke, Fallon. I need you to go on a date with this man."

"You want me to do what?" I was reeling, or maybe I was just stalling. I'd heard him loud and clear.

"Please, Fallon, don't look at me like that. I just… I need you to do this for me. I owe a guy a big favor—"

"And I'm supposed to be the favor? Is that it?" I slammed my fork down on the table, the sound of metal clattering hung in the air. My father had crossed a line. I hadn't realized there'd been a line, but there it was, and he'd clearly leapt right over it.

I'd been his shoulder to cry on when he should have been mine. At the ripe age of nine years old, I'd juggled making my father's coffee in the morning, cooking up my own lunch for school, and serving up dinner for him when he got home from work. I'd even gotten an apartment and opened my vet practice just a few blocks away from him so I'd be nearby in case he needed me. But this—it was too much. My father knew damn well I'd taken a leave of absence from the dating game ever since Jake. I wasn't ready. And to be thrown back into the game because he owed someone a favor? It was just too damn much.

"Please, Fallon, I need you to do this for me. If you don't... if you don't, they're going to ruin me."

Oh no. So that's what this was about. "You said you were done with all that shady stuff. Dad, you promised."

After my mother died, things had gotten strange. Strange people started showing up at the house day and night—men in suits who looked nothing like the few cop friends Dad used to bring around. They talked in whispers, and it wasn't until many years later that I understood what all those whispers were about. Money. Favors. Protection. When I'd finally confronted him on it the year I graduated college, he'd said all that stuff was over. Ancient history. But he had lied.

"Look, Fallon, I'm sorry. I never meant for anything I did to come back on you, but I need you now. I need you to do this for me. Please, baby girl, will you do this for me?" he asked with eyes that seemed a little waterier than they had a moment ago.

It could have been an act. I certainly wouldn't have put it past my father to lay on the sympathy act nice and thick. And maybe that meant I was just a sucker because I nodded, sighing as I sat back in my chair. Of course, I would do this for him. Because if I wasn't the one to take care of my father and help him clean up his messes, who would?

"Thank you, Fallon. I knew I could count on you."

Yup, he sure did. Good, old reliable Fallon to the rescue. But dear God, what I'd have given to be the one rescued for a change.

Chapter Five

Dominic

The scent of cheap liquor and cologne wafted through the air, like top notes that did little to conceal the body odor and acrid cigarette smoke smells underneath. The bar was filled with men who looked right at home here. Old men on the hunt for their lay of the day. Young men flirting with the pretty waitresses. One waitress, in particular, was damn pretty. Shy though; she kept her head down and stayed far away from the worst of the drunkards in the room. A difficult task given that there might have been just as much alcohol flowing through the veins of these men as there was blood.

This was definitely not my venue of choice, but I had a job to do. I'd been nursing the same piss-warm beer for ten minutes, waiting for my guest. The notorious Brute Hastings—not a guy who cared much about punctuality. And if I was waiting for any man other than Brute, there was no fucking way I'd still be here. Brute, the crazy motherfucker that he was, was a rare exception.

I swirled the beer around the cloudy glass, ignoring the glares I'd been getting since I walked in here. I stood out like a sore thumb in a slate gray Hugo Boss suit, but I didn't care. What did they expect me to do? Dress in old sweat- and grease-stained clothes? Even then, I'd need to give up showering for a month to really blend into the bar's patron motif. Just not fucking happening. I valued personal hygiene, and I liked the suits. They weren't just part of some mafioso uniform. Exquisitely tailored suits told the world I had style, and money, and that I was absolutely not a man to be fucked with. Easier, in my opinion, than having to teach them that lesson the hard way. I didn't have the luxury of time for that.

Although the men here weren't cut from the same cloth, they were dangerous. And they knew how to get a job done. Brute Hastings and his ragtag sons of bitches excelled in their craft. They'd been a benefit to the Luca family from the day they started working for us.

Ruthless. Tough. Like modern-day Vikings, but their steeds roared through the streets and could reach speeds of one-hundred and fifteen miles per hour. The bikers and the mafiosos had never liked each other in New York. But, in recent years, my father and I had come to realize they could be tremendously useful when we needed their brute force.

They weren't on the regular payroll—that wasn't the way Brute worked. Inconvenient at times, but I respected Brute and his men. They had a set of rules, values they lived by, just like us. And if we were going to wipe out that cartel, we wanted it done in Brute-style.

Right on cue, Brute strode in from the back of the bar and spotted me instantly—the benefit of sticking out like a sore thumb.

"Dominic, my boy!" he exclaimed, making his way across the peanut shell-covered floor with arms wide open.

I stood up and shook his hand when he reached the table. "It's good to see you, Brute."

He truly lived up to his name whether it was real or made-up. Even at my height of six feet and three inches, Brute towered over me, and his shoulders were twice as broad as the average man's. He wasn't an old man though. About my age, if I had to guess. And although bikers in this town wore leather cuts, Brute, the leader of the Old Dogs did not. Dressed in jeans and a V-neck, he looked like an ordinary man—albeit a big one.

"A round of the good stuff for me and my friend here, Ella, if you don't mind," he called to the pretty waitress who smiled gratefully and extricated herself from a group of young admirers to do his bidding.

Brute sat down, and I followed suit. Now that the patrons here saw me with their boss, his minions abandoned their evil glares and avoided eye contact like their lives depended on it. I smirked at the sight of it.

From his pocket, he pulled out a cigarette box lined with velvet then patted his pockets while the coffin nail hung from his lips.

When he came up empty-handed, I pulled out my lighter, flicked it open, and cupped the flame. He puffed in deeply and let out a satisfied *ah*.

"Could I offer you one?" he asked.

"Thank you, but I don't smoke. I quit a long time ago."

Brute chuckled. "That's funny for a guy who flirts with death on the daily, caring about his health."

His laugh was contagious. "What can I say? One less thing to worry about."

"So," he said as the laughter died away, "to what do I owe the pleasure of your company, my friend?" For some reason, he'd taken a liking to me. Maybe it was my sunny disposition? Bikers and mafiosos were generally like cats and dogs—not a good combination, even if they were forced to work together.

"I'm sure you've heard about the Free Bird's recent betrayal." There was no sense in beating around the bush. We were both busy men.

"For such a big city, news spreads fast. Of course, I heard about those idiots fucking you over. I know we're all bastards and brawlers, but would it kill them to have a shred of decency, for fuck's sake."

My sentiments precisely. I nodded.

"So, who do you need me to fuck up, my friend?" Brute flicked his cigarette in the small crystal ashtray at the center of the small table.

"We want to hit them hard and fast. We could go in guns blazing, but I think your team's particular skill set is exactly what we need."

"No one's ever called them 'my team'. I like that." Brute chuckled. "So, you're looking for a little… heat, are you? We'll teach them a lesson for messing with my buddy."

"Great. I'll see you there, *amico*."

***

Like the president in his motorcade, the McLaren was surrounded by the Old Dogs, and leading the charge was one of Brute's closest men. If nothing else, this was going to be fun. And I hadn't had a taste of that in eons.

"Now, I'm not one to question the Lucas," Brute said from the passenger seat of the McLaren, his large frame nearly spilling out of it. "But this is the last chance to change your mind, and all that shit."

"I've been called many things, *amico*, but indecisive isn't one of them." I laughed heartily, and he joined in.

The hustle and bustle of the city disappeared behind us. I didn't need to be here for this, but I wanted to be. Brute and his Old Dogs were capable men, so there was no reason to stick around and supervise. But I had never seen Brute in his element before. I'd heard countless horror stories of the things Brute had done, and I was wildly curious to see how it went down.

The Old Dogs were the fringe class, most of whom worked for drugs, booze, and, occasionally, cash. They didn't live in palaces like we did. But damn, did they have a knack for arson. And while we weren't looking for yet another war, we needed to send a message to Belemonte. A message that made it clear no one fucked with the Lucas without consequences.

The destination of the night was one of the Free Bird's main hubs, a large warehouse in a shitty area of town. The money we'd invested in our little intel gatherers had paid off. According to them, tonight was the perfect night for what I had planned. The Free Birds had just received multiple large shipments and would be hard at work cutting and repackaging their goods. What a scummy piece of shit, Belemonte. If you're going to sell drugs, at least make them pure, for fuck's sake. Too many people had died using Belemonte's cut goods, and that was just wasteful. Keep killing off your clientele, and one day, you'd have none left.

The streets were quiet and dark, with only a few riffraff wandering around. They weren't anything to worry about. The streetlamps were off, and as we stopped at the woven iron fence, we turned our engines off.

The man leading the charge pulled out a bolt cutter—where the fuck he'd been storing it, I had no idea. He cut the chains holding the front gate together like they were made of butter. The vehicles beyond the fence were abandoned, and we charged the building. A large parking lot on the right was filled up with one-ton vans—the kinds typically used for kidnappings. A decrepit warehouse took up most of the space on the property. Something told me the exterior was a façade to avert the eyes of police and citizens that passed by.

None of Belemonte's men were outside. Strange. That man was one cocky—and stupid—son of a bitch.

Brute spun on his heel and raised his sawed-off shotgun in the air—his signature weapon. "You know the drill, boys. If it moves, it dies. No one left standing but us. Wipe their stench off the face of this earth so they can meet their Maker!"

A little showy for my taste, but his men let out a battle cry so intense it was like they were standing on a battlefield, ready to lay down their lives for their fucking king. Brute sure as hell knew how to inspire his people.

Just as the ruckus died down, a shabbily dressed Free Bird stepped out from the warehouse. The signature patch of his people—a red bird in flight—was stretched tight across his flabby arm. "What the hell's going on out here?" he hollered.

Without a word, the group of Old Dogs approached the entrance and stopped a few feet short. Brute eyed the man up and down. "Hello, Chubs. We're the new landlords, and we're here to serve your eviction notice."

"Woah, buddy. You have the wrong property. I have about a million shipments to package and don't have time for this bullshit. Go along, or Harry will hear about this." Chubs held a cigarette between his lips, drawing drag after drag without pulling it away from his mouth.

Brute let out a thunderous laugh. "You think swinging that dickhead's name around is going to make me tremble in my breeches?" He shook exaggeratedly but stopped with a chuckle and spat on the ground next to him.

Brute was right. Belemonte was a piece of shit. He ran without rhyme or reason and thought he owned our streets. Back in the day, sure, he was a force to be reckoned with, but the drugs, money, and women ate his brain from the inside out. He'd lost whatever fucking mind he once had.

Chubs crossed his arms over his chest. "He'll hear about this and fuck you up, buddy."

"Oh, will he, buddy?" Brute cocked an eyebrow. "I don't think Belemonte will be hearing about this. Well, not from you, anyway." He paused as he watched Chubs inch his hand toward his pistol. It hung in a holster over his flabby hip. "Maybe he'll hear about it in the newspapers. Or in the morning, when he sees this place is up in smoke… buddy."

I chuckled under my breath.

Before he could pull out his pistol, Brute fired a shell square in his chest. One clean shot, and the guy fell backward as his cigarette tumbled next to him. Chubs was dead before he hit the ground.

I leaned against the wall to watch the show run its course. Despite my respect for Brute—the crazy, eccentric man he was—I was using him. He knew that. That's how things worked in the underbelly of New York. Business was business, and everything else came second. The Old Dogs would serve their purpose tonight. They'd do my dirty work without drawing any unwanted attention to the Luca family, leaving us free to make our next move. A move Belemonte wasn't going to see coming.

Brute ran back toward us. "Go grab the Molotovs, boys. Let's raise some fucking hell."

Ten of his men lit their Molotovs, but he grabbed a bottle from a blond boy who didn't look old enough to be allowed a beer at the sleaziest 7-11. Brute walked over to me, a gleeful glint in his eye.

"I'll give you the honorable first," Brute said, holding out the bottle.

"Well, I'll be damned. You really do have a soft spot for me," I teased. I nodded and took the bottle of liquor. Why the hell not?

While I walked up to the building, a few Old Dogs spilled gasoline along the warehouse's edge, on its walls, and through windows.

I raised the bottle in the air and chucked it then watched it explode into a vivid blaze of reds and oranges.

And then Brute's men began their assault.

"Make sure no one gets out," Brute roared. "Secure the perimeter, and burn it all to fucking ashes."

After the fiery assault on the exterior and the sound of Brute's shotgun, a few brave Free Birds tried to leave the building and make a stand. Not much of a fight though; they were shot down in seconds. The rest that tried to escape were executed.

The flames grew higher and higher. Molotovs flew inside and set it all alight as the air filled with a repugnant odor, a combination of smoke and burning narcotics—no fucking way that was good for the lungs.

I pulled out my pocket square and covered my mouth as Brute strode over, chuffed with a job well done.

"Now that's how you do it," Brute said with a smile that stretched from ear to ear. "You impressed, Luca?" There was some more shooting, but it was near finished.

I nodded. "You've done well, *amico*. I am in your debt."

There was some movement to the right where the vans were.

"Aw, shit, we hit the jackpot," someone exclaimed as the back of one van after another was thrown open.

"Boss, we got booze, drugs, money, and guns in here! We've hit the fucken' jackpot!" the blond kid said with his eyes nearly bulging wide open.

Brute scrubbed his fingers through his hair then raised an eyebrow at me. "It's your jackpot too, my friend. Want to split it fifty-fifty?"

I looked over his shoulder toward the goods. "It's all yours, Brute."

I knew how Belemonte operated, so I had no interest in his shit. Faulty guns, cut drugs, and repackaged moonshine.

"Well, shit. You're doing me a great kindness. Consider that debt you owed, paid." Brute turned around. "Round 'em up, boys. I'll call some of our men over to get the bikes. Get in these trucks and take them home!" he shouted.

"It was a damn fine pleasure working with you, Dominic." Brute put a hand on my shoulder and squeezed. "You take care of yourself. I know things are a little rocky right now, but you know you can keep me on speed dial if your family needs our firepower."

"I'll do that. Now, if you don't need anything else from me…"

"Nah, it's all good. You late for a hot date?"

I chuckled darkly. "Actually, I am."

Brute's eyes went wide. "My Dominic on a real live fucking date? I've never known you to wine and dine them."

True. Dating was messy and time-consuming. Better a no-strings-attached fuck, but this wasn't exactly an ordinary date—not that it was any of Brute's business.

Right on cue, the distant whine of sirens sounded. It was time to go.

"Ciao, amico."

"Goodbye, my friend. And good luck."

I walked back to the McLaren, listening to the crackle of flames and the roar of engines behind me. Sweet revenge. And if Belemonte wasn't certain before, he sure as hell would be now.

No one ever fucks with the Lucas.

Chapter Six

Fallon

"You're what?" Corinne shrieked. She shot up from the sofa in a flash, nearly spilling her wine.

"I'm… I'm going on a date," I admitted.

After my father left last night, I cleared the table and left the dishes unwashed in the sink. I headed to bed, but my eye lids felt like sticker paper. I watched the sun rise from my bed. When my alarm started ringing, I was pouring out my second cup of coffee for the day.

"Fallon, why didn't you tell me?" Corinne whined, grinning. "When is it? Who is it with? Oh, you called that guy with the dog, didn't you?"

She bounced up and down, jostling her perfect auburn curls.

"Ugh, that guy was as dumb as a doornail," I said, remembering the near-vacant look in his eyes.

She stuck her hands on her hips and gave me a comical glare. "Honey, you do know he doesn't need anything going on up top to be able to rock your world down below, right?" She waggled her brows as she stared meaningfully below my waist.

"Yes, I get the picture, Corinne." Even with my lack of sleep, I couldn't help but laugh.

"All right, so who's the hot date then?" she asked while excitement danced in her eyes.

I could understand her enthusiasm, but she didn't know the truth. And when I failed to join in, her face dropped and she put a hand on my shoulder.

"You do know a date is supposed to be a good thing, right?" she said with both eyebrows cocked. "A little romance, some good food… maybe a little naked nooky afterward, you know?"

I sighed—I couldn't help it. This date had nothing to do with romance, and there was no way in hell there'd be any "naked nooky" afterward. This was a "favor", not a booty call.

She took my hand in hers. "Why do you seem so upset? Shouldn't you be excited?"

Excited? Hardly. But since the date was in less than an hour, and I'd agreed to go, I needed to get ready. Time to confess and move on. "I don't know who it's with, Corinne, but I'm guessing it's some rich politician's son."

Corinne frowned, the recesses in her brows grew deeper. "You know how stupid that sounds, right?"

"It's a favor for my dad," I admitted, hating the way it made me feel all slimy inside. Did my father really not understand that this made me feel like a "thing" being offered up as payment? Or did he just not care?

She shook her head and crossed her arms over her chest. "A favor? A favor is, 'Hey, can I borrow a dress for a thing I'm going to?' or 'My car battery died, would you mind giving me a boost?'"

"Yeah, well, you know Dad."

She really did. She was the only living soul I'd ever told about what my father was like.

"Yes, and I know you're not a child anymore. He can't keep using you like this—it's a dick move, and you know it."

"I need to be ready in an hour. So, will you help me?" I said instead.

Corinne eyed me for a moment but couldn't keep a straight face. "Of course, I'll help you. What kind of stupid question is that?"

Corinne was silent as she led me down the hall to my bedroom and sat me down in front of the small vanity mirror in the corner.

"All right, I've reconsidered, and I think tonight is a great idea," she said with a wicked grin as she grabbed a brush and got to work.

"You do?"

"Absolutely. You said he's some rich kid, right?"

I nodded while she pulled and twisted my hair into intricate knots that seemed to stay in place by pure magic. She could have been a hairstylist to celebrities—not that I would have given up my best friend and hardest worker to Hollywood.

"All right, so here's what you're going to do. First, you're going to look so damn hot you'll knock this guy's socks off—I personally guarantee it. You're going to let him buy you a ridiculously expensive meal in some pansy-ass restaurant all while you drink in the appreciative looks from every man around you. And then, when the evening is over…" She smiled slyly, stabbing a crystal-topped bobby pin into the loose pile of knots gathered at my crown. "You'll let him kiss you good and thorough—because you need something for those long, lonely nights, hon. And then you'll turn around and let him watch your sweet ass walk away."

I laughed. "You seem to have this all figured out."

"Well, if it were me, I'd jump his bones if he was good-looking enough. But I figured you'd just give me the evil eye if I proposed it."

"You're… not wrong," I choked out through a continuous wave of laughter. Leave it to Corinne to be able to cheer me up, no matter the occasion.

"Your hair is done," she said, grabbing my hand and dragging me across the room to the closet. "Next, we move onto clothing."

She opened the closet door and peered inside before pulling out a dozen dresses on hangers from the back. All the dresses I owned, in fact. She tossed one after another onto the bed until she reached the eighth or ninth dress from the stack. A cream-colored Grecian-style dress. It was beautiful—I'd bought it on a whim not long before I found out Jake spent his lunch breaks with his secretary sprawled across his desk. Aside from trying it on in the dressing room, I'd never actually worn it yet. It fell just above my knees, and it was strapless aside from the gold braided cord that wrapped beneath my breasts and tied at the back of my neck.

"This is the one," Corinne said, shoving it at me.

She picked out a pair of twisted gold hoop earrings and a chunky gold bracelet to match the dress while I changed. She also dug out a pair of strappy high-heeled sandals from my closet floor. I put them all on obligingly, but when she took out her overstuffed makeup bag from her purse, I called a time-out.

"Haven't we done enough dressing me up like Barbie?" I whined, though there was no denying she'd done a good job. I barely recognized the woman staring back at me in the mirror. But I'd let Corinne do my makeup before and it felt like I had a pound of butter on my face.

"Just trust me, hon," she said as she took out a few brushes and palettes.

I pressed my lips together but sat still while she went to work. Surprisingly, she finished in two minutes flat.

"There," she said, stepping back so I could see my reflection.

The woman was a magician. A little mascara, a touch of highlighter on my cheeks and brow, and a bloodred lipstick that even made me think of all things dark and sinful.

"You look good enough to eat." Corinne nodded in approval. "I'd fuck you."

I blushed. There was no better compliment. "If you don't stop flirting with me, Corinne, I just might have to call this date off and spend the night with you."

Corinne winked at me and leaned in close. "You couldn't handle a night with me, babe," she whispered.

I laughed. But she was probably right.

Corinne checked her watch, and her eyes went wide. "Damn, time's up. You've got to go and make that rich boy drool."

"I'll do my best," I said, but really, what did I care whether some rich politician's son eyeballed me all night? "Love you, Corinne. I'll see you tomorrow. And please, make sure to lock everything and turn the lights off before you leave."

Corinne followed me out to the living room to see me off, and I made my way outside. But halfway down the stairs to the building's main floor, my hands started to tremble. Why the hell was I nervous? Sure, I hadn't been on many dates after Jake, but it wasn't like this was even a real date. *You can do this, Moore. Just get through the night, and you'll never have to see this rich snob again.*

When I got to the base of the stairs, leading to a hallway lined with pastel lime tiles, I gulped. One final push out of the building and onto the street where my blind date awaited.

But I did it anyway, no matter how much it scared me. I kept my eyes down as I walked outside, rummaging through my bag to ensure I had everything I needed. Cellphone? Check. Wallet? Check. Pepper spray? Absolutely. The three things a woman should never leave home without.

When I stopped near the curb, I finally looked up and the knots in my stomach twisted more. A limousine. A goddamn *limousine*. It was like a flashing sign that said, "Look at me, I've got money."

This night just kept getting better and better.

I glanced up at the window of my apartment, maybe hoping Corinne had tossed a lifeline down to me. Instead, her pretty face peeked out from behind the curtain. She shook her head then gave me an encouraging thumbs-up. So nosy. I scrunched my nose, chuckling.

A large man, built like a brick house, stepped out from the front passenger side of the money train. He wore a plain black suit that looked like it would rip if he flexed his arms too hard. His skin was either tanned or naturally olive.

"Ma'am," he said as he made his way past me to the very back of the garishly long vehicle. He opened the door and gestured for me to enter.

I stepped toward it, ducking my head, and looking inside.

"Oh, hell no," I said.

What the hell was *he* doing here?

Dominic, donning an impeccably crisp suit, sat on the far end of the seat. It was a warm gray sharkskin material, and it fit his Superman body to a tee. He stared off out of the window as if he didn't even notice the car door had opened. His pocket square was gold with red accents, which matched his maroon tie. Did he always wear suits? That had to be uncomfortable. Didn't he ever kick it back and wear sweats or something?

When he finally looked at me, his gray eyes made all the blood in my body rush to my fingertips. He practically licked his lips while he gave me a once-over. Warmth spread in my cheeks, I suddenly wanted to cover up. I dressed like *this* for *him*?

"Please, join me, Miss Moore."

"I'm not going on a damn date with *you*." I crossed my arms over my chest. Dominic's eyes settled on my chest, where I had accidentally squeezed my cleavage even closer together. Awkwardly, I let my arms fall back down to my sides.

"Yes, you are," he said in a voice that brooked no refusal. The look in his eye told me that he'd probably never heard the word "no" his entire life.

Just the buttery tone of this man's voice made the butterflies in my stomach explode. But I also wanted to pull his stupid silk tie and watch his stupid gray eyes bulge out. *What the hell is wrong with me?*

If I was being honest, though, I knew what it was. It was my most fatal dating flaw—my ridiculous fascination with men who knew exactly what they wanted and weren't afraid to make it known. Strong. Confident. Domineering, even. And one hundred percent a bad idea. Jake had been that kind of guy, and when he'd decided what he wanted was his twenty-year-old secretary, he'd had no trouble making it known.

But for now, I was trapped. I'd agreed to do this. So, with one final look back at my apartment window, I slipped inside.

I didn't know what to say to him. Did I say hi? What the hell would anyone else say in this situation? Corinne would jump straight into some great fun conversation that would leave everyone laughing.

Dominic turned in his seat to face me. The door closed behind me, and the limo's engine came to life.

"Fancy meeting you here, Miss Moore," he said with an amused twinkle in his eyes. "You look… nice." He spoke slowly while his eyes raked over my body.

This was Corinne's fault—she'd dressed me up like some sexy siren. "I know," I said bluntly, glaring at his suit, looking unimpressed while I secretly wondered how much it had cost, and if he had earned the money himself, or if he was just another spoiled rich kid.

"You look… expensive," I said with as much disdain in my voice as I could manage. He probably thought it was a compliment.

"Thank you," he said, but whether in jest or because he'd taken it as a compliment, I didn't know.

Silence stretched between us as the limo took us… wherever we were going. Every moment though, I could feel it—the tiny sparks snapping in the air between us. But why? Sure, the man was ridiculously attractive—really, there should be a law against rich pricks looking so good—and there was definitely something about the way he sat up straight with his chin tipped up just enough to say he was as confident as they come. But damn it, I knew better. I already knew this guy was a grade A jerk.

He grinned at me when the car stopped in front of a building. Both doors were opened by his… what were they? Bodyguards? Why did he need bodyguards? They were bodyguards, right? Normal people weren't that jacked for no reason. They had to be there for protection. When I joined him at the entrance of our destination, it was a shock to see how big they really were. Dominic was well over six feet tall, but his hulking masses for chaperones towered over him. Honestly, I was a little scared of them. They kind of looked ready to beat the living daylights out of anyone who looked at Dominic funny.

His two dogs followed us to the door and remained there when we went inside. The floor was packed with people—people who were clearly dressed better than I was. Elegant floor-length gowns. Enough diamonds to start up a Tiffany's franchise. Even the tables were better dressed than I was with their crystal glasses, shiny silverware, and lavish floral arrangements. Outshined by a dinner table—this was definitely not my night.

People stared as we were led through the building to a private room. A goddamned VIP area in a fine dining restaurant. My mouth was dry as a desert when we sat down, and I was about ready to crawl under the table when I caught sight of the view outside the floor-to-ceiling windows next to me. It was breathtaking. A wide open view of Jamaica Bay. The city lights painted a magnificent picture on the surface of the water while the sound of the soft, gentle lap of waves slipped through the glass and wrapped around me like a cocoon.

"It's beautiful," I whispered in awe.

"It is," he said, though there was no wonder in his tone. The view didn't impress him; he'd probably seen it a thousand times, sitting right here across a different girl every time.

The cocoon slipped away, and I ripped my gaze away from the tranquil scene outside.

"Impressed, Miss Moore?" he asked, like the answer was obvious.

"Please don't call me that. I'm not your middle school teacher," I snapped at him. I had a name, and he knew it, so why couldn't he use it?

"My apologies, *Fallon*. What's got you so grouchy?"

"Grouchy?" I raised an eyebrow at him, but he just smiled. "I'm not."

"Well, you're being awfully short with me."

"*Well*, maybe I'd be a little less 'short' with you if you hadn't been such a dick that night."

He put a hand to his chest, his palm flat against it. "*Me?* An asshole? I don't know what you're talking about."

"I called you a dick, not an ass. There's a difference," I huffed.

"Hmm," he said with a devious grin. "It's good to know you're well-versed in male anatomy."

I opened my mouth to retort, but words escaped me. *Damn it.*

If that wasn't bad enough, the smug smile on his too-handsome face clearly meant he knew he had me flustered.

But instead of pressing his advantage, he sat back in his chair. "Why don't we get some food and wine into you, beautiful? Maybe that will help take the edge off."

"Fallon. My name is Fallon," I ground out, but before he could come up with another snide comment, the waiter came to my rescue.

The waiter wore a tuxedo and had recommendations for wine pairings for the meals we chose. I ordered something that was in a different language and had to point at the menu instead of saying it out loud. There was nothing quite like feeling inferior to a freaking menu.

"Something wrong, Fallon?" Dominic asked as the waiter left our table.

"Nothing," I said. "I'm just not used to ordering food from a menu I can't read."

He frowned at me, and it made me want to punch him right in his chiseled jaw. "Are you trying to tell me you've never had a fine dining experience before?"

I shook my head.

"Your father never brought you to places like this?" He seemed genuinely perplexed. Did he not realize that not every family had the money to spend hundreds of dollars on a single meal?

"Never," I said with my nose in the air. There was no way I was going to feel bad about my modest upbringing. My father had provided for me as well as he could. At least, that's the lie I chose to believe.

"I suppose you're in for one hell of a treat. I bet you'll love it. If you don't, then I lose," he said, flashing me a thousand-watt smile.

"What do I get for winning?" I glared at him.

"What does your heart desire?" He took a sip of his drink and eyed me over his glass. I wasn't quite sure how a person's eyes could be screaming "sex" but if eyes could do that, his definitely were.

I had to look away. Again, I was saved. Our food arrived. They didn't bring only what we ordered, but an entire spread that filled the table. I had to admit that if nothing else, the food looked Instagram-ready.

While we ate, Dominic asked about my work, my friends, if I had any pets, and all the other lame questions people asked on first dates, like it was some sort of interview. From the way he looked and acted, I expected him to be the sort to constantly talk about himself.

"So, what did you think?" Dominic asked as the waiter cleared away what was left of the food. "Did I win the bet?"

"I didn't realize we were betting."

"We were. And since you look thoroughly pleased by the meal, I think it's fair to say I won," he said with a smug grin that was almost cute.

"I will admit I've never eaten anything quite so good," I conceded.

His smile turned devilish. Nothing "cute" remained. "Then I think it's only fair that I collect my winnings," he said.

Before I could ask what he was talking about, he swooped in. His lips pressed against mine with enough force to know this was no quick victory kiss, but not quite so hard that I couldn't have pulled away if I'd wanted to. Which I did… and yet, I remained there as his tongue plied against the seam of my lips, and tiny tremors of something dark and forbidden shot through me. Dear God, what the hell was I doing? I must have lost my mind because I opened for him, but the moment I did, he pulled away.

He sat back in his chair unruffled and picked up the small dessert menu that had been left on the table.

"Ready for dessert?" he asked, glancing up from the menu. Though he kept a straight face, I could see it there in the corners of his eyes—the smugness that came from knowing he'd thrown me for a loop.

"Yes," I said, sitting up straight and acting like I wasn't the least bit flustered by that kiss.

He held up a hand, and a waiter came running over within seconds. Saving me from another embarrassing attempt at the menu, Dominic ordered for me. Then he nodded at the waiter who bowed before leaving.

"You're not having dessert?"

"I don't like sweets," he said, clearing his throat.

A thick silence fell upon us.

"So, um… I've told you plenty about me. What about you?" I said, decidedly ignoring the thick tension that seemed to strangle me in place.

"What about me?" he said, cocking an eyebrow. Even the guy's eyebrows were stupidly sexy. Was that even possible?

"How about, what do you do for a living?"

He looked away and cleared his throat. "I do odd jobs here and there."

The guy hardly struck me as unemployed. "What kind of odd jobs?"

"This and that," he hedged.

I rolled my eyes. "Okay, how about, why did my father set us up on this date? What kind of favor is that?"

"Your father arranged our date as a favor to my father. And as for why… Would you believe I found you to be the most intriguing woman I'd ever met the other night? That I wanted to get to know you better?"

The guy had been a primo asshole that night, and nothing about his demeanor hinted that he found me to be anything other than a giant pain in his ass.

"Who is your father?" I asked since the other line of questioning was getting me nowhere.

"He's an important man. He thought it was time I got back into the dating… scene."

Oh.

So, Dominic didn't want to be here any more than I did. His father had pushed him into it too. For just a moment, I felt a spark of something more than attraction to this man. It was a spark of camaraderie that I hadn't expected. Dominic had been avoiding dating, just like me, and here we both were, forced together by our fathers.

"He thought I'd spent enough time hopping from one woman's bed to the next, and insisted I try something… different."

Ssss. Just like that, the spark fizzled out like a Dr Pepper being cracked open. Dominic didn't avoid dating to avoid getting hurt; he avoided dating so he didn't have to worry about being tied down to one woman. Just freaking wonderful. A rich playboy.

"Well, don't let me keep you from your bed-hopping," I said with more bitterness in my voice than I'd intended to let slip through.

He eyed me strangely, like I was a puzzle he couldn't quite put together right. "You asked me a question, and I gave you an answer. It seems a little unfair that you're glaring daggers at me over here."

Maybe it was unfair of me, but too fucking bad. He was just another jerk who slept with every cute little thing he spoiled with his money and fancy restaurants.

"Sit down, Fallon," he said in that same voice that made the butterflies in my stomach go wild.

I hadn't even realized I'd stood up, but I had no intention of sitting back down. "Don't tell me what to do." I slammed my open palms down on the table. "I don't know who the hell you are—clearly, you don't want to tell me—and I don't know what you want with me, but this date is just a farce, and it's time for it to be over." I grabbed my wallet from my purse, withdrew a few bills, and threw them on the table. I had no idea if it was too little or too much, but I couldn't stand to be in a room with him any longer.

"I'm your ride, Miss Moore." He sniffed loudly. "*Sit down.*"

There was that tone again, and though a teeny tiny part of me sparked to it, it damn sure wasn't enough to keep me in this man's vicinity any longer. "I would rather walk home on hot coals than spend another minute here with you, Mister… Oh hell, I don't even know your last name. Goodnight, Dominic."

I turned away and strode out of the restaurant, keeping my eyes down and pretending there weren't dozens of Chanel-laden people staring at me.

Chapter Seven

Dominic

"Fuck!" I roared, chucking the glass of whiskey in my hand across the room. I watched it smash against a wall opposite me, but somehow, it did nothing to alleviate the frustration coursing through my veins.

This wasn't how tonight was supposed to go at all. The woman had my blood boiling within just a split second of opening her mouth. I'd wined and dined her, just like a guy's supposed to do—and at the best restaurant in the city, no less. I groaned, my jaw clenching tight.

Maybe it was time to call it and do things the easy way. Send our guys to grab her one night when she was closing up the clinic? Have them bring her to the family home and keep her there? My family wasn't really down with kidnapping, but sometimes things just needed to be done—whether they fucking liked them or not. I sure as fuck didn't want to get married. Why the hell wasn't someone trying to wine and dine, and sweet-talk me into the fucked-up state of matrimony? The reason: because it was just something that needed to be done—whether I liked it or not. Maybe it was time Miss Fallon Moore learned about doing what needed to be done.

I dropped down into the chair behind my desk and scrubbed my fingers through my hair. Maybe I could rub out the memories of the monumental failure of a date and forget I'd ever agreed to Douglas Moore's ridiculous plan. Perhaps I could erase the memory of Fallon in that sexy-as-fuck dress. And the way she toyed with her bottom lip when we walked into that restaurant, clearly out of her element. And the way her eyes flared with blue fire when she got pissed off. Scrub it all away, and do this the way it should have been done.

It was the smart plan. But as I tried to plan it in my head, Fallon's eyes popped up there and wouldn't leave. Innocent eyes, like Sofia's, in a way. Neither of them had been polluted by the cold, dark world I lived in. Sofia never would be; she'd died sweet and innocent. But if I did this, it would all be gone for Fallon. No more innocence. No more believing in fairy tales or fucked up fantasies, or whatever the hell it was that made her look pure and untainted even in that crazy sexy dress. There would just be the real world. My world.

"Fuck," I groaned, not for the first time in the past hour. The woman was maddening, but I couldn't do it. And that left me backed into a corner with only one way out: I was going to have to romance the hell out of the infuriating-as-hell Fallon Moore. And that meant finding a way to repair whatever had sent her storming out last night.

Fucking hell, this was going to suck because I knew just where to start.

With worms squirming beneath my skin, I yanked out my cell phone and hit the speed dial for Leo. Leo. The last guy I wanted to turn to for help at the moment. Unfortunately, Leo was also the only guy I could think of who had a way with women beyond getting them into bed.

He picked up on the second ring. "Hey, Dom. What's up?"

"I need some damage control." I could feel a headache growing in the back of my skull.

"Damage control?" he said, the tone of his voice changing in an instant from laid-back to high alert. "What happened?"

"Nothing happened," I snapped, still chewing on the words I was going to have to spit out eventually.

"Okay… So, what's up?"

"I fucked up last night. I just need some help patching it up."

"Last night? What are you talking about? You were with that Moore girl… Whoa, hold on."

I could hear Leo laughing despite his attempt to cover up the mouthpiece. Goddamn son of a bitch.

"For fuck's sake, Leo. Could you please try to take this seriously for a minute?"

"Okay," he said, trying for serious but falling about a mile short. "So, the great Dominic Luca is having lady trouble, is he?"

"I'm not having 'lady' trouble. If you've got a woman looking for a good fuck, I'm your man. But flowers, walks on the beach, and that shit…"

"All right, I get it. And because I'm such a good brother, I'm going to help you, but it'll cost you." He really was enjoying this, wasn't he?

"Cost me what?" I spat.

"Oh, I don't know. I'll stick this favor in my pocket for a while and get back to you. For now, why don't you tell me what happened?"

And so I told him everything, from the moment Fallon walked out of her apartment to the minute she stormed out of the restaurant.

"So, you basically told the poor woman your only interest was in getting laid as often as possible… and you're surprised the date didn't go well?"

When he put it that way, it didn't sound so good. But I'd only been trying to be honest—a new leaf and all that shit.

"All right," Leo said, putting on his serious tone—about fucking time. "Here's what you're going to do…"

***

In the morning, I made a few calls, and my men brought everything over within an hour. I took a deep breath, got in my car, and drove as fast as I could to her apartment. Like some stalker, I waited for her outside of her second floor walk-up. Its brick face was hideous, decades old and crumbling. Although not necessarily in a bad area, I wouldn't predict a real-estate boom in here in the next fifty years.

The apartment door opened, and I stepped into view. Like last night, she was rifling through her bag and just kept walking. She bumped right into me and let out a little scream.

It was damn cute, but I did my best not to smile at her discomfiture. I didn't need Leo to tell me that was a bad idea. I cleared my throat and stepped back to give her space. "Hi Fallon," I said with a lopsided grin.

Fallon gave me the same look as last night, the look that said she wouldn't be terribly opposed to giving me a hard shove into traffic. "What do you want? Didn't I tell you that I'm not interested?"

"Well, technically, you didn't." I chuckled, my hands behind my back.

It looked like she wanted to laugh, but she didn't and let out a sigh. "Fine. What is it?"

"I think we got off on the wrong foot. I was an idiot. No, I was a dickhead yesterday, and when we met."

She looked me up and down, lingering on my crotch before her gaze met mine.

"You were definitely a total dickhole." On any other woman, that potty mouth would have been a turnoff. On Fallon, it was really fucking cute.

"Okay, hear me out. I wasn't lying when I said I haven't exactly been the relationship-type guy up until now, but the thing is, I'd like to be. And I like that you're not just beautiful, but you're witty and kind and passionate about the things that are important to you… like the animals you work with." I was speaking out of my ass, and I felt like a schoolboy all over again, fumbling over my words. "I'll make it right."

I could feel the tension around her begin to dissipate while her expression turned contemplative rather than contentious. She was considering it. Leo had been right that honesty dressed up with a few compliments was a good way to lead in. The strange thing was, though, I hadn't had to search for the compliments. Fallon really did seem to be all those things. It was too bad she also had the temper of a firecracker, or maybe this marriage thing wouldn't have been the worst damn idea in the world.

"All right, let's say I'm considering it. How do you propose we move forward?" She raised one perfectly arched eyebrow, but she was in. I could feel it in the spark that had reignited in the air between us.

Just for good measure, though. "I'll answer one question"—since she'd been so keen on answers last night—"But the rest will have to wait until we go on a date again. Deal?"

She nodded and couldn't stop the quiver of a smile that turned up the corners of her pretty lips. "Deal."

"My family are investment bankers," I said, though the lie tried to stick in my throat. "I was embarrassed to admit it to you because you were right that night at the vet office. I grew up spoiled, and I didn't want you to think less of me because I do work my ass off. Everything I have, I've worked myself to the bone for." It was true that I'd worked my ass off, so there was some semblance of truth to my lie. Did that make it better? And why did I care? I was standing here, practically begging her to give me another chance. Wasn't that enough? I didn't beg anyone for anything. I took what I wanted, when I wanted.

"Thank you," she said with more sincerity than my lie deserved. It made an unfamiliar feeling bubble up inside me that seemed an awful lot like guilt.

Thrusting the feeling aside, I pulled out the bouquet of flowers I'd been hiding behind my back. Leo had said roses, but my mother loved lilies, and that had felt like the right way to go. "I brought you a peace offering," I said.

The way her eyes lit up told me I'd made the right choice. Roses were boring, and I had a feeling Fallon was anything but boring.

"They're beautiful," she said, as she pressed her nose between the bright pink blooms, breathing in the light, sweet scent.

"You're beautiful," I said, not because it was part of the script, but because it was true.

She smiled. "All right, you're out of the dog house… for now."

"So, you'll give me one more chance?"

She pressed her lips together, and her expression turned serious.

"If I'm an asshole, you have permission to punch me in the dick," I joked, putting up my hands in mock-surrender, partly to try to convince her, but partly just because I knew it would make her smile.

And finally, one of my jokes made her laugh. It was loud, and it was unrestrained, and full of warmth and light.

"All right, Dominic, I will give you another chance. I do understand what it's like to have a parent pressuring you. But no more clamming up every time I ask you a question. If we're going to do this, then I'd like the chance to get to know you. Deal?"

"Deal," I said, smiling at the way she'd turned the tables. "I won't let you down, limone."

"Limone?" she repeated, her blonde waves glittering off the sun. She tilted her head and scrunched her nose as if she'd just eaten a Sour Patch.

"Oh, would you look at that?" I said, glancing at my watch. "Our time's up. I'll see you around. I'll text you a date and time."

I shoved my hands in my pockets and walked off before she could respond.

The hot air that drifted up from the vents from the underground subway turned to steam as it rose up around me and combined with the cold morning air. Without looking back, I got in my car and sped off. The encounter left me feeling humiliated, but maybe not as much as I'd thought it would. I'd accomplished what I'd come here to do, and now I had business that needed tending.

***

The nightclub was on neutral ground, but I was still treated like royalty the second I set foot inside it. I sat down at a table near the bar and watched as the prettiest waitress—a blonde with a killer rack and an ass to match—headed straight for me.

"What can I get for you, handsome?" she asked, batting her pretty eyelashes at me.

"A whiskey, straight up, please," I said then turned to watch the door, waiting for my men to arrive.

The blonde returned with my drink and a knowing smile, but if she was hoping for anything more than money for the drink and a hefty tip, she was out of luck tonight. It had been a long day, and I had one last job to do. My body felt sluggish, like I was trudging through mud with each step I took.

My men joined me at the table a few minutes later and didn't bother ordering anything for themselves. Last call was soon, and we needed the place empty.

Girls too young to be drinking and men too old for the girls finished off the last of their poison. The lights turned on and burned my eyes, like the start of a migraine. Seeing a nightclub under bright light, even an upper class one, didn't feel right. It was filthy and seemed wrong without its dark and dingy atmosphere. Waitresses did the last bits of cleaning, turned the chairs over, and set them atop tables. They counted their tips for the day, some left looking defeated, and others like they were on top of the world. The ones brave enough to dress the most scantily were the happiest, and the blonde seemed the happiest of them all. She gave me one last hopeful glance, then turned away, tucking her night's earnings into the bra beneath her low-cut shirt.

"Excuse me, uhm, sir," a manager said. "We're closing."

"I know. We won't be leaving," I said, not bothering to make eye contact. I downed the rest of my drink.

"It's past two in the morning," he said, stuttering.

"Then go home, chum," I said. "We'll lock up."

When I finally looked up, recognition dawned in his face. His eyes darted between me and the four men sitting around the table. Sweat beading down his forehead, he scurried off without another glance.

"Right. Looks like everyone's out. It's time," I said, standing up, as my lapdogs followed suit.

I started toward the bar, which spanned the length of the back of the club. Behind the shelves was a mirror, and I caught a glimpse of my reflection. Damn. I looked exhausted. The dark circles under my eyes made me look like I'd died a week ago. Oh well, dead men walking could still get a job done.

The door to the left of the bar led to a staircase, which went up to an office. The prick who owned the place overlooked the dance floor from his desk through double-sided glass. Voyeuristic creep.

He was still in his office, his back to us as he hunched over a sleek glass desk. The rest of the room matched with the modern centerpiece. Stainless steel artwork on the walls, graphite suede wingback chairs. It all seemed a bit pretentious to me.

The globe-shaped lights overhead glinted off the bald circle at the top of the man's head while thin tufts of hair stood on end all around it. His sport coat was about two sizes too big for him, making him look like a balding child in adult clothing.

Bradley Miller had been causing problems in the community for as long as I could remember, beating up hookers, selling drugs to kids. I was a teenager when I first heard about some of the shit he pulled, and his name left a sour taste in my mouth.

I nodded at my men, and Marco, my favorite, who had the temper of a Rottweiler, took his baseball bat to a glass shelf against the wall. It shattered into a million pieces, and the sculptures, books, and trinkets crashed to the ground.

"What the fuck?" Miller screamed, nearly falling out of his chair. He spun around to face us and slammed his laptop closed.

My big Rottweiler smashed a vase off of a table, shattering the coffee table.

"Bradley Miller," I said.

"What the hell are you doing? Who are you?" he asked.

Any other day I would have been pissed that he didn't know who I was, but I was in a giving mood so I wasn't going to punish him for the disrespect.

I walked up to his desk, the glass crushing beneath my Cordovan shoes. I stopped just short of his desk. He probably had an interior designer who'd told him the glass would make the room feel bigger. It was smudged with fingerprints.

"Wouldn't you like to know?" I said. "I don't think you're in the position to be asking me any questions right now."

"What do you want? Money? I can get you money!" he whimpered. The buttons of his shirt looked like it was just about ready to pop off, while the loose skin of his turkey neck draped above his yellowed collar. If I didn't have a stomach of steel, it would have made me gag.

I laughed, the sound so loud and boisterous it filled the room. Over the years, I had learned that it was one hell of a tactic to make people uncomfortable. Miller slicked back his graying hair with sweaty palms.

I wiped a fake tear from my eye when I stopped laughing. "Money? You think I want your filthy money, you piece of shit?"

My men walked up on either side of him while two stayed behind. Marco, my baseball bat boy, eyed the glass desk with such ferocity like it was a piece of meat dangling over a lion's head. He really liked smashing things, and that's why I'd gotten him that baseball bat with his name embossed on its sweet spot. It read "Marco" in cursive, and it was the last thing many men saw before it connected with their faces and knocked their lights out.

"Then what is it?" Miller mumbled. He was terrified, like a little Chihuahua, I would have said, but that would have been a disservice to Bullet's recent bravery.

"You've been a bad, bad boy, old man. Word around town spreads fast," I said.

"W-what? Is this about that incident with the waitress? I already handled that with HR!"

I pinched the bridge of my nose. How long was his list of sins, really? "Our women talk. And they've had a lot to say about you."

His eyes widened as reality set in.

"Good boy. It's finally clicking, isn't it?" I said.

He nodded his head limply.

"How many women have you beaten since you started using our services?"

"Your services?" Bradley said. "Fuck. You own the brothels, don't you? Look, man, I can pay you for the damage. How much? Ten thousand? Twenty? Fifty? Whatever you want, I just need this to be kept silent."

He thought he could buy me? What a fool. Nevertheless, I nodded to Marco to stand down just to see what Miller would do.

He stumbled across the room and yanked a painting off the wall. His fingers shook as he fiddled with the combination on the cheap-as-shit safe concealed there. His password was one-two-three-five-four. Dumbass.

Miller desperately pulled out stacks and stacks of hundreds. I could see the sweat that had beaded up across his forehead drip down his temples and over his bushy eyebrows. He tried to wipe the sweat away with one hand while he fumbled to gather the stacks of Benjamins in his arms. Some fell to the floor as he made his way back to us and dropped it onto the desk.

"H-here. Is this good?" he asked.

I picked up one of the stacks tied together with a rubber band. My fingers felt slimy just touching his dirty cash, and I couldn't help but wonder how many women he'd exploited to get it?

I tilted my head left to right, though I'd never had any intention of taking his filthy money. "No."

Bradley visited our brothels many times, beating and torturing our women, but he spaced it out, rotating between dozens of brothels all over Queens, thinking he could disappear and never get caught. But I did.

The women who worked at our brothels deserved respect. The work was tough enough, and having the likes of Miller hurting our women wouldn't stand. We didn't operate our brothels like others did. We took a cut of the money, of course, but we paid for the women's healthcare and taxes. In the eyes of the law, our girls were formally employed, and they would never be thrown in a cell because our grounds were heavily protected—thanks to Douglas.

I nodded at Marco to give him the go-ahead. I appreciated men like Marco who could understand what it was I wanted without having to say a word.

With a sinister smile, he raised his bat above his head and smashed it down into the desk. Miller backed off from the glass, his eyes wide with fear. If he didn't want this to happen, he shouldn't have been such a depraved piece of shit.

"Bad deeds don't go unpunished in this town," I said. "You've done too many wrongs for us to turn a blind eye. A fistful of dollars won't fix the sick shit you did."

"Please, man! I-it's just my wife and I h-have been having p-problems for years... and I-I need something for... my needs. Y-you can understand that as a... man, right?" Miller said.

How dare he compare himself to me? Miller wasn't a man; he was an animal, and rabid animals needed to be put down.

Two of my men pinned him against the window that overlooked the club. He tried to fight it, but they were far too strong for him.

"The only way to make this right is to get rid of disgusting vermin like you. Repeat offenders don't get cured overnight." I paused, looking him over. "I don't care that your wife doesn't want to screw you. She has good reason not to, considering the shit you're into. I'm just glad you don't have any daughters."

Marco connected a swing with Bradley's right knee, resulting in a satisfying crack. He howled in pain but my men held him in place, stopping him from dropping to the ground.

"You owe us a lot of money, but that's the least of your problems. It's about what's right. And wrong."

His eyes narrowed and his face turned red. I could see the veins throbbing in his temples. And there it was. Stage two, anger. "Who the hell are you to be my judge and jury? You've never done any wrong in your life?"

"I've done many, many bad things, but I've never exploited the innocent."

I walked up to him and looked down at the pathetic rolls of useless flesh. His brow was coated in a layer of sweat. I balled my fist, cocked back, and rammed it into his face. The force shot his head backward into the window behind him, shattering the glass.

He roared in pain, but with his arms held firmly, he was powerless to escape it. "The Novas will hear about this!" he seethed, resorting to threats.

"I don't think they will. Did they blackmail you into being your protection?" Fucking coward. I punched him again, this time, in the stomach.

He groaned while his body tried to double over, but he was trapped.

"Let me guess. You had several attacks, robberies, and assaults at your club. And then, magically, one day, the Novas came to your rescue, offering protection in exchange for money?"

"How the fuck… did you know that?" he croaked out between gasps.

"Because that's what us scumbags do." I shook my head. The reminder of the Novas exhausted me to the bone. They weren't much of a problem just yet, but they could be.

I stepped away and left Marco and his boys to it. Bats, the back of guns, fists, and boots. My job here was done.

"I'll see you tomorrow, Marco. Leave him alive, leave him dead, I don't care," I said over my shoulder, "You be the judge, jury, and executioner."

"Hmm," his deep voice came from behind me.

I left, went home, and wearily fell into bed half-dressed.

Chapter Eight

Dominic

The gentle evening breeze was too warm. The lap of the waves against the shore was too loud. The vague briny scent of the seaweed and water had somehow managed to infuse itself into every bite of the risotto in front of me. And the woman sitting across from me had spent the past ten minutes pushing food around her plate with her fork. What the hell had I been thinking?

I'd seen the way Fallon had stared out at the bay from inside the restaurant on our last date. This was supposed to be perfect. A private dinner on the outdoor patio of a five-star restaurant, overlooking Jamaica Bay. It had started out all right. The way she'd smiled, the way the light of the moon had shone in her wide, excited eyes. I wasn't sure I'd ever seen anything more beautiful.

Now, we were quiet, uncomfortable. This would have been so much easier if the end goal was simply to get her into my bed. As much as she seemed to dislike me, her body didn't. I could see it in the liquid heat in her eyes when she looked at me, and I could feel it in the air that was practically combusting between us. But this wasn't supposed to be about sex. It was supposed to be about something more. The problem was I didn't fucking want more. I wanted Fallon naked in my bed, and tomorrow, I wanted to move on. That's what I did. That's what I was good at. Trying to converse with a woman who was as sweet as sugar one minute and as sour as lemon the next drained the energy I didn't have to spare.

"So, um, what's your favorite color?" Fallon asked, still pushing food around on her plate.

"My favorite color?" Just great. Now we were resorting to small talk? And even if I wanted to jump on board this pathetic train, I didn't have a favorite color, probably because I wasn't in the sixth grade anymore.

"Red." The word slipped out unbidden. Red like all the blood I'd cleaned off my hands. Red like the bloodshot eyes that stared back at me in the mirror some mornings. Red like the rage that clouded my vision sometimes. That was apparently my favorite color. Then again, it was also the color of Fallon's dress that was hugging her curves and offering a tantalizing peek at the upper swells of her breasts. It was the color of the lipstick she wore that shined like the juiciest thing I'd ever seen when she swept her tongue across her lips.

"What's yours?" I asked because now I was curious, not really about her favorite color, but why she'd chosen it.

"Blue, like the sky and the ocean," she said, nodding toward the water. "They're both so big, but I could stare at them endlessly and never tire of it. It's calming, I guess." She shrugged then smiled a little awkwardly, like she'd said more than she'd been expecting.

The sky and the ocean? This woman was too innocent for her own good. Next, she was going to tell me she spent her free time picking daisies and chasing rainbows.

"Don't you think so? That it's calming, I mean," she asked, looking up at me with a hopeful glint in her eyes. I wondered if she had any idea that everything from her eyes to her expression to the way she sat gave her away. She wasn't very good at hiding her emotions.

"No, I don't find a vast endless sky calming. I find it boring," I said and then wished I hadn't when the strange hopeful look in her eyes fizzled out.

But someone needed to burst her bubble. She was never going to fit into my lifestyle the way she was now, and she would never make a good wife to a Don. My mother was sweet and kind, but she was also practical and ruthless when she had to be. She was wise enough to see the world for what it was and not dress it up with rainbows and daisies. Maybe Fallon needed to be shaken up.

"The sky isn't comforting because everyone looks up at that same blue sky, and that doesn't put me at ease. Murderers, rapists, corrupt politicians, pedophiles; they all look up at your blue sky, and I find no comfort in that."

She tilted her head just a little and her brow furrowed. "But by that way of thinking, Mother Teresa looked up at my sky, and so did Gandhi, and Martin Luther King Jr., and every good person who ever lived. There has been just as much greatness looking up at my sky as there has been evil men." Her hands moved as she talked, and there was a passionate light in her eyes that I could only describe as breathtaking. "I'd rather look at the wonder of something than the misery of it."

"Even if that leaves you blinded to the filth of our world?" I goaded, though I wasn't quite sure why except that there was something mesmerizing in the way her eyes lit up, and I wasn't ready for it to disappear yet.

"I'm not blind. I'm fully aware there is both good and bad in this world, but I'd rather not focus on the negative when there's nothing I can do about it."

"Not focusing on it doesn't make it go away. It doesn't stop bad things from happening."

The light in her eyes disappeared. She sat back in her seat. Even her shoulders slumped just a little. If I could have taken my words back, I would have, but that pissed me off. I was Dominic Luca; I could say whatever the fuck I wanted to say.

"I know bad things happen," she said in a voice that seemed smaller now, sadder. "But if I only ever focused on the bad things, they'd swallow me up."

The sadness in her voice ate at something inside me, and I felt the craziest urge to fix it. To do something to bring back the light in her eyes. But as I stared at the beautiful woman who'd gone back to pushing food across her plate, I couldn't think of a thing to say, not that it was my goddamn responsibility to make her happy. It wasn't my fault she was naïve enough to think she could bury her head in the sand and pretend bad things didn't happen.

Fortunately, our waiter appeared at just the right moment. "Is there anything else I can get for you, Mr. Luca?"

"Another bottle of wine, please." Fallon spoke up before I could respond.

The waiter glanced at me, and I nodded, sending him on his way.

"It seems we agree on something," I said when we were alone again. More alcohol certainly couldn't hurt.

She smiled victoriously, though I wasn't sure what it was she thought she'd won. "You see? There you go, looking for the good even in our miserable situation."

I laughed, and she joined in, and it seemed for the moment, a truce settled over us.

She took a bite of her risotto she'd managed to push around so much it was one giant mess in the middle of her plate. She closed her eyes and let out a quiet sigh as she slipped the fork out of her mouth, so it must have tasted all right. But damn, the woman had lips that could fill even a monk's head with dirty fantasies. And I was no monk.

She swallowed and then her tongue darted out to lick her lips, and my cock stirred inside the confines of my pants.

She glanced up and caught me staring, not that I had any intention of looking away. The crackle of sexual energy in the air grew louder. She could hate me all she wanted. She couldn't deny the chemistry between us was explosive.

The waiter returned, and I motioned for him to leave the bottle on the table without taking my eyes off Fallon. Though she sat perfectly still in her seat, I could feel her squirming beneath my gaze. And I liked it.

"Why are you looking at me like I'm part of the meal?" she asked, cocking what I'm sure she hoped looked like a disapproving eyebrow at me once the waiter had left.

"Am I? Do you want to be eaten, Fallon?" I asked with a wicked grin.

Her eyes widened just a little, then she glanced down at her plate, trying to hide her response, but she wasn't quick enough. I'd seen it. I'd seen the flare of heat in her eyes, and I'd heard the quiet hitch in her breathing. We might have come from two different worlds, but some languages were universal, and Fallon's body was speaking plenty. Maybe it was time to take advantage of it before we wandered into even more dangerous territory than favorite colors. God only knew what naïve notions the woman had wrapped up in favorite animals or days of the week.

"Why don't we take the bottle to go?" I suggested, but I was already getting to my feet. I didn't really care if the bottle came with us or not.

She looked up at me, and I could see the battle going on in her head by the look in her eyes. And I knew the moment she'd settled it by the way her throat muscles worked as she swallowed hard.

She stood up, sweeping her tongue across her lips, and that small movement did me in. Maybe I couldn't stand this woman's ridiculously innocent views or the way she had to argue with me on everything, but her body, I had absolutely no objection to. I wanted it, and if that wasn't good enough reason—which it was—sex could be one hell of a tension breaker. Maybe once we'd fucked each other's brains out, we'd both be too mellow to argue over useless shit.

I wrapped my fingers around her wrist and tugged her toward me until her breasts pressed against my chest. I kept hold of her wrist, pressing it against the small of her back and using it to push her more firmly against me. She gasped, and her gaze shot up to meet mine as the hardening length of my erection dug into her abdomen through our clothes. What I wouldn't have given to rip them off and have her right here on the table. But there was no hurry. The longer I could draw this out, the longer it would be before the battles started up again.

So, I focused on her lips, covering them with my own. Hers were still moist from the number of times her tongue had flicked across them, and they immediately brought to mind her other lips, the ones I'd be parting with my tongue before the night was over.

She pressed herself closer against me as I swept my tongue along the seam of her lips, and I could imagine the changes going on in her body; her nipples hard from arousal and friction, her clit engorging in anticipation of what was to come.

I pulled my lips away just enough to see her face. "Look at me," I said. Her eyes were closed, but I wanted to see what was going on in them, and like the good girl I'd hoped she would be, her lids opened, and she stared up at me with dilated pupils.

I'd just leaned in for another taste when movement from the patio door caught my attention. Expecting it to be the waiter, I nearly dismissed it, but the woman in black with long, dark hair and a predatory light in her eyes was no waiter. I knew this woman, and she was heading this way.

Oh fuck. I was no dating expert, but I had a feeling that a woman I'd fucked and a woman I was trying to fuck, both in the same vicinity, was number one on the list of dating-don'ts—particularly when the woman I was trying to fuck was the one I also had to rope into a long-term commitment.

"Dominic Luca," she purred when she was still six feet away. "So, this is where you've been hiding." She looked pointedly at Fallon with disdain.

Fallon took a step back, but I still had her wrist firmly clasped in my hand.

"I don't hide, Emmanuella, and you know that," I said. The woman had been a mistake, far too interested in sinking her claws into a mafia man for the luxury he could provide her, but I'd made it clear after a lackluster fuck that nobody was sinking their claws into me.

She smiled, a sultry look on her face that I'm sure was supposed to be enticing. "I know a lot of things."

She was an attractive woman, no doubt, but she was seriously fucking with what I'd been about to indulge in. I could feel the heat from Fallon getting cooler by the second. I had the sinking feeling that her and I were going to be back on opposite sides of the battlefield by the time I got Emmanuella's ass out of here.

"Then I'm sure you know to go dig your claws into someone else," I said, but she made no move to leave.

"Don't be like that, Dominic. I don't mind if you want your friend to join us. A party for three?" she said, eyeing Fallon from head to toe. I didn't miss the way her eyes settled on Fallon's chest.

Fallon gasped, and I could imagine the indignant look on her face so well I had to stop myself from smiling.

No man in his right mind didn't give Emmanuella's kind of offer a moment's contemplation, but before she could read into it, I shook my head.

"Leave, Emmanuella," I said in a tone that brooked no refusal, and even she wasn't stupid enough to push me any further. She turned around with a huff and stormed back inside the restaurant to a table by the door where a man sat waiting for her.

I didn't need to turn back to Fallon to know Emmanuella had just managed to fuck up my night. I could practically feel the winds of the Arctic blowing off of Fallon.

"I can't do this," she said and tugged her wrist out of my hand.

"Everyone has a past, Fallon," I tried to reason with her.

"It's not your past, it's you," she said, throwing out her arms in exasperation. "I don't know what I was thinking. We have nothing in common. We come from two completely different worlds. Call me stupid and ignorant, but I'd rather be happy in my optimistic view of the world than live in your dark, dead one."

I sighed. My "dark, dead world" was reality. It wasn't my fault she was too naïve to see it. Besides, that wasn't even what she was pissed about.

"Admit it, you're jealous," I said, nodding toward the damned woman sitting inside.

"Jealous?" she railed.

The incredulous look in her eyes was enough to make me second-guess myself—not something that happened often. But that meant Fallon was seriously going to walk away from the chemistry between us because we had different worldviews? Was she insane?

"If you're not jealous, then you're crazy."

"Ha!" she scoffed. "Now who's being delusional? I'm not crazy, you're just pissed because you thought you were going to get your dick wet, and now you're in for a dry spell."

"If all I wanted was to wet my dick, I have no shortage of options," I said, glancing over at Emmanuella to make my point.

Fallon's eyes widened even more and her chest heaved with every deep agitated breath. This would have been far more entertaining if I could have stripped her and watched her rant and rave naked.

"You know what, Dominic, screw this. I hope you live a long, miserable life in your dark world." She scooped up her purse from the table and stormed off the patio. Half-stunned, I watched her disappear around the corner of the restaurant. No woman had ever walked away from me before. And this was the second time she was doing it. Fallon was fucking infuriating.

I left money on the table for the waiter and went after her. She could damn well stand outside the McLaren until I got there. But when I rounded the corner, she wasn't anywhere near my car. She'd reached the sidewalk and stared out at the passing cars.

"What the hell are you doing?" I barked at her once I'd caught up.

"I'm waiting for a cab," she said without turning to look at me. "Not all of us drive around in hundred-thousand-dollar cars."

A hundred-thousand-dollar car? Try four-hundred-thousand, not that it was relevant to this fucked-up conversation.

"You're suddenly opposed to my car?"

"No, I'm not-so-suddenly opposed to spending another minute with you. Goodbye, Dominic." She held out her hand, and a yellow taxi slowed to a stop.

I could have stopped her. Hell, if I'd really wanted to, I could have turned on the charm and had her naked and breathless beneath me before the night was over, but fuck it. I was done trying to deal with this woman whose sweet side just wasn't worth the bitter aftertaste.

I watched her get into the cab's back seat, tamping down the ridiculous urge to pull her back. And then I watched her drive off, refusing to even think about just how pissed my father was going to be when he found out what a total failure tonight had been.

For now, though, I just wanted to go home. For the first time in a long time, I had a hot date with a cold shower to get to, and I wouldn't want to be late.

Chapter Nine

Fallon

"Why the heck are you so secretive about Mr. Rich Boy?" Corinne prodded.

Maybe because Mr. Rich Boy turned out to be Mr. Playboy, I thought to myself.

We had a Moyen poodle in today with fur as white as snow. She was averse to being groomed, so I needed Corinne's assistance to pull it off without being nipped. Snowball hated both baths and nail clipping, so we had to be careful when it came to her service.

I sighed, pausing to look at Corinne. "It's complicated. And I don't know."

"If you don't tell me, I'm not bringing you brownies ever again," Corinne said.

She was an avid baker, and I was her taste-tester for every new sweet treat. Her brownies were the best I had ever tried—pecan nuts, dark chocolate, the inside moist and fudgy.

"How dare you threaten me with something like that?" I gasped. "I thought we were best friends."

I stuck my bottom lip out as I took small hair cutting scissors to clean up the poodle's legs.

"Okay, maybe that was a little too far." Corinne sighed. "I just don't think it's fair you're keeping all the juicy stuff to yourself. You usually tell me everything, even the embarrassing things."

I gave the little snowball one last spritz of deodorizing spray, a kiwi and strawberry scent per her parent's request.

"You've been such a good girl, Snowball," I cooed. "Let's get you back to your kennel. Mom and Dad should come pick you up soon."

Corinne huffed and waited for me in the staff room. It was lunchtime, so one of our part-timers took over for the next half hour. It was only noon, but it felt like I had been on my feet for twenty-four hours straight. Corinne's face was flushed with disappointment.

"Come on. How bad could it be?" she asked.

Corinne took our lunches out of the small fridge and slid mine toward me.

"It's bad."

I couldn't stop thinking about the stupid, drop-dead gorgeous bitch who'd practically thrown herself at Dominic right in front of me. What kind of guy had women who actually did that?

"I told you about the time I went back to a Tinder date's house, and I got so drunk that I somehow managed to pull his sink out of the wall while doing a quick before-bang cleanup. There. I told you something stupid. It's your turn," Corinne said.

"I don't even know where to start."

I picked at the garlic in my pasta as images of a certain woman's long and dark mane flashed behind my eyes.

"You've been acting weird ever since you had those dates with him," Corinne said. She narrowed her eyes at me.

"Okay. Fine. The first date was a total disaster. He took me to that fancy restaurant down by Jamaica Bay. But he was stupid and arrogant, and he was mean. So I left," I said.

"Then why the hell did you go on a second?"

"Because he came to me, asking me to give him another chance. It was… it was like Jake all over again, so I crumbled."

"Oh, hell no," Corinne said with a sigh. "Don't do that again. Not another Jake."

"No. Don't worry about that. It's different. He's different. He's the most handsome man I know, and he can be sweet, and there's just something about him," I said, thinking about the confident set of his shoulders and the don't-mess-with-me look in his eyes and the crazy things it did to my insides, but not willing to share those details with Corinne just yet. "But he makes me so angry that I want to pull my hair out."

I told Corinne about everything—the risotto, what we talked about, what he was like, the menu I didn't know how to read. As I went on, Corinne's smile grew wider and wider.

"You didn't go on the second date because he manipulated you with flowers and cheesy lines. You went because you have the hots for him," Corinne said matter-of-factly.

"No! No, I didn't!" I ignored the way my cheeks grew warmer because it wasn't entirely untrue, if I was being honest. Dominic might have been a dick, but he was a hot dick. I would have had to be blind not to notice.

Corinne eyed me closely, leaning her face toward me.

"Corinne, I don't think you quite get my point here… I can't stand him," I said as much to myself as to Corinne, shoving any thought of pants or dicks or any of Dominic's other body parts out of my head. "He's a typical rich boy who expects every woman to climb in his bed. And unlike most men, this guy actually has women who'll do it."

Corinne popped a crouton in her mouth, chewing loudly. "Uh-huh. Okay. Whatever you say, honey pie."

"Seriously. I called Dad after that train wreck of a date and told him I was done paying his favor. But he told me he'd actually bartered me for three dates! Three!" I dropped my head on the table. "I'm spineless, right?"

"You can't wait for your next date, can you?" Corinne poked my arm.

"I'm only going for Dad. Captain Spineless, remember?"

"No, you're not. But, honey, honestly, your dad's a grown man. Maybe it's time you start letting him handle his own problems."

I merely shrugged.

"Yeah, I know." Corinne flashed me a small smile and laid her hand on mine. "Then just take it for what it is. Free dinner with a hot guy. If nothing else, it beats an ordinary night at home. We can make fun of it after."

Maybe my love life sucked, but I had the best friend in the whole world.

***

The morning sun spilled bright and hot through my bedroom window. I'd passed out the moment I walked through the door last night. Apparently, I'd slept right through my alarm. The pounding on my front door, though, was bringing me wide awake in a hurry.

I flung my legs over the side of the bed, wrapped myself in a satin kimono, and dragged my feet to the door.

Looking through the peephole, I saw Corinne's face smiling back at me. She knocked again, and the sudden thud so close to my head made me jump, but I unlocked the door for her. She had a giant paper bag in each arm, both of them brimming with baking ingredients and kitchen tools.

"You seemed so down yesterday, and I couldn't stop thinking about it. I know you probably would have spent the whole day in bed, so I've come to mother you," Corinne said. She pushed past me into my apartment.

Corinne and I kind of looked after each other, but she was the one with the amazing maternal instinct for the people she loved. She could tell when someone was struggling and when they needed a pick-me-up. After my breakup with Jake, Corinne helped me get back on my feet. She'd been there for me even when I tried to push her away.

Corinne made herself at home in the kitchen, unpacking the bags she brought while a smile tugged at the corners of her lips.

I stood in the narrow archway that led into the kitchen, leaning against it. "Don't you have plans today, hon?" I asked. "You don't have to—"

Corinne lifted her finger to my mouth without looking up at me. "Pssh."

"But—"

"Nuh-uh," she said. "Stop arguing. I'm doing this and you have no choice in the matter. You got me?"

She pressed her lips into a flat line as she glared at me. She looked so damned cute when she was trying to be serious, I couldn't keep it in. Out of nowhere, laughter bubbled up my throat and burst out.

Her eyes went wide, which only made me laugh harder, and then her serious expression gave way to mirth, and she joined in, dissolving into laughter until both of us were clutching our stomachs and tears leaked from the corners of our eyes.

It was a long time before I could rein it in, but when I did, it was almost cathartic, like the moment I finished a vigorous exercise and all my muscles sagged with sweet relief.

"I needed that," I told her, wiping the tears off my face.

"I know," she said with a shrug, then turned her attention back to her bags of goodies like nothing had happened.

"Just give me a minute to get dressed, and I'll be with you."

"I knew you'd crumble," Corinne said.

When I came back to the kitchen in a pair of tights and a T-shirt, Corinne had two champagne flutes in her hands.

"Mimosas usually get the juices flowing for you," she said. She gestured for me to sit across from her by the breakfast nook where we could both work on the baked goods in the same space.

"It's early," I said. "But I'll never say no to mimosas."

"That's my girl. And no, it's nearly afternoon."

I took a deep sip, gulping down a few times before taking in a deep breath. "What's the occasion, really?"

"My friend's having a hard time and she's not telling me everything," Corinne said. "Here, start on creaming the butter and sugar. I'll zest and juice the lemons."

Thanks," I said while tears stung my eyes. It always happened when she did things like this, taking care of me in a way I hadn't experienced in a long time. "I'm sorry I didn't tell you from the get-go. It's just such a strange situation because my dad's so desperate for this to work."

I measured out the soft packed sugar and regular white, leaving the butter for last. When that was done, I began whisking the mixture until it was fluffy.

"It's okay, hon. Why do you think I brought all this stuff? We're gonna be slaving away in the kitchen all day and get your mind off of things," Corinne said.

My bottom lip quivered. Corinne and I reached our hands over the table and gave each other an affectionate squeeze.

"Dominic makes me so confused," I finally admitted after a long period of silence.

The clean, sharp scent of citrus filled the apartment. She had just finished zesting and juicing three lemons. On the menu today was lemon cookies. They were soft, and cakey, and would have a lemon-flavored glaze drizzled over the top. Corinne brought ingredients for my favorite cookies, confident that it would butter me up.

"There it is." Corinne looked up at me with a smirk. "And why is that?"

"I think he's a despicable person. No, that's a little harsh. We just don't get along, right?" I said.

Corinne nodded as she measured out the dry ingredients of the recipe.

"My mind doesn't like him, but my body does. God, that sounds pathetic, doesn't it?" I cringed as I spoke. I was not the kind of woman who let herself be led around by her hormones, but here I was, letting myself get wrapped up in the way Dominic's tall, broad frame filled out a suit. The way his heat had seeped right through his suit and into my body when he'd held me against him. The feel of his lips, even the way he'd grabbed my wrist and not my hand. Everything about him seemed to ignite me in one way or another.

"I still haven't seen a picture of him," Corinne said, waggling her brows.

"We haven't cozied up enough to be taking selfies together. And something tells me he wouldn't be into being photographed, anyway." I handed her the bowl of creamed butter, and she dumped the wet and dry ingredients together.

"But that's not all, hmm?"

I nodded, but my thoughts were all over the place, and I worried my words would come out in a jumbled mess. "Even though we argue, it's kind of a breath of fresh air, in a way. I have the guts to stand up to him. I speak my mind. And the conflict is… thrilling." I hadn't really understood what I was feeling until I got the words out, but it kind of made sense now.

"So, that's why you're doing it. You're bored. You shouldn't be beating yourself up over it. Go on this one last date and enjoy it for what it is—some silly drama."

"I guess so." I didn't love the idea I was doing this just for cheap thrills, but it felt better than thinking I was letting myself be led around by my vagina. And it was even better than doing it because I was just too spineless to stand up to my father. And really, didn't I deserve the occasional cheap thrill? "I haven't done much with my life but work and hang out with you the past few years, huh?"

"Yep. I get more action and suspense in a weekend than you do in a month," Corinne added.

I huffed, crossing my arms over my chest. "Come on, now you're just rubbing it in."

Corinne put her hands up in front of her. "Sorry, sorry. But seriously, don't be so glum. So what if you find the confrontation fun? I'd love to be in your shoes, honestly."

"Is that only because he's a potential billionaire playboy?" I squinted at Corinne.

"Okay, yeah, sure. You got me. Maybe you could send him my way if things don't work out." Corinne stuck her tongue out at me.

"And get my sloppy seconds?" I made an exaggerated sound of disgust. "Gross."

"Hey, I haven't had the best luck. Maybe someone like him would be exactly what I need." Corinne lined a baking sheet with paper and had me help roll the cookie dough into balls. She made a double batch, as she usually did, because she knew what our plans would be for the day: Binge-watch *Supernatural* and eat ourselves into our respective food comas.

And we did exactly that. Thanks to Corinne, I already felt better about a third date with Dominic. I just needed a little excitement in my life. Someone to spar with. Unlike my father, I didn't have to care if I hurt Dominic's feelings—not that I was entirely convinced he had any feelings to hurt. And the fact that he was drop-dead freaking gorgeous, well, that was just a nice perk.

One more date. One more chance to go another round in the ring with the man who seemed to excite me and frustrate me to no end. And then I'd never have to see Dominic Luca again.

Chapter Ten

Fallon

"Can I help you?" I asked the tall, dark-haired man, dressed in a suit and an expensive-looking trench coat, who'd just walked into the clinic.

I'd spent the entire day working off the mimosas and lemon bars Corinne and I had consumed, and I just wanted to go home. Unless this guy had an animal in need of emergency attention, the clinic was closed for the day—hence the "Closed" sign that hung in the front window of the building.

"You're a good veterinarian from what I hear," the man said from where he stood just inside the doorway. He had no animal with him, but maybe he'd left his dog in his car while he came inside.

"I am," I said because it was true. I had my flaws just like everyone else, but I was good at my job.

"I'm pleased to hear that," he said, leaning a shoulder against the wall. "Too many people take a lackadaisical approach to their work these days, wouldn't you agree?"

"Um, I guess so." Beyond the strange conversation, something didn't feel right. I wanted to shrug this guy off and tell him we were closed for the night, but something had me holding my tongue. It was the way he'd kept his eyes focused on me from the moment he'd walked in the door. Most people smiled politely and then looked around at the waiting area and the posters on the wall, and even squinted a little, trying to get a glimpse of the rooms beyond the reception desk. But not him. He just kept staring at me, and it sent a prickling sensation down my back.

"Is there something I can do for you?" The sooner I could get this guy out of here, the better.

He smiled broadly and pushed away from the wall. "Indeed, there is," he said, walking toward me with a slow, easy stride.

The urge to backstep away from him was potent, but I held my ground. It was probably all in my head. It wasn't like there was an epidemic of veterinary clinic robberies going around.

"You can keep doing exactly what you've been doing," he said. "It's important, you know? Caring for those that cannot care for themselves."

"I mean, do you have an animal you need looked at? That's why you're here, isn't it?"

"No." He laughed, the humor in it nonexistent. It was deep and dark, and it made my palms feel sweaty. "I care for those that cannot care for themselves as well."

I swallowed hard, unable to stop myself from taking a step back.

He stopped laughing, and something just as dark as his laugh flashed through his eyes. "My name is Tony. It was a pleasure to meet you, Miss Moore," he said, extending his hand.

The last thing I wanted to do was take it, but I forced my hand to clasp his, hoping this meant he was leaving. He shook my hand once, then held me there for just a moment. His hand felt cold and rough against mine.

When he finally let go, I couldn't hide the sigh of relief that slipped out. He nodded to me then turned and strode back out the door.

I leaned heavily against the reception desk for support. My legs were shaking, and my heart was racing. I spritzed some alcohol on my hand, rubbing vigorously.

The moment I heard the click of a car door outside, I crossed the room and locked the clinic door. Even though part of me wanted to scurry back to the desk, I forced myself to watch through the window as the man pulled out of the parking lot and drove away.

I stood there for a moment after, half-expecting to see the car come squealing back into the lot, but it never did. I shook my head and laughed at myself. While it might have been strange, it wasn't like any harm had come to me. Still, I was more than happy to grab my purse from the back room and lock up for the night.

I glanced around once as I scurried across the parking lot to my car, but there was no sign of him. Of course, there wasn't. He was just a guy who'd been a little off his rocker.

I'd managed to get my heartbeat back to normal by the time I arrived home. Unfortunately, the first sight I saw as I slipped into my parking spot was my dad's squad car. Out of the pot and into the frying pan. My nerves were just too frazzled for this tonight.

Nevertheless, I smiled weakly at him as he got out of his car and followed me up the walk. He followed me inside and up to my apartment, heading across the living room while I locked the door, then jiggled the handle just to be sure. I'd long since accepted it was a bit of a neurosis, but I had no intention of changing it. Better safe than sorry.

"Tough day, Dad?" I asked, noticing he'd headed straight for the liquor cabinet and poured himself a drink.

"I just need a drink. That's all," he said.

"You know, there's like a dozen bars between your place and mine. They probably would have been quicker."

"I've just come to check in on my daughter," he said, looking disgruntled. "But, yeah, it's been a long day." He gestured for me to join him on the sofa.

"What is it you want, Dad?" I asked. I was already on edge, and I just wanted him to spit out whatever he'd come to say.

"I came to see my beautiful daughter. Am I not allowed?"

I almost scoffed but managed to hold it in. I loved my dad, but I wasn't so blinded by love that I didn't notice he only ever came here for a reason.

"Dad, if you're not here for anything important…" I prompted, hoping to get the ball rolling.

He sucked down the rest of his drink and poured another.

"Okay, okay. I just… I wanted to apologize for pushing so hard with the Luca boy."

A lump formed at the back of my throat, and I had to swallow it back to force words out.

"Thank you," I said, reaching out to cover his lined hand with mine. It wasn't often my dad apologized for things, but—

"So, I just want to make sure you're on for the next date…" he said, cutting into my thoughts, but the look in his eyes was just a little too hopeful.

"I knew it." I drew my hand back. The chuckle that slipped out wasn't jubilant or sarcastic. Really, it just sounded sad. "Not that it's any of your business, but no, we didn't…"—I raised my hands to make air quotes—"…'hit it off.'"

His eyes widened in panic. "But… but you have to."

"What?" Since when did this dating agreement mean things had to end up with some kind of happily ever after?

"I mean, Dominic is a good man, Fallon. I'm sure if you just gave him a chance—"

"What the hell, Dad? You said you owed a guy a favor, so I went out with Dominic, just like you wanted, and it didn't work. We're not compatible, end of story. What is it you want from me? Am I supposed to keep going out with a guy I can't stand? Do you want me to marry the jerk?"

Dad's face lit up like I'd come up with the best idea of the century. "Well, you know—"

"You can't be serious!" I said, sitting up straight.

His expression fell, and his eyes turned pleading. "I just need you to do this, Fallon. Give it a little more time, all right? For me?"

So, he hadn't really come to apologize. He was just here to make sure I didn't back out of whatever deal he'd made. I wasn't proud of it, but part of me wanted to make him suffer, to make him think I was calling the whole thing off right here and now. But looking at my father's frantic face, I couldn't do it.

I wasn't normally like this. I'd graduated at the top of my class in college, established my own vet practice, and lived a relatively productive life. But when it came to my dad, I would always be the little girl who only wanted to make her father happy, her only family left.

I sighed and leaned back on the couch, staring up at the ceiling.

"Don't worry, Dad, I'm not backing out on our third date just like I promised," I said. The relief that washed through him felt like a freaking tsunami.

He took another swallow of his brandy.

"That's my girl," he said, patting my knee.

Yup, that was me. The little girl who would never stop jumping through hoops and bending over backwards to please him.

"I'm sure he'll change your mind about him, Fallon. You'll see. I've heard he can be quite charming."

Charming and ornery and devastatingly handsome and frustrating as hell. Dominic Luca was every good and bad thing, all wrapped up in one crazy gorgeous package. He should have come with a warning sign tattooed across his forehead, but I couldn't wait to spar with him again.

Chapter Eleven

Fallon

Once I'd reassured my dad I wasn't dropping Dominic just yet, it was unsurprisingly easy to corral him toward the door and send him on his way. He'd hugged me before he left, and the little girl inside me had rejoiced even as I cringed over her enthusiasm.

But I didn't have time to worry about the ever-present conflict inside me when I had less than thirty minutes left to get ready. *He* was going to be here soon, and I could already feel my mind putting on its boxing gloves, gearing up for the battle that was about to ensue.

At the same time, though, other parts of me were revving up. I could hear his deep voice in my ear, feel his firm, full lips against mine, and see the heat in his eyes when he looked at me. I could imagine the perfect fit of his suit across his broad chest and wondered about the body beneath it. Was he in good shape or totally ripped? God, how I would have loved to find out. I couldn't help but think about what would have happened if that woman hadn't interrupted what we'd started on the restaurant's patio.

Would he have taken me back to his place? Would he have stripped me naked and demanded that I keep my eyes on him while he made me come with wickedly talented fingers? Would he have pinned my arms above my head while he thrust deep inside me over and over again? Or pinned my hands behind my back while he fucked me from behind? So many possibilities, and every one of them sent heat to my core.

Pressing my thighs together against the pulsing onslaught of arousal, I stepped beneath the shower head and pointedly ignored the way my nipples pebbled beneath the flow. I didn't have time to pay attention to my throbbing clit, nor would I give it the satisfaction of giving in to the fantasies that played behind my eyes like a porn reel.

I washed, rinsed, and dried as perfunctorily as I could, then dashed to my bedroom to pick out something to wear. It had nothing to do with the thought of Dominic's heated gaze on me that had me choosing a halter-style black dress that plunged low in the front. And certainly, the image of him ripping it off me wasn't what had me slipping into the laciest, skimpiest black bra and panties I owned. *Yeah right.* Even I wasn't falling for my own bullshit.

By the time I was dressed, I only had a few minutes left to run a brush through my hair and sweep a bit of mascara across my lashes. I could hear the knocking at my door as I dabbed on the juicy, dark red lip gloss that made my lips look like they belonged on a centerfold. They were my favorite feature, and I wasn't above playing them up tonight. Corinne had taught me well after all.

At the door, I wasn't quite prepared for the sight that greeted me. Dominic, of course—but he wasn't dressed in what I'd come to see as typical-Dominic style. No custom-tailored suit this evening, he was dressed in a black V-neck T-shirt and a pair of jeans that hugged him in all the right places. And just to make sure I had to work extra hard not to drool, I could see the hard, chiseled planes of his chest beneath his shirt and had no doubt now that this man was *ripped*.

I looked up, only just realizing I'd had my gaze roaming all over him.

The hungry look in his eyes, I was sure, mimicked my own, but he wore a knowing grin.

"Thanks for the compliment," he said before I could open my mouth.

I pressed my lips together and tried to look incredulous. It didn't work. He laughed. He was freaking laughing at me, but it was just what I needed. I could feel my mind stretching in its boxing gloves, like hands warming up for a fight.

I leaned forward and looked down the street, making an exaggerated show of looking left, then right before leaning back inside.

"Waiting for someone?" he asked, though he didn't sound the least bit perturbed.

I crossed my arms over my chest. "Just wondering when the rest of your fan club is going to show up."

His smile only grew broader.

"Jealous?" he asked, waggling his eyebrows.

"Only in your fantasies, Dominic," I said.

He scoffed. "In my fantasies, you have a lot less on, and jealousy is the last thing on your mind."

Asshole. Part of me was pissed and would have loved nothing more than to slam the door in his face. The other part, though, couldn't deny the rush that came from arguing with this man.

I rolled my eyes. "I envy the people who've never met you," I quipped. "Shall we get this over with? Or were you hoping for a date right here in my doorway?" I asked, cocking a brow.

His smile fell, but the look in his eyes grew hotter. "I had something else in mind, but if you'd rather invite me in…"

Round one goes to him, I guess.

I stepped outside and shouldered my way past him, not oblivious to the firmness of his chest beneath my arm. I could hear him laughing under his breath behind me, but he followed me to his car and opened the passenger door.

We were both silent as he turned onto the street and merged with traffic, like we'd gone to our corners and were regrouping for the next round.

There was no way I could have anticipated it, though, when he pulled into an empty lot not ten minutes later. The parking lot of a miniature golf course. What the hell? Somehow, I just could not picture this man swinging around mini-putt clubs at wooden windmills.

"What are we doing here?" I asked as he pulled into one of the many empty parking spaces.

He shrugged. "I thought that since restaurants didn't seem to be our thing, maybe we'd have better luck with something out of the ordinary."

I could "do" dinner in a restaurant, but I hadn't played miniature golf since I was a little girl. I cringed because I was so going to make a fool of myself.

"I don't think so, Dominic," I said.

This was not what I signed up for.

"Chicken?" he asked, rolling his eyes.

"You know if you keep rolling your eyes, you might eventually find a brain in there." I smirked.

But still, I got out of the car when he came around and opened the door. If I chickened out, it felt like I'd be handing round two over to him without a fight.

He took my hand and led the way toward the entrance. It was a building, not much more than a shack, but it was locked, and there were no lights inside.

I was just about to sigh with relief when he withdrew a key from his pocket and slipped it into the door's lock.

"Do you own this place?" I asked as the key turned in the lock and clicked open. It seemed like a strange business venture for an investment banker.

He laughed. "No," he answered simply as he pushed open the door and led us inside.

"Then how…?"

If he'd stolen the key, I'm walking home. It's not like I haven't done it before. There was no way I was going to spend the night in jail for an ass-hat.

"Let's just say I'm borrowing it for the night," he said with a wink that made my insides quiver.

I relented, following him inside, trying to prepare myself for an hour of humiliation. And just like I'd expected, I *sucked*. Tennis, racquetball, or even basketball, I could have held my own, but miniature golf was not my sport.

We'd made it through the first half dozen holes of the course, and whatever was par for each one, Dominic had come in way under. I, on the other hand, had a score that was approaching the triple digits. He hadn't laughed once, but I could almost feel it bubbling up in his chest, and the mirth in his eyes was just too damn happy for what I'd seen from him thus far.

What was worse was that minute by minute, I was becoming less interested in the sparring match and more cognizant of the pull of the fabric across his chest and the flex and bunch of his shoulders and biceps with every swing.

All right, pull it together, Moore. I'd hit the ball four times, and it had sailed right past the hole every time. This was hitting an all-time low on the humiliation scale. One stupid ball in one stupid hole—was it really so much to ask?

I lined up the club, ignoring the man who was grinning from ear-to-ear beside me—I could just feel it. I exhaled, then swung the club and hit the ball, but right away, I could tell I'd hit it too hard. The ball sailed past the hole, rolling to a stop a good twelve inches beyond it, glinting cheekily at me in the moonlight.

I glared at the traitorous ball. "'He's still alive. They hit him with five shots, and he's still alive'," I quoted aloud.

Dominic's head shot up. "You've seen 'The Godfather'?"

I laughed. Dominic didn't strike me as the kind of man who surprised easily. "Of course. Who hasn't?" Did he think I'd been living under a rock for the past two decades?

"What did you think of it?" he asked, his eyes searching my face.

It felt like I was wading into another sensitive topic, though I couldn't imagine how. Dominic didn't strike me as a die-hard movie fanatic. "I don't know," I said cautiously. "I guess I thought it was all kind of sad."

"Sad?" he asked, and for the first time, it didn't feel like there was an argument hiding behind his question. He looked genuinely perplexed.

Still, I was going to tread carefully. As much as I'd been looking forward to sparring with him, I liked this more. "I mean, they spend their entire lives worrying about absolutely everything. Enemies, police, even the people closest to them. Not to mention the guy inherited a 'kingdom' he didn't even want."

The furrow between his brow deepened. "But what about family?"

"What about it?" I wasn't following.

"It was paramount to the plot. They fought for each other, died for each other. They *trusted* each other."

I'd never thought about it. "That's true," I conceded. I'd always paid attention to the murder and the fighting and the gunfire in the movie. I'd never given much consideration to the theme of family loyalty that was inherent in the movie's plot.

Dominic's jaw dropped open exaggeratedly. "Holy shit, did you just agree with me?"

I smiled. "Well, I wouldn't go quite that far. I didn't completely *disagree* with you. My father is the chief of police, though, so it would kind of be a disservice to him to speak too highly of loyalty among criminals, right?" I laughed, but he didn't join in. Just like that, it felt like I'd pressed some invisible button.

"Cops aren't all heroes," he said with a shrug, but his shoulders seemed more tense than they'd been a moment ago. "Sometimes they're worse than criminals."

Tension shot through my body, straightening my spine. "Now you're kind of making jabs at my father. He may never win 'best dad of the year award', but he's still a good person. Deep down," I said, though even I could hear the lack of conviction in my voice.

"See? That's exactly what I mean by loyalty, Fallon. No matter their flaws, you defend family to the end."

Dominic, the family man? I never would have suspected that. and somehow, the revelation had me lowering my gloves. "Yes," I said. "I see your point."

There was no overexaggerated jaw-dropping this time. He smiled, but there was something that looked an awful lot like gratitude in his eyes. Could it be he was thanking me for the concession I'd made?

"What do you say we call it a tie?" he offered, looking over at my cheeky ball. He had to be wondering just how many more swings it was going to take for me to sink it.

"I swear the ball is cheating," I said, giving it the stink-eye.

"Then we can't have that," he said, taking the club from my hands and dropping it on the ground.

And then there was only hard muscle and smooth planes as he pulled me against him and captured my lips with his own. They were full and firm, and when his tongue pressed against the seam of my lips, demanding entry, I obeyed. I parted for him as his grip on me tightened, molding my curves to his hard frame and making my nipples tighten almost painfully.

His tongue slipped in, and I could taste him. He tasted like coffee with a smooth undercurrent of something sweetly vanilla, like whiskey. My tongue sought his, seeking to take his taste inside me, to feel the buzz of the caffeine and alcohol running through my own veins.

His hand slid down to the small of my back, and when he used it to bring me even closer, the long, thick length of him pressed against my abdomen, and my clit began to throb.

He leaned away, and it was all I could do to keep the quiet whimper from slipping out at the loss.

"I think it's time to take you home," he whispered against my lips.

Home? He had to be kidding. I didn't want to go home. I wanted him here. Now. I didn't care that we were in the middle of a miniature golf course. We could have been standing in grand central station at rush hour, and it wouldn't have mattered.

He smiled knowingly as he took a step back and held out his hand. I wasn't sure if I wanted to slap it away in frustration or grab it and yank him back to me, but I did neither. I slipped my hand into his grasp and let him lead me back toward the parking lot.

Had it just been another sparring match? An opportunity for him to win another round? Maybe it was his way of training me to agree with him. Wouldn't that just be great?—I'd begun the evening as Fallon Moore and ended it as Pavlov's dog. And yet, I'd felt the proof of his arousal hard against me. If he was trying to train me, he was salivating over the lesson just as much.

He locked the shack's door behind us, and I followed him to his car, but as I moved to get in, he grabbed my waist from behind and leaned in close.

"Don't worry, Fallon. I'm going to fuck you," he whispered against my ear, sending tiny bolts of electricity throughout my body.

"I just thought I'd be gentlemanly enough to get you home first," he said, then grazed along my earlobe with his teeth.

If I'd felt tiny jolts of electricity before, I'd just been struck by a lightning bolt. Whatever else Dominic might have been—irritating and demanding, to name just a few—he was damn good at whatever game he was playing.

He released me, and I practically fell into the passenger seat.

Conversation eluded me as he got behind the wheel and revved the engine, or maybe I just wanted him badly enough, I wasn't willing to risk it turning back into a sparring match. *Not being led around by your vagina, huh?* a voice taunted from the back of my mind. I didn't like the voice very much. It was even more irritating than the cheeky golf ball.

Chapter Twelve

Dominic

Fallon was silent the entire drive back to her apartment, and after staring at her for the past hour on the miniature golf course—Leo's idea, of course—I wasn't about to say a thing to fuck this up. I was already cursing whatever chivalrous bullshit had stopped me from having her right there on the miniature golf green. Every time she'd bent over, the deep V of her dress had fallen away from her breasts, and every time she'd stomped her foot in frustration, they'd jiggled tantalizingly. Fuck, how I wanted them in my hands and in my mouth. I'd even had a thought or two about sliding my cock between the firm, perfectly shaped globes. It wasn't my fault every part of her just looked so damn fuckable.

I maneuvered the McLaren into an empty parking space in front of her building then pulled the key out of the ignition and reached for the door.

"I haven't invited you up, you know?" she said with a coy smile as she unfastened her seat belt.

"But you're going to." Because every pore of her body was screaming *sex* just as loudly as mine.

"Am I?"

I cocked an eyebrow at her and met her heated gaze. "Are you trying to tell me you're not wet for me right now?"

Her blue eyes darkened, and I didn't miss the way her thighs clenched together. Instead of answering, she tore her gaze away and moved to open the car door.

I chuckled as I got out and came around to offer a hand. Maybe it looked like a chivalrous move, but really, I just wanted to touch her.

I pulled her up, and then closer, watching her pupils dilate as her lips parted in anticipation. I'd intended to leave her wanting, but the temptation of her glossy red lips was too potent. I touched my lips to hers but made no move to delve deeper. I wanted her to come to me. I wanted her to show me she wanted it just as badly as I did. And she didn't disappoint.

Her tongue darted out, but instead of demanding entry like I'd done to her earlier, she swept the tip of her tongue across the seam of my lips, beseeching me to open for her. Such a good girl.

But I was done playing around. I wanted Fallon. Now.

Just as she began to lean up on her toes, I pulled back.

She let out a quiet gasp and looked up at me with her lips still parted and arousal flashing in her eyes. It took a monumental effort to lead us toward her building's front door rather than fucking her right there on the hood of my car.

Inside, she led the way up a flight of stairs, and I hung back just enough to take in the view of her slim legs and swaying hips.

At the door, she fumbled with the key in the lock, but eventually managed to get the door open. Inside, she closed the door behind me, locked it, then rechecked the locks.

I almost laughed. Who she had in her apartment with her now was a hell of a lot scarier than anyone that could come through that door. But she didn't need to know that, not yet. One day soon, she'd have to know. I'd almost forgotten that tonight wasn't just about getting into Fallon's incredible body. It was about trying to manipulate her into believing this was more than just sexual attraction.

I followed her across the apartment to the arched doorway that led to her small kitchen, but before she'd stepped into the room, I lunged for her, pressing her body into the doorjamb behind her at the same time I delved for those incredible lips. They were warm and soft and pliant at the moment, just like the woman they belonged to, and I'd never been hungrier for anything more.

"Wine?" I asked against her lips, trying to grasp for something to slow this down.

She nodded, clearly confused. "I have wine, I guess, but you're not going to like it." Something shifted in her. Arousal still flared in her eyes, but the set of her shoulders had changed.

"Why wouldn't I like it?" I asked, leaning back in to kiss a path down her jaw to try to soothe whatever I'd inadvertently set off.

She shrugged even as she tipped her chin up higher to allow me better access. "Because it didn't cost half my year's salary," she said, and though her voice came out a little breathless, there was a scathing undercurrent in her tone.

I paused at the junction of her jaw and her neck. "You think I can't like something unless it cost a fortune?"

Did she really think of me that way? Sure, I liked the finer things in life, but I wasn't a fucking snob. I leaned away and looked down at her. I couldn't help but notice the new light that was flashing in her eyes. Not just arousal, it was something else.

And then it hit me.

She was enjoying it. Some part of her was getting off on all the tension that flew back and forth between us. During our previous two dates, she'd made me angrier than any woman had before. But it had been a fucking game to her?

Maybe it was time to play a game of my own. One that would teach her that if she played with fire, she was going to get burned.

Without warning, I lifted her off the ground and sat her up on the kitchen counter, stepping between her parted thighs until her panty-covered pussy pressed against my abdomen. I could feel the damp heat of her against me, and it made my cock jerk and my mouth water.

"Dominic—" she started, but I swooped in and covered her lips with my own. There would be no more talking, no more opportunities for her to try to goad me into a pointless battle.

I reached for the knot of her dress behind her neck and pulled it loose. The sides of her dress fell forward, revealing black lace that barely concealed her breasts. I could see her dusky pink nipples peeking through the fabric. My length stiffened even more, wanting to break free.

With a flick of my fingers, the clasp of her bra gave way. The moment it fell, I palmed her bare breasts, feeling her supple flesh in my hands.

She gasped against my mouth as my fingers grazed across the tight peaks of her nipples, drawing even tighter, begging to be suckled into my mouth.

I ignored their plea and shoved the hem of her dress up to her waist. More black lace, but as big of a fan as I was, it needed to go. I slipped my thumbs beneath the thin sides of her panties and pulled hard, leaning away to watch as the fabric molded to the contours of her pussy.

She moaned, sending tiny vibrations through my lips, but with one tug, the fabric gave way, and I ripped the tattered lace off her.

I stared down at my prize, the blonde, perfectly trimmed landing strip that led to her engorged clit and her slick, pink folds.

"I want—" she began.

I kissed her again, silencing whatever she'd been about to say no matter how much I yearned to know. What was it she wanted? For me to finger her? Lick her? Fuck her?

I ran a finger along her slit, feeling the way her folds parted for me, urging me on to her wet center. But instead, I moved to her clit, pressing two fingers against her and loving the way she writhed against them, begging me to move, to rub, to do something other than remain there motionless. If I refused to move, would she groan in frustration? Or would she work her body against my fingers, bringing herself to the brink?

I darted my tongue into her mouth, sweeping along her teeth before gliding along her tongue. She writhed against my fingers, not enough to get her where she needed to be, just enough to tease herself, to keep her on a slow climb.

My fingers moved, seemingly of their own volition, rubbing once, twice. Her hips jolted, and she moaned into my mouth, a sound that shot down to the base of my spine and made my cock jerk appreciatively.

I rubbed her again, and then again in slow, languid circles, but the way her body responded was like I'd pressed a vibrator against her clit. Her breathing picked up, and her moans grew louder. Damn, she was loud. Over and over, I circled her clit, feeling her body near the top of her climb in record time.

I was supposed to stop. I was supposed to leave her desperate and pleading and more frustrated than she'd ever been before. But I didn't want to stop. As her skin flushed and her moans turned to cries, I wanted to see her topple over the edge. I wanted to see her body writhe as her orgasm shot exquisite pleasure through every inch of her body, and then I wanted to bury my cock hilt-deep inside her while her slick walls spasmed with aftershocks.

Fuck games. Fuck fire. I wanted Fallon. Now.

My phone vibrated against my thigh from inside the pocket of my pants. *Fuck, not now,* I cursed silently, knowing whatever it was, it was no social call. I slowed my pace on her clit, but there was no fucking way I was stopping as I pulled out the phone and put it to my ear without looking at the ID. I kept my eyes on Fallon, watching her writhe, listening to the frustrated moan that slipped from her lips.

"Get out of there—now," my father barked from the other end of the line.

I froze. We weren't at my apartment; we were at Fallon's.

"Dominic?" she whispered as I withdrew my fingers, cursing whoever was after us for interfering when we'd been so close.

"We need to leave," I said, still silently cursing while I picked up her bra and handed it to her. The black lace panties were a lost cause.

"Why? What's going on?"

I opened my mouth to lay it out for her but hesitated. I couldn't do it. Even after fighting with her over her naïve view of the world, I couldn't bring myself to burst her bubble, not yet. For some fucked up reason, I wanted to let her hold onto it for every moment I could.

"Fallon, I don't have time to explain. Please, don't argue with me, not now. Just trust me."

"Trust you?" She looked skeptical.

"Right, you probably shouldn't." I tried for humor, but it fell flat. "We need to get out of your apartment right now."

She was silent as she covered up and then fastened her dress behind her neck, but I could see all the emotions in her eyes. The lingering arousal, the fear, uncertainty. But somehow, she managed to pull herself together, and she nodded.

I waited until the last possible moment, until she'd slid off the counter and there was nothing left to do, before pulling the gun I kept in the holster at my ankle.

She gasped but didn't say a word.

I held out my hand, not really a comforting gesture, but to keep her close and keep her behind me. She stared at it warily. There wasn't time for this. But when she looked up at me, searching my gaze, I let her. There was probably a whole lot there she wouldn't want to see, but I was certain what was shining brightest was the need to get her out of here. To keep her safe—even if that meant I really needed to get my head examined.

But seconds passed, and we were out of time. Whether what she'd found had satisfied or not, it was time to go.

I led her across the living room, unlocked the door, and peered out first. No sign of trouble in the hallway. I tugged her with me, keeping her behind me as I started down the hallway, listening for any sign of danger. Down the stairs and out the front door.

No sign of trouble, but the prickling sensation at the back of my neck spoke volumes. Something was coming.

I got her down the walk and into the car without spotting anything out of the ordinary, but it didn't matter. My intuition was never wrong.

Behind the wheel a moment later, I squealed out of the lot, watching in the rearview mirror for any sign of a tail. I stared into every car we drove past, looking for a familiar sinister face or the telltale glint off the steel barrel of a gun. But even though I found nothing, I pushed down harder on the gas, feeling the approach of danger like a tidal wave behind us.

"It'll be all right, Fallon. It's just a precaution," I said at some point after realizing she'd been talking. Anger and panic were flashing in her eyes in equal measures, and her chest heaved with the overflow of emotion. But I had no room in my head to pay attention, not when every inch of me was on high alert, watching, waiting. Ready for whatever tried to come at us.

We made it to my condo without incident. Now, all I had to do was get in touch with my father or brothers to find out what the hell was going on and where to go from here, but for now, the condo was safe enough. I'd had all the windows fitted with bulletproof glass, and I had a whole arsenal of weapons hidden in my bedroom closet.

Fallon was silent as we left the car for the safety of my condo, but I could practically feel the thoughts flowing rapidly through her head like lava. As much as I'd wanted to postpone bursting her bubble, I was beginning to suspect it had been a bad call. This woman was about to erupt, but there was no time for her to go up like a pyroclastic cloud. We'd made it across the city just fine, but it wasn't over yet. I could feel it.

Inside my condo, I pulled out my phone and texted Leo. "I'm home. What's going on?"

"Our father will be there any minute," Leo texted back.

Fuck. "I've got Fallon here," I wrote, noticing the way she stood ramrod straight with her arms crossed over her chest in front of me.

Seconds passed, and then Leo texted back with a goddamn emoji laughing so hard it had tears coming out of its eyes. *Stronzo!*

"Dominic, what's going on?" Fallon said a little hysterically, willing to be silent and patient no longer. "I came with you. I did what you said. You've got to tell me what's going on."

I opened my mouth to respond without a fucking clue what I was going to say.

And then my front door opened, and my father strode in with two of our men on his heels and two men taking point outside the door.

My father looked furious. Fallon looked like she was ready to erupt.

This was going to be a disaster.

Chapter Thirteen

Dominic

My father walked across the living room and sat down at the walnut dining table while his men stood at attention on either side of him. Though his eyes were livid, he spared a glance at Fallon, and something in his countenance softened. Pity? No, it was more like sympathy, not something my father often spared for strangers.

Fallon's eyes had widened, and though I could still see a storm brewing inside her, she was silent. Did she recognize him? My father had appeared in the newspapers more than once, usually over donations our family had made, but occasionally in speculation over his role in New York's underworld. Fallon was a smart woman. If she hadn't put it together by now, the revelation was coming soon, and there wasn't a damn thing I could do to mitigate the fallout. Not now with an obvious crisis on my doorstep.

My father's gaze swung back to me. "Tony's father is dead, and Tony believes you're responsible for the murder." My father was not one to mince words. He crossed his arms over his chest like he was waiting for an explanation.

Indignation shot down my spine, but I held my tongue, not because I had to, but because my father wasn't the kind of man who demanded respect; he earned it. And he had earned mine ten times over.

I'd heard Fallon's small gasp from behind me, but it had to be all business right now. Dealing with Fallon would have to come later.

"Why would he think that?" I asked, crossing my arms over my chest and leaning against the tall column that separated the dining room from the living room. It made no sense. Tony's father might have been an asshole, but Tony was a hundred times worse. I had no interest in taking out the old man, and even if I did, I was smart enough not to start a war without preparing for it first.

"One of the Novas saw you at Bradley Miller's club. Miller ended up dead, and Tony's father wound up dead not long after. It's crude reasoning, but Tony has never been known for his rapier wit, has he?"

I scoffed. The man was like a hand grenade with a faulty pin. He could explode at any moment without rhyme or reason.

"And now he's seeking revenge. It's not just business now; it's personal," my father explained what I'd already figured out.

"And I imagine Tony's putting the weight of the Novas behind his vengeance?" I asked, though it wasn't a question. Of course, the volatile prick was going to use every weapon in his arsenal to exact his revenge. Besides, while his father had kept him in line, Tony had been itching to try to take down the Lucas for a long time. Now that his father was dead, this was nothing more than an excuse for a battle over territory.

"Tony?" Fallon piped up. It was the first time she'd said a word since my father had walked in here.

He and I both glanced at her.

"*Sì*," my father said. "I said Tony. Why, *signorina*?"

His jaw was hard-set, but there was the slightest softness in his eyes as he spoke to her. It would have been easy to miss. If I hadn't seen every side of my father, from his rage to his kindness, it was possible even I would have missed it.

And though I could see the fear and confusion still shining bright in Fallon's eyes, she swallowed hard and opened her mouth. "A man named Tony came to my clinic a… a few hours ago, actually."

A red haze settled over my vision. I clenched my jaw and balled my hands into fists.

"What did he want?" I asked before my father could respond.

Fallon winced.

"What did he want, Fallon?" I softened my tone, my heart pounding in my chest.

"Nothing. He said something about us both caring for things that can't care for themselves. Then he shook my hand and left."

"Dominic," my father called before I'd realized I'd taken three steps toward the door.

This was my fault. By putting Miller down for what he'd done to our girls, I'd set off a chain of events that had put Fallon on Tony's radar. But as much as I wanted to put a bullet in that fucker's brain, this wasn't about me. It was much bigger.

It was a goddamned fucking war.

Fallon stepped forward. The way she moved reminded me of a bird, ready to dart at the slightest provocation, but she kept walking until she stood just outside the dining room.

"You're Vincent Luca," she said to my father then her tongue darted out to lick her dry lips.

"*Sì, signorina,* I am. My apologies for not introducing myself sooner," he said with a gracious nod.

Her gaze flickered to me, then back to my father, but in that brief moment, I'd seen it. She'd put the pieces of the puzzle together, and now she knew who I was. She stared at me as the fear and confusion in her eyes gave way to something else. Not anger, but something just as potent. Something that made my insides twist painfully.

Betrayal.

She took a step back, and then another. I wanted to reach for her, but really, there'd been no other way for this to end. The moment my father had called me, it had been written in stone.

"I'm afraid I'm going to need you to stay with us, *signorina,*" my father called to her. His tone was polite, but the undercurrent of steel was unmistakable.

She paused, stealing a glance toward the door. "Why?"

I cringed. *Fuck, don't do it. Don't say it.* But I kept my mouth shut because I knew the stakes. The time to woo Fallon into believing this was some sort of romance had come to an end.

"Because you have a very important role to play, Miss Moore," my father said then motioned for her to take a seat at the table.

She eyed the chair like she thought it might have been rigged to explode, and her feet remained firmly planted where they were.

"Sit down, Fallon," I said in a tone that brooked no refusal, remembering that she wasn't as opposed to following my commands as she liked to think.

Her feet moved slowly, almost grudgingly, but she obeyed, pulling out the chair opposite my father and perching at the edge of the seat.

I looked at my father, and a silent exchange took place.

Let me do this, I told him.

Are you sure? he asked.

I nodded then crossed the dining room to the liquor cabinet against the wall. I grabbed a bottle of scotch and three shot glasses. I filled them up and downed my own in one gulp.

"Drink up," I told Fallon. She was going to need it as much as me.

She picked up the glass, eyeing it just as warily as she had the chair, but took a tentative sip and then another. Fortified for the moment, she placed the glass on the table and looked up at me.

"What role?" she asked, swinging her gaze back and forth between me and my father. Her blue eyes had turned a shade darker when it landed on me, but when she spoke, her voice came out as little more than whisper.

I straightened my shoulders, stiffened my spine, and met her gaze.

"You and I have to get married," I said, not bothering to mince words.

She stared at me like I'd spoken gibberish then blinked slowly.

"Like an arranged marriage? You've got to be joking." She scoffed, but the sentiment didn't quite reach her eyes.

"My son isn't joking in the slightest, *signorina*," my father said.

Fallon blanched. All the color drained out of her face. Even her lips got paler. I'd always thought that cheesy thing where women fainted in old movies was bullshit, but she looked on the verge of passing out.

"A marriage between a Luca and a Moore solidifies our... relationship with the police force," my father explained, but I knew there was no point. His words might have been making it to her ears, but they weren't getting inside her head.

"You want me to just marry you? You want me to just hitch myself to some guy in the mafia?" she said, her voice an octave higher than usual.

"It isn't a matter of 'want', *signorina*. It is what must be done."

But she wasn't listening, and I had to hand it to her. The woman had nerve to sit across the table from Vincent Luca himself. Fortunately, my father was fierce, but never cruel. He sat back, sipping on his scotch, and waited for Fallon to come to her senses.

But instead, her eyes widened. She looked up at me. The fear was gone. The confusion. All that remained was the sharp, piercing glare of betrayal.

"The Godfather… all that bullshit about family… it was all an act. You were just feeding me lines." She paused then added with a roll of her eyes, "Investment bankers my ass."

"No," I said. "It wasn't an act, Fallon."

On the miniature golf course, it had been an opportune moment to press my point, but I believed every word I'd said about loyalty. It was the most important thing in the world. It was the only reason I was standing here, willing to tie myself to a woman who dared to look at me like that. No one else who dared to question my loyalty would have lived to tell the story.

She grabbed the glass in front of her and tipped it back, draining every drop, and while my father sat back in his chair and his shoulders began to relax like the storm had just ended, I knew better. The storm hadn't even begun. This was Fallon just getting warmed up.

"No," she said, slamming the glass down on the table. "Absolutely not. I am not a *thing* that you can claim for your own purposes. I will not marry you." Her eyes snapped with fury, and color had come back to rise high on her cheeks, like angry slashes from a painter's brush.

"You don't have a choice in the matter," I said matter-of-factly. It was better to dispel whatever notion of free will she was holding onto now. It was less cruel in the long run.

"Really? What are you going to do, Dominic? Drag me kicking and screaming down the aisle?" Fallon pursed her lips.

"Yes," I said, squaring my shoulders.

Her jaw dropped open. "You… you can't be serious."

"Dead serious. You thought all that loyalty talk was an act, but it wasn't. There is nothing I wouldn't do for my family, Fallon. Nothing."

It hadn't escaped my notice that my father was near bursting at the seams, biting down on his lip to hold back his laughter, but it shone in his eyes. *Glad my misery could be so damn amusing.*

Fallon shot to her feet. The chair scraping across the marble floor reminded me of the first long rumble of thunder. The storm had begun.

"There's no way in hell I'm going to marry you. That's just insane," she railed, throwing out her arms.

"What's insane is thinking you have any say here, Fallon. Your life has been decided for you, the same as mine," I said with a shrug that belied my real feelings on the subject.

"Like hell it has," she spat.

And then she ran. She stumbled at first, giving away the fear that was making her legs tremble. But still, she was fast. Across the living room in three seconds flat, she threw open the front door, but jerked to a stop when the two men there pointed their pistols at her face.

"Stand down," I roared, but the sight was surreal. The glint of steel so close to the lips I'd kissed. "For fuck's sake, get the goddamned guns out of her face."

I batted their guns away from her while my stomach roiled like I'd been punched in the gut. I couldn't remember crossing the room. She'd opened the door, and then I was there, ready to rip the two men apart limb from limb if they fucking dared to threaten her again.

I grabbed hold of her arm and led her back across the room. Her body was trembling, and the color had drained out of her face again, zapping her fight, at least for the time being.

At the table, she sat down with nothing more than a gentle press on her shoulder. I poured her another glass and thrust it into her hand.

"Drink," I said, and she obeyed, tipping it back while she cast furtive glances at the closed front door. I could only imagine how that moment had been burned indelibly in her mind, and it had come because of me.

The room was silent until my father sighed and placed his hands down on the table.

"There's been enough commotion for one day," he said then turned to address Fallon. "You'll stay here where you'll be safe, *signorina*. The outlook may be bleak now, but the sooner you come to accept what is, the sooner you can move on, at peace with what must be."

She looked at him but didn't say a word.

"When?" I asked.

Fallon's shoulders stiffened.

I didn't want the answer any more than she did, but I didn't bury my head in the sand. Ever. It never kept the bad shit from happening.

My father glanced at Fallon then back at me.

"One week. With Tony ready to wage war, we can't wait any longer than that."

I nodded. It didn't sound like much time, but my father was giving Fallon a gift whether she wanted to acknowledge it or not. There was no reason he couldn't proceed with a wedding this very day, so if he was offering up seven days, he was giving her time to come to terms with this abrupt turn in her life.

I looked down at her. Her lips were pressed in a flat line, her hands were clenched in her lap so tight her knuckles were white, and I could feel the hatred rising off of her like steam.

She looked up to meet my gaze. Her eyes were blue flames, ready to combust at any moment—seven days or not.

Chapter Fourteen

Fallon

They kept talking. I could hear the voices pass back and forth across the table, but it was just sound. Not words. I had no room in my brain for their words.

Dominic had lied to me. My father had lied to me. It felt like the entire world had lied to me. And two men had just had guns pointed at my face. The man I'd nearly slept with an hour ago had turned out to be a murderer. A thief. An animal. And my father had known it all along. *This* was the favor. This was the reason he'd lit up when I'd made some stupid comment about marriage. This was how he'd used me to settle whatever he owed this family.

I looked up at Dominic then at his father. They didn't look like killers, or maybe they did. I'd always gotten the feeling there was something dangerous about Dominic. Apparently, I should have trusted my instincts and ran as far away as I could. *Is this what I get for listening to my vagina?*

Now, I was trapped. I was just supposed to marry this man like my life, my choice didn't matter. Nothing mattered.

"Fallon!" Dominic shouted at precisely the wrong moment.

I flew to my feet, slammed my hands down on the table, and glared at him.

"You've been sitting here for twenty minutes looking like a zombie," he said.

Twenty minutes? I'd figured it was much longer.

I could feel myself coming apart. I was like a funnel cloud, spinning faster and faster.

"Isn't that exactly what you wanted? A mindless zombie who will do whatever you want?" I goaded him.

"Do you think—" Dominic began, but his father held up his hand, and he stopped talking.

I spun around to face the man who'd interfered with the fight I desperately needed, but I snapped my mouth shut, biting back the words I'd been about to spew out. I didn't know this man. It was one thing to spar with Dominic. But this man, Vincent Luca, was just as dangerous as his son, if not more. I had no way of knowing how short his fuse was or what he was capable of.

I turned to the front door, but I already knew what happened if I tried to go through it. A cold shiver shot down my spine, remembering the glint of the guns that had been pointed right at me.

But still, I felt like a caged animal, and so I did what any caged animal would do. I ran for the nearest way out.

There was no escaping the apartment, at least for the moment, but I needed to get away from the table, from the men who were holding me captive. I strode down the hall, past the bathroom on the right and the bedroom on the left. Finally, in the room beyond it, I found a neutral space, a guest room, perhaps. A guest? Ha! More like a prisoner, but I strode inside nonetheless and slammed the door shut.

The bed, covered with an ivory bedspread and a half dozen pillows, was the only furniture in the room aside from a dresser and a bedside table. I supposed it was better than a stone-floored jail cell, but it was still a prison.

My legs threatened to buckle, but I forced them to carry me across the room to the window. Dominic's apartment was too high up for me to jump, but maybe I could wave my arms around like a lunatic and get someone's attention. Would they help me? If I convinced them to call the cops, would it do any good?

But like he could read my mind, Dominic threw open the door.

"What are you doing, Fallon?" he asked as his gaze swung back and forth between me and the window. But he made no move to stop me.

My shoulders sagged. Of course, he didn't bother trying to stop me. What good would it have done if I convinced someone to call the cops? They'd just drag me kicking and screaming to the chief of police. My father. Who would then just serve me back to the Luca family on a silver platter.

"Unless you've come to tell me I'm free to go and I never have to see you again, I want you to leave."

"Fallon, I—"

"Don't talk to me," I snapped, but the dangerous light that flashed in his eyes sent a cold shiver down my spine. This man wasn't just "Dominic" anymore. He was the son of the don of the Luca family.

Instead of him lashing out in any of the terrifying ways I could suddenly imagine, he turned and walked out of the room, closing the door with a quiet click behind him.

Abandoning the window, I plopped down on the floor. I was still wearing the stupid black dress I'd put on just hours ago. I was still panty-less because he'd ripped the scrap of black lace off me. My traitorous clit pulsed in memory, but I dug my fingernails into the palms of my hands and shoved the memory away.

This was like some terrible nightmare, but instead of being trapped by monsters, I was trapped by something far worse. Something that paraded itself around as a decent human being. There was nowhere I could turn for help.

I stared down at my hands. They were bare now, but in a week, there would be a ring on my finger. In my mind's eye, I could see it there, wrapped around my tanned skin like a noose, glinting at me, laughing at me as it choked the life out of me.

I squeezed my eyes shut and looked away, tucking my hands into the skirt of my dress like I could hide them from what was coming. I stared up at the window, looking out at the sky that had begun to lighten to a dismal gray in the early light of dawn. Tiredness tugged at my eyelids, but I fought it. Asleep, I'd have no defense against *him*. But then again, what was he going to do? Walk in here and take away my freedom? Turn me into a prisoner?

So I laid my head down against the plush carpet. The bed was right in front of me, but it felt wrong somehow, like I'd be declaring my acceptance if I used it. I turned away, rolling to face the window, and stared up at the lightening sky. The faintest orange hues had begun to infuse the dismal gray, but I closed my eyes to shut it out and let sleep drag me down into an abyss where there was no

Dominic. No Vincent Luca. An abyss where I was still free, and no man, no matter how powerful he was, got to dictate what my life would be.

I didn't know how much time had passed when the light thud of footsteps passed my door and brought me awake. Unlike most mornings, there was no haze over my mind. No moment of pulling myself away from the sticky tendrils of sleep. The footsteps belonged to Dominic.

I was lying on his floor.

And I was a prisoner in his home.

A door closed somewhere in the hallway, and a moment later, I heard the muffled sound of a shower running. My treacherous mind filled in the blanks. Dominic tugging off the black V-neck. With his arms stretched up over his head, I could imagine every ridge and plane of his torso. Then the button and zipper of his jeans. I could see his thumbs hooking into the waist of his jeans and pulling them off while his chiseled glutes flexed as he moved. Every inch of my body felt sensitized. The hem of my dress tickled my thighs, and I could feel the rub of the fabric against my chest as I breathed in and out.

I squeezed my eyes shut, not that it helped because the images were playing behind my eyes, not in front of them. But it wasn't my fault he was built like a freaking god. And no matter how much my body responded to him, I could still hate him. I was done being led around by my vagina.

No longer tired, the carpet that had seemed so plush a few hours ago felt rough beneath my cheek. I sat up, but halfway up, it hit me.

Dominic was in the shower. There'd been no other sound, nothing to suggest there was anyone else here. I stood up slowly, creeping toward the door. Images of the guns that had been shoved in my face flashed through my mind. They could still be there, but as I looked around at my prison, it was a chance I had to take.

I grit my teeth as I turned the handle, begging the thing not to make a sound. Once out of the room, I closed the door behind me, silently thanking it when it barely made a click. I tiptoed down the hall, past the bathroom where I could still hear the water running.

My legs felt like jelly, and my heart pounded like it was trying to burst out of my chest, but I made it out to the living room. Twenty more steps, and I was home-free. One after another, I crept across the living room on silent feet, but blood was whooshing so loudly in my ears, I didn't realize the shower had stopped until the bathroom door clicked open. Without thinking, I spun around.

He stood outside the bathroom door with a towel slung low around his hips. The rippling eight-pack across his abdomen still glistened with moisture, and I couldn't stop my gaze from following the droplets that dripped down the hard jut of his hips and disappeared into the towel's edge. Even my fantasies couldn't have conjured up this kind of perfection.

"Go ahead, open it," he said, nodding toward the door. "I'd recommend not charging through it, though."

He was too confident. Too damn cocky. If I opened the door, I had a feeling all I was going to get was an eyeful of cold steel. It was strange that even in the warmth of the apartment, I imagined the steel of a gun was cold.

"Let me go," I said with more bravado than I felt. Still, I straightened my shoulders and drew up every ounce of hatred I felt for this man, letting it shine clear in my eyes.

"You know that's not going to happen, Fallon. You're here as much for your own safety as anything else. Tony Nova is a dangerous man."

I scoffed. "A dangerous man? And you're what? A saint?"

The muscles in his shoulders tensed, and his jaw ticked.

"I may be a lot of things, but don't ever compare me to him," he said then turned away and headed down the hall, out of sight.

My breath came out in a whoosh, and I sagged against the door. Now that I knew those men were still there, I could practically feel the cold of their guns seeping through the wood.

A dangerous man in here, dangerous men out there; I felt like I was trapped in a minefield, waiting for one wrong step.

I hadn't moved when Dominic returned a few moments later. He was dressed in typical-Dominic style. A three-piece suit that highlighted the breadth of his shoulders. The black of his shirt seemed to darken his eyes so much they looked like storm clouds.

He walked straight to the kitchen, and though I couldn't see him from my vantage point, I could hear him fiddling around in there. The quiet glug of a coffee maker filled the silence a moment later, and the rich, dark scent of coffee wafted through the apartment. He'd tasted like coffee when he'd kissed me. I'd been so hopped up on arousal, I'd wanted to draw the taste into me and feel it buzzing through my veins.

"Coffee?" he called out like I was an ordinary guest in his home.

I didn't answer him, but he appeared a moment later with a black mug, filled to the brim in his hand. He stopped at the edge of the living room, holding out the mug.

"I left it black. You don't seem to be in much of a sweet mood today, *limone*."

If he thought I was going to waltz over there and accept the mug graciously, he could think again. I was more tempted to take it just so I could dump it on him. Tempted, but not quite brave enough, it seemed. I remained where I was with my back against the door.

"Suit yourself," he said, retreating back to the kitchen.

A sizzling sound broke the silence a moment later, and a sweet, buttery scent mingled with the coffee aroma in the air. My stomach rumbled, and I was grateful I was too far away for him to hear it. I was hungry, but there was no way I was accepting anything he offered—assuming he offered anything at all. Maybe after rejecting the coffee, he'd decided I was on my own. Then again, it wouldn't look very good if he was dragging a starving bride down the aisle.

Or maybe there wouldn't be an aisle. Plenty of marriages now were just civil proceedings, no church, no aisle. It would be a far more practical solution just to use whatever justice of the peace they had in their pocket.

A tiny part of my heart ached like someone had taken a gouge out of it. I'd always dreamed of a big wedding in a pretty church. Not that it mattered. In none of those fantasies had I been forced into marriage by a freaking Godfather wannabe.

"Breakfast is ready," he called, but he didn't come out this time. "Unless you've decided to go on a hunger strike."

I could hear the amusement in his tone.

Now, I was just going to look like an idiot if I didn't eat. *Fine*. But eating didn't mean talking. He wasn't getting one damned word out of me.

I stomped across the living room and into the kitchen. There was a small wrought-iron table for two set off to one side, and he'd placed two plates of pancakes down on it.

I raised my eyebrows. I'd never pictured scary mafia guys with aprons on in the kitchen.

"Don't look so surprised," he said, seemingly reading my mind. "My mother was very particular about raising her children right, and apparently 'right' meant making sure her sons knew their way around a kitchen."

I scoffed. Raising her children right? I could just imagine it: cooking lessons at nine, gun practice at eleven, and how to be a big, scary asshole at noon.

"You can say whatever you want about me, Fallon. She's off-limits, understand?" he said, crossing his arms over his chest and looking at me expectantly.

I nodded, more because he'd caught me off-guard than out of any sense of agreement.

"Good." He sat down at the small table and waited for me to take the seat opposite him.

I waited for him to dive in before turning my attention to the food on my plate. The pancakes were warm and buttery with just the perfect amount of crisp around the edges. It pissed me off that it seemed he really could cook. At least his mother had done something right, even if she had raised her son to be an animal.

"I'll be away for the day." He spoke between mouthfuls, and my hopes soared. "But don't worry, there will always be someone close by," he finished, dashing my hopes to shreds.

The food in my stomach turned to lead. I pushed away from the table and stood up. He made no move to stop me.

"Fallon," he called when I reached the doorway.

I paused but didn't turn around.

"That man could have killed you. I won't take that risk again no matter what you may think of me."

I didn't bother to respond. What was the point? If he'd really been so concerned about me, he would have stayed the hell away from me from the beginning. I returned to the guest room and closed the door, then just stood there, listening to the clatter of dishes, the footsteps down the hall then back to the living room, the sound of the front door closing.

Finally, I was alone. It should have been a relief. It should have been the closest to normal I'd felt since he'd dragged me out of my apartment last night. But the click of the door had gone off like a switch in my head, opening the floodgates, and it all came pouring out.

Sobs wracked my body, clambering up my chest and out my throat. The sound came out loud and harsh in the silence of the apartment, but I couldn't hold it back. Hot tears streaked down my cheeks as I sunk to the floor in the middle of the room. I wrapped my arms around my knees, tucking them close to my chest like somehow, if I could hold on tight enough, I could hold myself together. But I couldn't. More sobs, more tears. He'd stolen my life. How was I supposed to be okay with that?

I cried until my body ran out of tears and my chest hurt from the sobs that had wracked it relentlessly. I mourned for the life that had been taken from me until everything inside me gave way to a cathartic numbness that started in the core of me and worked its way out to the tips of my fingers and toes.

I didn't feel angry anymore, or hurt. My heart felt like it had been anesthetized. This wasn't acceptance, it was indifference. A temporary reprieve that would wear off just as surely as the numbness that came from lidocaine.

The apartment was still silent. I stood up on unsteady legs and crept out into the hall, listening, but he hadn't returned. I walked into the living room, taking stock of my surroundings, but it didn't feel like enough. I could see the tall, dark wood entertainment cabinet against the wall, but I wanted to know what was inside it.

It wasn't really curiosity that compelled me to open it, or to wander throughout the apartment, snooping through every drawer and cupboard I came across. Nor did I harbor any real hope of finding something that would help me out of my predicament. It felt more like I was orientating myself to my surroundings.

The kitchen, the dining and living room. The linen closet in the hall and the bathroom. When I came to Dominic's bedroom though, I stopped, hovering with my toes on the threshold. To become familiar with my surroundings was one thing; to look through his private things felt too personal, and I had no interest in getting personal with him. So, I moved on, continuing my investigation in the second spare bedroom.

The sun had begun to wane by the time I'd finished exploring, and still, he hadn't returned. I was tempted to try the front door again, but whether because I was smart or a coward, I dismissed it.

I looked down the hall into the open bathroom door. I was warm, and my skin was covered in a light sheen of sweat from all my exploring, and I really needed a shower. But to use his shower?

I shrugged. If he didn't want me using the shower, he should have put one of his stupid lackeys in front of it.

Chapter Fifteen

Dominic

"They shot up her apartment."

Leo was on the other end of the line, but he'd chosen a bad time to call. I'd just left Fallon's apartment with eleven bullets in my pocket. Eleven bullets I'd found on her floor and buried in her walls. No shattered windows. It meant that the Novas' lackey had walked right into her apartment and started firing.

I squealed out of the parking lot, cutting in front of the slow Ford that had been inching up the street. He began honking his horn. I slammed my foot on the gas and sped past him.

"But both of you got out of there," Leo said, his tone confused.

"That isn't the point," I growled.

"Then what is the point, *fratello*?"

"They could have killed her."

"Hm, not good. All those wedding invitations you would have had to cancel…" He sighed a melodramatic sigh.

I opened my mouth then closed it. Who gives a fuck about wedding invitations?

I hadn't given a single thought to the wedding, to the marriage. I'd only thought about *her* body lying lifeless on her living room floor. Her blood on the carpet, her sapphire eyes staring unseeing at the ceiling, her lips colorless and cold.

My stomach turned, and a strange feeling shot through my chest.

"Exactly," I lied. "They could have ruined everything, Leo. This marriage has to happen."

Leo laughed. "So, that's the story we're going with, huh?"

"It's not a story. It's—"

"All right, all right. If you say so. What do you need?"

"There's a store across from her apartment with a camera out front. It's a digital feed." I tapped my fingers on the steering wheel as I spoke.

"I'm on it," he said. He could be a pain in the ass, but I could always count on him.

"*Grazie*, Leo."

"Non c'è problema, fratello."

I hung up the phone and dropped it onto the passenger seat. I scrubbed a hand over my face and lightly tapped my foot on the brakes.

I'd been heading in the direction of Chianti to find Tony. I'd deal with him—I had no doubt about that—but there was no way I'd make it back out alive. There was no room in my life for dumbass moves. Ruthless, always, but never stupid.

All I could do was wait for Leo to do his magic. It was one of Tony's men, no doubt, but which one?

Twenty minutes passed, and then thirty. I was just about ready to come out of my skin by the time my phone rang.

"Did you find him?" I asked as soon as I answered the call.

"*Sì*. I found the guy who did the shooting—Cosimo De Carlo. The asshole practically posed for the camera." Leo chuckled. "But who told Tony about Fallon in the first place? *Non lo so*. I'll keep digging."

"*Grazie*, Leo. You do that. I'll see if I can't motivate our shooter to talk." I was just about to hang up the phone, but Leo kept talking.

"Dom…?" he said, and then silence.

"What is it, Leo?"

"We've got a war coming at us. Why are you going after some lowly soldier of Nova's?"

It was a fair question.

"It's just something I have to do," I said simply.

He laughed, but at least he was wise enough not to comment.

"I've texted the shooter's mug shot and address to you. Any chance you want backup?"

"No, not this time."

***

I pulled up in front of the decrepit four-story walk-up. The brick was old and crumbling in spots. Faded and broken shingles littered the ground. This place was a dump.

Two children in ragged clothes played on a makeshift hopscotch a few yards away, and a man sat on the steps of the building next door, smoking a joint. He had an old-fashioned boom box next to him, and it blared out garbled noise that I was fairly certain was supposed to be music.

Perfetto. The garbled noise would help cover up the sound of gunfire—even from the fourth floor.

I waited until I was inside the squalid building to pull out my Sig then climbed the old linoleum-covered stairs. In the hallway, more music came through the walls from one of the apartments, but as I neared my destination, the sound grew quieter.

There was no noise coming from inside De Carlo's apartment. It was possible he wasn't home.

I turned the handle slowly, expecting to find it locked, but it wasn't. *Coglione.*

The door opened without a squeak, like it wanted its occupant to suffer for his own stupidity. Inside, the scent of gone bad food and filth overwhelmed my nostrils, so potent it stung my eyes. A narrow garbage-littered hallway led to a tiny kitchen on the left and to a living room on the right.

No sounds came from the kitchen, so I crept toward it to make sure it was clear. The room was empty, though it was a wonder the room hadn't been overrun by vermin. Dirty dishes in the sink and on the counters. Old food spilled on the floor.

I strode back toward the living room, and there he was. The back of De Carlo's ugly head. He sat on a brown threadbare sofa with his arms sprawled across the back of it and a beer in one hand. Since the sofa was faced the other way, he couldn't see me. Not yet.

No weapons sat on the chipped and stained coffee table in front of him, but the gun was here somewhere. The gun he'd fired inside Fallon's apartment. The gun he would have used to kill her had I not gotten her out of there.

It would have been so easy to put a bullet in the back of the fucker's greasy head. One shot to his brain stem. But I wanted answers, and having to draw this out didn't bother me in the slightest.

I raised my Sig and fired a bullet right through De Carlo's hand. The bottle he held exploded as he roared and then shot to his feet. He gripped his hand tight to his chest while his glazed eyes met mine.

"What the fuck?" Recognition dawned in his eyes as the crimson pooled in his chest.

"I was about to ask you the same question. Have a seat," I said then fired a shot into his kneecap.

He crumpled to the ground as he screamed. With one hand and one leg out of commission, he scrambled back awkwardly.

"It was nothing personal, man. I gotta work, same as you."

I scoffed. "If you'd come at me, De Carlo, I would have paid you the same respect. I would have put a bullet in your head, and the score would have been settled. But I saw the bullets you fired. Very messy. Very… indiscriminate, wouldn't you say?"

He looked at me like he couldn't figure out what I was talking about. Maybe I needed to use smaller words.

"You shot up that apartment like you didn't care what you hit, but I cared, so now we have a problem."

His eyes widened. "The girl? I didn't shoot her. I swear, no one was there."

I chuckled. "Of course, no one was there, but that isn't the point. You didn't know she wasn't there until you'd finished shooting up her apartment. Correct?"

He pressed his lips together. His whole face had turned red with pain, and his hands shook against his chest. "So, you're just gonna kill me slow?"

"I could," I said with a shrug. I wasn't squeamish. Slow and painful didn't bother me. "Or you can give me a name, and I'll make it quick."

There wasn't a third option.

He was inching his way toward the TV stand against the wall. The scratched doors were crooked, but I had a feeling there was a perfectly functional weapon stashed inside.

I raised my gun and made a fresh hole through his shoulder.

More screams. More blood. "What do you want?"

"I told you, I want a name," I said, leaning against the living room wall then thinking better of it. The walls were probably crawling with insects.

"It was Tony—Tony Nova. He told me I gotta shoot up that place. He told me… he told me he wanted you dead, and…"

"And what?"

He cringed, squeezing his eyes shut like he was waiting for the final blow. "And the girl, too."

With Fallon dead, Tony wouldn't have to worry about her being married off to Dante or Leo to seal the deal with Douglas Moore. Strangely, the thought of her marrying Dante or Leo didn't thrill me either. But that meant Tony knew about the marriage arrangement, and he'd be going after Fallon full-force to stop it from happening.

"I want to know how Tony knew about the girl. Who gave him that information?"

De Carlo's eyes widened. "I don't know. How the hell would I know that?"

There was no reason Tony would have shared his source with De Carlo, but sometimes, even lowly minions overheard their bosses talking.

"All right, I believe you, De Carlo," I said.

He let out a sigh of relief.

Then I fired a bullet right between his eyes.

Chapter Sixteen

Dominic

It had been a long day. All I wanted to do was collapse, but I had a feeling my new roommate was going to try to get in the way of that.

With a heavy sigh, I nodded to Leandro and Salvo, the two men who'd spent the past twelve hours sitting outside my door, and walked inside with a gym bag in one hand.

I half-expected to find her in the middle of the living room, glaring daggers at me, but she was nowhere to be seen. The bathroom door was closed, though, and I could hear the water running.

Images of Fallon, naked and wet, bombarded my mind, sending a hot jolt of arousal through my veins. I'd had her naked, her legs splayed, on the verge of orgasm less than twenty-four hours ago. I wondered what she'd do now if I walked in there and joined her in the shower. Would she push me away? Or would she succumb to it, setting the stage for the best angry sex of her life?

The water shut off while I stood there, hesitating. I scrubbed my fingers through my hair. It would have been better if she'd been ugly—a hump, a few warts, and maybe some hideous scars would have made it so much easier to get her out of my mind.

The bathroom door opened, and she stepped out with a towel wrapped around her, tucked between her breasts. She gasped when she saw me and took a step back, hovering between the bathroom and the hallway. Her hair was dripping wet, her eyes wide, her lips parted in surprise. A walking, gasping fucking fantasy come to life.

Her eyes were no longer blue flames. It surprised me—something I rarely felt. It was too much to hope she'd come to terms with our situation. It was more like she was in some sort of trance.

I looked her up and down because I would have had to be dead to not pay any attention to her slim thighs or the curve of her waist, or the way the edge of the towel had been tucked so carelessly between her breasts, it could come loose at any moment.

The sparks were snapping in the air, just like they were this morning when it had been her eyes grazing over my half-naked body. She'd stood there frozen in her sexy black dress, and I'd known for a fact she'd had no panties on beneath it. It would have been so easy to thrust her up against the wall and fuck her senseless, just like it would be no difficult task now.

I took a step toward her, and she remained where she was. Another step and then another, and I could see her throat muscles working as she swallowed hard. Her chest rose and fell faster, loosening the towel's edge, but it stayed there, taunting me, like it was suspended in space.

But when I stopped right in front of her and reached for the towel, the trance-like glaze in her eyes evaporated.

"Dominic, don't," she whispered.

I dropped my hand, but I didn't move away.

"I won't do this," she said, though it sounded like she was trying to convince herself as much as me. "You can't treat me like a prisoner and expect me to fall all over you. What you're doing is wrong. I'm a person, not an object for you to own."

With every word, her voice grew stronger, and her sweetness gave way to bitter anger. Though I didn't miss the way her body tensed as I drew closer, she was looking at me like I was some vile creature.

I stepped back. Maybe the princess would get off her high horse if she knew just how close her hot little ass had come to being blown to pieces. I reached into my pocket and withdrew the eleven small crushed pieces of metal.

"You're welcome," I said, dropping them at her feet.

She looked down, squinting at the fragments on the floor.

"Just in case you're curious, I retrieved those from your apartment walls."

"My walls?" She paused. "That's why you dragged me out. That's why…"

She swallowed hard as her face lost some of its color.

Maybe now she'd realize that my apartment was a safe haven, not a prison.

"And this is my life now?" she said, her voice once again an octave too high while she motioned to the bullets on the floor.

That wasn't the point I'd been trying to make. The point was she was alive. She was safe. She was breathing. She was here.

"There are people shooting at me… shooting at me because of *you*. That man… he wasn't after me. He was after you. If I'd never met you, he would never have known about me."

"What do you want me to do? Turn back time?" I clenched my jaw.

She was right. It was my fault she'd been in danger. But none of this was my choice any more than it was hers.

"I want you to leave me alone. I want you to let me go, and I never want to see you again." She glared at me while her chest heaved with every deep breath.

"No can do, *limone*, but don't worry, as soon as we're married, you can lock yourself away in here and never lay eyes on me again if you so choose," I said then turned and walked away.

Inside my bedroom, I closed and locked the door, then proceeded to pace back and forth across the long stretch of hardwood flooring at the foot of the bed.

I let out a groan. She was lucky I wasn't a lesser man, or I might have been tempted to strangle her just to stop her from spewing her senseless bullshit. Nobody fucking talked to me that way.

Maybe I just needed to give her more time, I tried to reason with myself as I loosened my tie and tossed it on the bed. If I was in her shoes, maybe I'd be just as pissed off as she was. But then again, I *was* in her shoes. I sure as fuck didn't want to marry a woman who not only annoyed the hell out of me but wanted nothing to do with me. But my family needed this, so there was no question to it.

Loyalty came first.

Family came first.

But who does she have to pledge her loyalty to? a voice taunted from the back of my mind. It hit me like a sucker punch. Fallon had no one. No mother, no siblings, and a lousy deadbeat prick for a father. My father, my mother, every one of my siblings; we would die for each other in a heartbeat. Would Douglas endure so much as a hangnail for his daughter?

I sat down at the edge of the bed and tugged off my shoes. While the woman still pissed me off to no end, perhaps I'd expected too much of her. Maybe she was entitled to her anger. And maybe for once, it was my turn to get off my high horse and try to help her through this.

I laid back and closed my eyes. Helping her might have been the right thing to do, but not tonight. I was too tired to deal with any more of her antics.

***

I should have known Fallon would fight me, that she'd make it impossible to try to help her. She had locked herself in the guest room by the time I got up in the morning. I hadn't seen her since—and it had been two days.

She wasn't always in there. I had no doubt that when I left the apartment, she came out of her room. She might have tidied up after herself and washed dishes to make sure she left no trace, but I knew.

It had been amusing at first, like I was living with an oversized mouse who kept eating its way through the strawberries and grapefruits in my fridge. Now though, I'd just about had enough. I was done waiting around.

I sat on my sofa in the living room, waiting for the inevitable confrontation. I made sure I had nowhere I needed to be today, and the mouse couldn't hide out in her room indefinitely. It pissed me off, though, that for the first time, I understood the thrill she'd gotten from fighting with me. Outside, I was as cool as stone, but inside, I was cracking my knuckles and rolling my shoulders, preparing for battle.

An hour passed before I heard the telltale click of the door and then the quiet footsteps shuffling along the floor. I remained perfectly still as she left the hallway, headed for the kitchen.

She'd made it halfway there before she noticed me. Her breath caught in her throat, but she kept going, either too hungry or too stubborn to abandon her scavenging for food.

She was wearing the same black dress—she'd washed it at some point. The washer and dryer had been used, but my housekeeper hadn't been in yet this week. If she wasn't so stubborn, I would have told her about the duffel bag of clothes I'd grabbed for her from her apartment. But knowing she was still walking around panty-less didn't bother me in the slightest.

I waited while she rummaged through the fridge then returned with a bowlful of fruit.

"Stop," I said when she started back toward the hallway, and despite my irritation, I loved how her feet froze like her body couldn't help but obey me.

"What do you want, Dominic?" she asked while her eyes darted back and forth from me to the hallway.

"I want this bullshit to stop now," I said, standing up and taking two steps toward her.

She laughed, but it came out a touch on the maniacal side. She was all fire and fight today.

"Whenever you're done with me and you're ready to stop keeping me here against my will, just let me know."

I clicked my tongue. She made it sound like I'd kidnapped her and was keeping her here for my own depraved desires.

"Do you think I want this?" I barked which made her jolt.

"You're the one keeping me locked in here, aren't you?" she spat, loud enough that she couldn't hide the slight tremor in her voice.

"I'm keeping you here to keep your ass safe. And I'm marrying you because I don't have a fucking choice. I'm just as trapped as you are, Fallon. Do you really think I want to marry you?"

She flinched like I'd cut her deep.

She opened her mouth but then closed it as if she'd thought better of it.

"What do you mean you're just as trapped?" she asked, and though she still looked angry, there was genuine curiosity in her gaze.

"I mean this marriage is my father's idea, not mine."

She was silent, like she was actually taking the time to process that information.

"But you're just going along with it?" It came out like a question, but it didn't sound much like one.

Still, I nodded. "It's important to my family, and I meant it when I said loyalty was everything. I'd do anything for them, Fallon."

She winced like I'd hurt her again. "Even take away my choice, my future?"

"Yes," I said quietly because I wasn't proud of it. My family needed this, and I would do anything for them, but in the past, it had always been my safety at stake, my life on the line. Not someone else's. Not *hers*.

"I thought one day if I ever married, it would be to someone who loved me, to someone who put me first, who didn't use me. Someone who wasn't…" She trailed off, leaving the words unspoken, but I could see them in her eyes even as she tried to hide them from herself.

"…like your father?" I finished gently.

"Don't say that. You don't know him." Her eyes flared, but it wasn't anger, it was denial.

"Yes, I do know him, *limone*. And I know you deserved better."

She scoffed. "Better? Like you?"

"No, not like me," I said, balling my hands into fists.

I thought of how she saved Bullet's life. I thought of the relief that washed over my father's face when I told him Bullet was going to be fine. I thought of how Bullet wasn't the first dog she's ever saved.

She deserved to be able to do that for the rest of her life. Not be trapped here, constantly worrying if a bullet was out there waiting for her, waiting to be shot through her heart.

But blood *is* thicker than water.

"But you're still going to go through with this." There was no inflection in her tone, no question in her voice.

"You'll want for nothing," I said like it was some consolation prize, but we both knew it wasn't true.

She would forever want one thing, and it was the one thing I couldn't offer her.

Chapter Seventeen

Fallon

All night, I tossed and turned while Dominic's words followed me from one nightmare to the next.

"You'll want for nothing."

I dreamed of sitting like a China doll atop a veritable sea of gold. I dreamed of money and gems filling up the apartment, surrounding me until there was no room left for air. I dreamed of falling in a deep, dark hole where I was crushed, little by little, by rubies and emeralds and diamonds. They glittered so prettily as their weight ground my bones to dust.

But sometimes, every once in a while, he was there in my dream beside me, gasping for air or screaming beneath the weight of his fortune.

He didn't want this marriage either. I didn't feel sorry for him. He'd chosen to accept his bondage rather than fighting for my freedom or his own. But I did feel something. Maybe it was envy. Not for his money or his power. I didn't care about those things. But he felt such a bond to a whole group of people that he would sacrifice himself for them.

Would I have willingly offered up such a sacrifice for my father? As much as I wanted to believe I loved him that much, I knew the real answer. I knew that there were limits to the lengths I'd go, just as there were limits to what he would do for me.

The front door of the apartment opened, and I jolted a little in my seat. I was sitting at the small dining table in a pair of tights and a T-shirt I'd found in a duffel bag Dominic must have left outside my door. *My* door—how quickly I'd come to see a room in his home as my own.

He walked into the kitchen, but before I could decide whether or not I was talking to him today, he held out his hand.

"Come with me," he said.

Panic shot out from the core of me, making my hands tremble and my heart pound a frantic beat. His father had said seven days. I had days left before they forced me to marry him.

"I'm not dragging you down the aisle yet, Fallon. I promise," he said, holding out his hand a little further.

He could be lying, but it didn't feel like it, and more than that, what would be the point? He could throw me over his shoulder like a caveman and drag me wherever he wanted. And damn, I hated how much the idea excited me as much as it pissed me off.

Reluctantly, I took his hand and followed him to the front door. A tiny thrill shot down my spine at the prospect of getting out of here, even if the reprieve was only temporary.

The thrill dissipated, though, as he drove me across the city. No matter how many times I asked, he wouldn't tell me where we were going.

"You've got to be kidding me," I said as he slowed to a stop in front of a big building with a sign that read *Shooting Range* in large black letters across the front. "A shooting range, really?"

It seemed like a bad idea on his part to "train" a woman to fire a gun when that woman might very well be tempted to use that gun on him. Then again, if he wanted to take that risk, then so be it.

He smiled smugly. "It doesn't matter what I teach you, Fallon. You'll never be able to outgun me, so don't even try," he said like he'd read my mind. I really wished he'd stop doing that.

As if he wasn't the least bit worried about what harm might come to his person, he slid out of the driver's seat and came around to open my door.

He led me inside the building, but no one stood at the reception counter. Strange. And even stranger was that not one person tried to stop Dominic from leading me through the door on the left to a large room that was segregated in rows with paper targets hung at the end of each one. Shouldn't someone have stopped him from walking around like he owned the place? Then again, it seemed like no one stopped the Lucas from doing anything—not if they wanted to keep breathing.

He closed the door behind us and placed the case and the box he was carrying down on a small table. He stood there with his hands behind his back and an expectant look on his face.

"What?" I asked when he made no move to explain.

"It's for you. Open it," he said with a smirk as he motioned to the case on the table.

"What is it?" I raised an eyebrow at him.

After unfastening the clips, I lifted the lid and looked in. A sleek black handgun rested on top of dark gray foam.

A humorless laugh bubbled up and slipped out. "A gun? Is this some kind of joke?"

But there was nothing humorous about Dominic's expression.

"Why are you giving me a gun?" I asked.

"It's a gift, Fallon. But I'd like you to keep it on your person wherever you go," he said, apparently forgetting that he hadn't let me leave his freaking apartment on my own. "It's a Springfield Hellcat—the name seemed fitting."

He winked at me.

Damn it, no one should make my legs feel like jelly like he could.

"It's a semiautomatic, compact, and easy to conceal. It's got a thirteen-round extended magazine. It seemed like a good idea, considering how bad of a shot you're going to be." Another smug smile. The man was insufferable.

"We'll see about that," I said, picking up the gun. I'd seen people use guns plenty of times on TV. How difficult could it be?

I stormed toward the nearest row with a target strung up at the end.

"You might want to load the gun before you try to shoot it," Dominic called to me, making me swallow back a scream. And I was not blushing. Definitely not blushing.

I stomped back toward him and held out the gun, doing my damnedest to look bored. It felt like I fell about a mile short when he took it from me, released the clip, and made an overexaggerated show of loading each bullet. When he was finished, he slid the clip into place and handed it to me.

Without a word, I stormed back, trying to pull up every gun fact I could recall. Fatal shootings, gun violence, gun laws; plenty of those sprung to mind, but not one useful tidbit about what the hell to do with a gun. *Wait!* The gun would have a safety on it. I needed to remove the safety or the thing wouldn't fire. All right, that was something.

I turned to face the target, surreptitiously glancing at the gun in my hands, searching for what might have been the safety mechanism. Next to the trigger was a small circle, like a button. That had to be it.

I pressed it then wrapped both hands around the gun and raised my arms up in front of me. I couldn't believe I was really going to do this. A week ago, I'd been a veterinarian who was more likely to take part in a march against gun violence than fire a gun in some stupid shooting range. But here I was, and there was no way Mr. Al Pacino over there was walking out of here with that smug look on his face. I would slap that look off of his face if I had to.

I focused my attention on the target in front of me—jeez, it seemed really far away—then squeezed the trigger.

The crack of the gun went off like a thunderbolt in my ears. I flinched at the sound.

When I'd recovered enough to squint at the target, I wanted to curse even more. Not a mark. The bullet hadn't even grazed the outer edge of the target. *Shit. Shit. Shit.*

I could feel Dominic's eyes on me, but there was no way I was going to look at him. I didn't want to see the stupid smug look on his stupid face.

Instead, I stared at the target and raised my arms again. *You got this, Moore,* I pep-talked myself, ignoring the fact I wasn't going to be a Moore for much longer.

One breath. Two. Three. I squeezed the trigger, prepared this time for the earsplitting crack, but the bullet made it no closer to the target. *Damn it.*

"All right, Annie Oakley," he teased, coming to stand behind me. "How about you let me teach you before you end up shooting me by accident?"

"It wouldn't be an accident," I muttered under my breath.

I remained still when he moved in closer. So what if I wasn't an expert marksman? I'd spent my adult life trying to help things, *not* hurt them.

When he positioned himself right behind me, his arms on either side of me and his chest pressed against my back, tingles shot through my whole body. And it seemed with him standing so close, he was using up more of the oxygen in the room, making me work harder for every breath.

He leaned in closer until his lips were right next to my ear.

"Breathe with me," he whispered, and the sound traveled right through me, settling low in my abdomen.

I closed my eyes and tried to do as he said, focusing on the rise and fall of his chest against my back and breathing in tandem. But it was difficult when I could feel the gentle exhale of his breath against my neck.

He reached out from behind and repositioned my fingers on the gun, making it sit more comfortably in my hands. His fingertips grazed mine, I could feel the roughness of his thumb as it smoothed over mine.

"Just focus." His voice was a whisper, releasing my hands. "Now… fire."

As if my hands had been trained to obey him, I squeezed the trigger, trying to ignore everything but the target far in front of me.

A loud crack. The recoil that shot my shoulders back hard into his chest.

I did it! The bullet landed far from center, but I could see the small hole right through the paper, maybe eight inches off from the bull's-eye in the middle.

Forgetting myself entirely, I *whooped* in triumph.

"You did it," he said, hugging me from behind and making me forget all about the target. There was only the heat of his body. The feel of his powerful arms around me. His warm breath against my neck.

"Do it again," he said, letting go just enough so I could reposition my stance.

I tried to focus through the haze of heat that was wrapped around me. It made my muscles weak despite the coil that was winding tighter in my core.

"Do it," he whispered, breathing warm air against my neck.

I squeezed the trigger, and the bullet found its mark, a little closer to the bull's-eye this time.

Instead of celebrating, I leaned back harder against him, searching for his lips. I wanted to feel them against my ear, my neck.

"That was better," he breathed. "With enough practice, you might be almost as good a shot as me one day."

As good of a shot as him? He was an expert shot, wasn't he? How old had he been the first time he'd held a pistol? The first time he'd fired a shot? The first time he'd killed a person?

I surged away from him as a sharp shiver charged down my spine like my spinal fluid had been replaced by liquid nitrogen.

"All right, Annie Oakley. It's my turn," he said, stepping in front of me.

"Don't call me that," I hissed, just as frustrated with my body's own response to him as I was with the man himself. "I have no interest in being an expert at killing people."

He turned to look at me with his eyebrow raised. "You might have no interest in going on a citywide killing spree, but I guarantee that the day you've got a gun pressed to your skull, you won't have any qualms about killing the motherfucker."

He spun back around, raised his gun in front of him, and emptied his whole clip straight through the bull's-eye.

"Contrary to what you seem to think, I'm not a cold-blooded murderer," he said, holstering his gun. "But I won't die—or let the people I care about die—just so I can pretend the world is full of fucking sunshine and rainbows."

"I never said you were—"

"I know what you think," he snapped. "Your eyes give you away every time." He took the gun from my hand and returned it to the case on the small table.

I had no idea why I felt like crap when he was the one who killed people and did God only knew what else.

"I'm sorry," I said through gritted teeth because it was absolutely insane that I was apologizing to the Undertaker.

"No worries, *limone*," he said, shutting the case and flicking the clips into place. "I think that's enough training for one day. We should go."

I followed him out of the room, back through the reception area to his car. He opened the passenger side door for me without a glance, but as I slipped inside, he caught my wrist and pulled me to him. His lips were on mine before I could make sense of what was happening. Warm and firm, he tasted like coffee with just a hint of scotch. I didn't know what it was about the combination, but it never ceased to draw me in, to make me want to delve deeper.

Heat coursed through my veins, lighting a fire between my thighs as his tongue slipped between my lips, gliding along my tongue.

This was wrong. Some part of me knew it, but I was just so tired of caring.

I grabbed onto his shoulders as he released my wrist and took hold of my hips.

He pressed me back against the passenger door until he'd molded every part of me to his hard frame. A hard frame I could so easily picture now after seeing him when he'd walked out of the shower. The smooth planes of his chest. The wide breadth of his bare shoulders. The rippled perfection of his abdomen.

I slid my fingers down and slipped them beneath his jacket as he pulled his lips away and started a hot trail down my jaw. His lips were warm, and his breath whispered against my skin, sending tiny sizzles of current throughout my body.

Without missing a beat, he slid his hands beneath me and lifted me up, then placed me down on the trunk of his car.

"Open your legs," he said against my skin, then he pressed himself between my thighs as I complied. Closer and closer, until nothing but thin clothing separated us.

His lips continued down my neck, but as I tipped my head back to give him more access, I caught sight of the black car across the street. Inside it, a man sat in the driver's seat, staring right at us. And in the car behind it, another man was watching us.

A cold tremor fired down my spine despite the heat that was pumping through my veins.

"Dominic?" I said, angling away from him. "We need to leave."

He sighed and stepped back, his hands still on my hips. "What's wrong, *limone?*"

"There are people watching us," I whispered.

Were these the men who'd shot up my apartment? We were out in the open. Nothing could stop them from killing us right here and now. My shoulders slouched like my body thought it could make itself small enough to disappear.

Dominic followed my gaze then barked out a laugh. "They're my men, Fallon. They're not 'watching' us. They're watching out *for* us so I can focus on more… enticing distractions."

Some of the cold chill began to evaporate, but it had been enough to shock me to my senses. This man was part of the mob. He was keeping me against my will. What the hell was I doing making out with him?

"We should go," I said even though my body railed in objection.

He muttered something under his breath. It sounded an awful lot like "sweet and sour", but I had probably heard him wrong.

When he stepped back, I slid my feet to the ground and made a beeline for the passenger side door and practically tumbled into the front seat. It was so much easier when the line was drawn clearly in the sand, and we stayed on opposite sides of the battle. It was too confusing when he crossed the line, when he touched me and kissed me and made me forget about everything but the feel of his body against mine. It made me soft, it made me weak.

Those were dangerous things to be in the company of a killer.

Chapter Eighteen

Fallon

Dominic was silent on the drive back to his apartment. Despite the electricity that seemed to buzz in the air all around us, he seemed completely unfazed by it.

Could anything rattle this man? I wondered.

He pulled up in front of his condo and handed his keys over to a valet. I followed him out of the car, but I lingered outside the passenger door, staring up at the building. It had no bars on its windows or guards patrolling its perimeter, but it was a prison nonetheless.

My prison.

I wasn't ready to go back in yet.

"Come on, Fallon," he said after a moment, but I ignored him. I had no doubt I was just as much a captive outside as inside, but at least out here, my walls were invisible.

"Now," he said in that tone that seemed to make my feet move of their own volition.

Maybe my feet were just smarter than the rest of me. The man probably knew a hundred different ways to kill me without anyone being the wiser. Really, after all the times I'd fought with him, it was a wonder he hadn't put those skills to use. All those mobster guys in movies seemed to have perpetually short fuses. It was strange then, that Dominic had never lost his temper. Strange, and disconcerting. It would have been easier if I could have fit him neatly into a mold I recognized. Much less confusing, and at least then I could know what to expect.

He led me to the elevator and up to his condo.

"*Signora* Luca is here," one of the men who guarded his door like a Doberman said as Dominic moved to turn the handle.

He paused, and his shoulders stiffened. He turned to look at me, eyeing me warily.

Suddenly, I knew what could rattle the unshakable Dominic Luca: his mother.

"You can say whatever you want about me, Fallon. She's off-limits," he'd said my first morning in his home.

It was a strange side of him to see, and it bothered me. Not because it somehow made him more human. In any other situation, it would have been a relief to see he wasn't just a coldhearted killer. But because, on the other side of the door, stood a woman to whom he was loyal. A woman for whom he'd do anything. He'd murder for her. He'd die for her. He'd take away my life for her.

Something about the way he was looking at me pulled at my stupid heart. This woman mattered to him, and he worried I would mistreat her. It stung that he would think I'd lash out at the woman to spite him, almost enough that I was tempted to do just that. Almost.

But even though he was just as stuck with me as I was with him, he'd tried to soften the blow today. He'd taken me out of my cage and put a weapon in my hand. I had no doubt his intention had been to make me feel more empowered… even if we both knew I didn't have a hope in hell of outgunning him.

I nodded, though I was sure it wasn't necessary. The man seemed to be able to read my thoughts all on his own.

Then he flashed me a small smile and opened the door.

I wasn't quite sure what I'd expected—maybe a woman with cold eyes and a hard-set jaw—but the beautiful woman who sat in the plush armchair in Dominic's living room definitely wasn't it.

She was tall and slim with high cheekbones and the most soulful dark eyes I'd ever seen. Her dark hair was lightly streaked with silver, and she wore it up in a simple knot at the crown of her head.

She stood when we entered the apartment, smiling first at Dominic and then at me. There was something so genuine about her smile, it sent a comforting warmth through my veins.

She crossed the room and embraced her son, standing on tiptoes to reach her arms around him despite her height.

She stepped back and looked at me. "You must be Fallon, *cara mia*," she said. "I am Maria, Dominic's mother."

And then she hugged me. She hugged me just the same as she'd hugged her son, with her arms wrapped tight around me and her cheek pressed against mine.

Something twisted in my chest and a sob bubbled up, but I swallowed it back. It had been so long since a mother—anyone's mother—had hugged me this way.

She let me go, but her hand was still on my arm, and turned to Dominic. "And now, my son, it is time for you to leave."

She shooed him toward the door. He smiled indulgently, but at the same time, I could sense the way he was assessing me, looking to see if I would breach the silent agreement I'd made.

Seemingly satisfied with what he found, he nodded. He held a hand over his heart like he'd been wounded. "A man can tell when he's not wanted."

Could he really? Because it seemed he hadn't taken the hint when I'd practically screamed it at him.

"You're wanted plenty, Dominic," Maria said with an impish grin. "Just not here, not right now."

He flashed a boyish grin, and then he was gone.

"Come, Fallon, I brought you something," she said, leading me to the small wrought iron table in the kitchen. A pretty box sat in the center of it. She sat down at the table and opened it up while I took the seat across from her. Inside, the box was filled with tiny decorative cakes. The sweet aroma was almost enough to send me on a sugar high.

"They look incredible," I said, and they smelled even better.

"*Grazie*," she said, placing a small plate for each of us. "I like to bake." She shrugged her shoulders. "I bake for my boys all the time."

"But I thought…" I trailed off, remembering our first date.

Maria shot me another impish smile. "You thought correctly, *cara mia*. Dominic has as much of a sweet tooth as this table, but he doesn't know I know that. He thinks he's been fooling me all these years."

I laughed. It seemed this kind woman had a dark side. "And you don't mind playing along one little bit."

She shrugged. "Well, let's just say a woman needs to have her fun, *sì?*"

"What's it like?" I blurted out without thinking. I'd had no intention of getting personal with this woman, and yet, so quickly, it felt like the easiest thing in the world to talk to her, almost like I was talking to Corinne.

My heart clenched, thinking about my best friend. Would I ever see her again? Would I ever be allowed out of this apartment on my own?

"What do you mean?" Maria asked.

"I mean… being married to someone… to someone who…" Now that I'd started, I couldn't seem to get the words out.

"Being married to a man like Vincent?" she filled in for me.

I nodded, still having a difficult time with words.

"It's not easy, particularly in the beginning," she said. "My marriage was arranged, like yours. My family is much like the Lucas. And I won't lie to you, I hated Vincent at first. I wanted a life of my own, *si*? He stood in the way of that, and I resented him for it."

Yes, exactly! I didn't want to be forced to give up my whole life.

"But like with all things, I got over it."

"Just like that?" I pressed.

"No, of course not. It took time." She laughed, a sound that reminded me of wind chimes, while her eyes were far away. "We fought more than we talked that first year. Much more."

Is that what was in store for me?

"I don't want this," I said, not because I expected Maria to do anything to stop it, but I needed to say it out loud and it not fall on deaf ears like it had with Dominic.

"I know you don't," she said, placing a hand over mine. "It may be hard to believe, but I promise that if I thought this marriage was a bad choice for either of you, I would speak up. I have done things…" She trailed off and looked down at her hands. It felt like she'd traveled to some far-off place, maybe to some distant memory before she came back to me. "I have done things to protect my family." She met my gaze with a hard determination that told me this woman was no fragile doll. "I will protect you as well, Fallon. You will be part of the Luca family very soon."

Part of her family? She squeezed my hand, but it felt like she'd wrapped her slim fingers around my heart and squeezed it. It had been so long since I'd felt like part of a real family.

The men who'd murdered my mother hadn't only stolen my mother but my father as well.

I stopped recognizing my father the moment my mother took her last breath.

"Thank you," I whispered and then dug into one of the mini cakes before the tears in my eyes could spill over.

I didn't want this marriage any more than I had a moment ago, but I wanted what she was dangling on a hook in front of me. To be a part of something, to belong somewhere. Maybe I could even understand Dominic's commitment to his family when I looked at it through Maria's eyes.

When a person had something so valuable, wouldn't they do everything in their power to hold onto it, to protect it? That was loyalty, after all—the willingness to go to any lengths for another person. And Dominic was willing to go to the ends of the earth for his family.

***

I was lying on the sofa when the front door opened and a sliver of light spilled across the living room. It was the only light in the apartment. I'd been drifting in and out of sleep for the past two hours. I couldn't say for certain what had kept me on the sofa rather than retreating to the room I'd claimed as my own.

The door closed, shutting out the light and shrouding the apartment in darkness. I could have scurried off to the bedroom. If I crept quietly enough, he might not even know I'd been here, but I stayed where I was, listening as his footsteps strode across the living room toward the kitchen.

He moved more slowly than usual, but if it weren't for the strange metallic scent that followed him, I might not have thought anything of it. As a veterinarian, I'd spent plenty of time around blood; the smell was unmistakable.

I sat straight up. "Dominic?"

He stopped walking. "Go to bed, Fallon."

I stood up, searching for the light switch in the dark while my imagination went wild. I could picture him there with a dead body slung over his shoulder, dripping blood along the carpet. Or maybe he was carrying a human head in a bowling ball bag—that was a mafia thing, wasn't it? *Oh god.* As my fingers found the switch, I hesitated. Did I really want to see what hideous thing he'd brought home?

Then I remembered him sneering at me about burying my head in the sand, and I flicked on the light.

There was no body slung over his shoulder. No bowling ball bag in his hand. There was blood. On his shirt, on his hands, even splattered on his jaw. My heart raced, and my stomach roiled violently.

I rushed at him, running my hands over his jaw, down his chest, his abdomen, searching for the source of the blood. He'd been shot. Someone had shot Dominic. It seemed crazy. Impossible. This was Dominic Luca!

I reached for the waist of his pants to untuck his shirt, now frantic because I couldn't find the damn source of the blood.

He put his hands over mine, stopping me. "Fallon, what are you doing?" He cocked a brow and flashed me a small grin.

Damn it. Had he lost so much blood he was delusional? I pulled my hands out of his grasp and resumed my search, yanking the hem of his shirt out of his pants.

"If this is your new way of greeting me when I get home, I can't say I'm opposed to it," he said.

I rolled my eyes. "Where the hell is it, Dominic?"

"You might have to tell me what you're looking for, *limone.*"

"The bullet, damn it. Where were you shot?"

He sniggered. "I wasn't shot."

What? I dropped my hands.

"I appreciate the concern. It's a bit unexpected, honestly, but it isn't my blood, Fallon."

I took a step back. "Then… then whose blood is it?"

"It belonged to the man who told Tony about you." He met my gaze, holding it like a vise. "He won't be needing it any longer."

"Is he…" The word got stuck in my throat, but it didn't matter. I could see it in his eyes.

"Yes, Fallon. He's dead."

I should have yelled at him, berated him, something to tell him what I thought of the vile thing he'd done, but words eluded me. I couldn't find them because, in truth, I didn't know how I felt about what he'd done. He'd murdered a man, and now he stood in his kitchen, covered in blood, without any remorse. It was wrong, and yet, he'd killed the man who had no regard for my life, who had handed me up on a silver platter.

"It's not so black and white sometimes, is it?" he said, but his voice was gentle, not scathing or mocking.

"I don't know what to say—"

"Nothing, *limone*. You don't have to say anything. I did my job, nothing more."

But it felt like more than that. Or maybe I just wanted to believe it was more than that. It would explain why I leaned up on my toes and pressed my lips against his. I could feel the stickiness of the blood on his chest against my arms. All I could smell was its coppery tang. But Dominic's lips were firm and warm.

"Thank you," I whispered as I leaned away, and then I hurried to my room.

Chapter Nineteen

Fallon

I stood in the middle of the marble-floored bathroom in a long, white satin dress. It hung prettily off my shoulders and fell all the way past my toes like it was trying to envelope me completely. Swallow me up.

In a few hours, it would all be done. I'd be married.

"Married," I said to my own reflection in the wide mirror. I could see my mouth forming the words, and I could hear my own quivering voice, but I still found it difficult to believe.

An arranged marriage.

I wondered if this was how the brides from centuries before me had felt, trembling in the hours leading up to a life sentence from which there was no escape.

Had wedding bells sounded like the banging of a gavel in their ears, condemning them to their imprisonment? Did their beautiful white gowns feel like orange jumpsuits? Did their expensive diamond rings feel like steel handcuffs?

"It's time, Miss Moore," a deep voice called through the bathroom door. One of Dominic's lackeys.

He and I were the only people still in Dominic's apartment, though I couldn't say what time Dominic had left. I didn't care. Our fragile truce had held up over the past several days, but today, white-hot flames blasted through my veins. This was my life he was taking away from me, even if he was just as trapped in this as me.

I stood staring at myself for another long moment, silently begging the woman in the mirror to get me out of this, to trade places with me, to do… something. But of course, she didn't. She couldn't. She was trapped as much as me.

"Miss Moore?" the lackey called again.

"I'm coming," I said, more to keep him from speaking to me again than to placate him.

I'd delayed all I could, but I knew there was no sense in trying to put off the inevitable. It was coming whether I wanted it to or not. I squared my shoulders, turned away from the woman in the mirror, and stepped out of the room.

The tall, dark-haired lackey stood outside the door, just far enough away I could get by him without having to touch him. He followed me down the hall and into the living room. I spun around before I reached the front door.

"What's your name?" I asked. This man was going to take me to the church, escort me inside. He was the closest thing to a wedding party I had. He was practically my maid of honor, and I didn't even know his name.

"It's Leandro, ma'am," he said with a curt nod.

"It's nice to meet you, Leandro," I said, even though it wasn't the first time he'd been here. I held out my clammy hand, and with a confused look, he took it, shaking it and then drawing back like he was afraid I was going to try to clock him.

"Have you worked for the Luca family for long?" I asked. It probably seemed like I was stalling. Maybe I was.

"Yes, ma'am," he said with another curt nod. "Seventeen years."

Leandro didn't look a day past thirty; he'd been working for the Lucas since he was barely a teenager. That was abhorrent, and it didn't do a thing to make me feel any better about this wedding.

I turned back toward the door.

"He's a good man, Miss Moore," he said before I could reach for the handle.

"Is he?" Dominic or his father had taken a teenager and turned him into a lackey, a goon. That wasn't my definition of "good".

"I can see what you're thinking, but you're wrong. My brother and I were living on the streets when Dominic found me, starving and half-dead from fighting for scraps. He and his family took us in, gave us food—"

"And all you had to do was pledge your allegiance and do everything they asked of you," I finished for him.

"No, ma'am." He shook his head. "My brother's a doctor in Syracuse these days. The Lucas paid for his schooling and everything. And me, I'm right where I want to be."

I looked down at my feet encaged in satin stilettos. Nothing about the Lucas made sense. I turned the handle and left the apartment with Leandro following close on my heels.

He opened the back door to the black Escalade outside the building, but I shook my head and climbed into the passenger seat. I didn't want to sit in the back seat like some rich businesswoman.

I could hear him chuckling under his breath as he got in next to me and started the car. He was still smiling as we pulled out of the lot.

"What are you smiling about?" I asked because it beat sitting in silence, stewing in my own thoughts.

"It's nothing, ma'am," he said.

"What?" I persisted, enjoying the distraction for the moment.

"It's just that, in my opinion, you and Dominic may be better suited for one another than you think."

My distraction fractured. Maria had said something similar, though what made any of these people think they knew me well enough to make that assessment was beyond me.

I turned to stare out the window as the city flew past me. This was it. I had no idea how far it was to the church, but I had a feeling I was moments away from sealing my fate. And just to be sure my misery was complete, Corinne's face appeared behind my eyes and made my heart twist.

She was supposed to be here. She was supposed to hold my hand and tell me I'd get through this even if it felt like an insurmountable task. But Corinne wasn't here, and I'd never felt more alone.

Too soon, Leandro pulled into the parking lot of a pretty chapel. It was at least a century old, made from stone, and its windows were all stained glass, each of them depicting a different religious scene. The grounds around it were lush green with pruned bushes near the church and a sparse forest of oaks and pines behind it. It was beautiful, peaceful looking, but despite the tranquil scene, every breath I took grew shakier. I felt cold despite the warmth of the bright morning sun through the car's window.

Leandro got out of the car without a word and came around to open my door. He took my hand and helped me down while I held up the hem of my gown with my free hand, trying to keep it from tearing or dragging in the dirt as I stepped down.

I laughed a little hysterically. Why did I care if I walked up the aisle in a mud-splattered dress?

I could hear voices coming from inside the chapel, but Leandro guided me around to a door at the side. It led to a small room with a plush sofa and two wingback chairs. There was a table between them, and a bottle of wine sat on it with a single wineglass beside it. *How nice.* It seemed I was allowed to get drunk before I joined myself irrevocably to a veritable stranger, and while it was tempting, I refused to humiliate myself that way.

I stared at the bottle of wine, watching moisture bead up on the bottle and drip down like teardrops onto the wood, one after the other.

"If you're all right, ma'am, someone will come for you when it's time," Leandro said from where he stood awkwardly in the doorway.

I nodded, not wanting him to leave but not wanting him to stay. I didn't want to be alone, but it wasn't Leandro I wanted with me. *Corinne,* my heart cried. It felt like I was drowning.

I turned away as the door closed, gasping for breath, but no matter how hard I tried, I couldn't draw in enough. I plopped down in the wingback chair, holding my head in my hands as I focused on one slow, deep inhale until my chest expanded and my lungs were full. I pursed my lips and pushed the air out. Then in, then out. I closed my eyes and imagined Corinne here with me, sitting next to me.

"*You can do this, hon,*" she'd tell me, and there wouldn't be a flicker of doubt in her eyes.

I can do this, I tried to mimic her in my head. *I can do this.*

My breathing returned to something that resembled normal, and though my heart was beating fast, it didn't feel like it was going to burst right out of my chest.

There was a quiet knock at the door that led further into the chapel, and it opened without a moment's pause.

It was Maria. She smiled at me from the open doorway. She looked so beautiful in a pale blue sheath with a matching silk scarf wrapped around her long neck. Her hair had been swept up atop her head, but not pulled severely, and loose tendrils had been left free to frame her gently lined face.

She came toward me, and my insides began to tremble.

"It's time, *cara mia,*" she said, laying a hand over mine and squeezing gently.

I opened my mouth but no words came out.

She leaned in closer and tipped my chin up to meet her gaze.

"It will be over soon," she said in a tone that somehow managed to banish the sliver of the loneliness that was threatening to crush me.

She understood what I was feeling. This woman knew what it was like to be bartered, to be a mere pawn in a transaction. But she'd survived, and more than that, she hadn't lost herself. No one could convince me that Maria Luca wasn't her own woman.

"Thank you," I said then forced myself to my feet. There was no way out of this. All I could do was move forward.

She nodded, looking me in the eyes for one long steadying moment. Then she left, leaving the door open behind her like she knew the monumental effort it would have taken me to turn that handle.

Still, it took me a few seconds to muster the strength to walk through the open doorway. The music started. *Wagner's Bridal Chorus*. I'd always imagined I'd walk up the aisle to the chords of *Songbird* by *Fleetwood Mac*, just like my mother had done. But it didn't matter. No part of this was the wedding I'd imagined.

I took a step. My legs felt wobbly, and out of nowhere, my father's face flashed through my mind. I'd been so angry with him, I hadn't even asked about having him here with me, but now I regretted it. He was supposed to be here, with his hand around my arm, keeping me steady. He was supposed to walk me down the aisle and kiss my cheek.

But instead, I forced myself to put one foot in front of the other. In all the movies I'd seen, the bride's movements were fluid and graceful, every step in perfect harmony with the music. My movements felt stilted and uncoordinated. I could feel every eye in the pews turn toward me. Eyes that belonged to people I didn't know, I'd never met. All strangers, staring at me as I marched to my doom.

I kept my head down, but out of the corner of my eye, I spied Leandro near the back. It surprised me to find comfort in his gaze. He smiled, just a quick quirk of his lips, but it felt like I almost had a friend amid this crowd of strangers. *That's my maid of honor.*

It was enough to bolster my courage, and I looked up. Right away, my eyes found Dominic. He stood at the front of the church, dressed to the nines like he'd just walked off the runway. He was looking right at me with storm gray eyes. He was beautiful, though there was nothing feminine about him, but to have said he was *handsome* wouldn't have done the man justice.

I couldn't interpret the expression on his face since he had it arranged in his unreadable mask, but what was he thinking? Feeling? He didn't want this any more than I did, but his shoulders weren't slumped dejectedly, he wasn't staring at the ground pretending he was anywhere but here. He stood unmoving, unwavering.

While I still cursed him for making me do this, his strength bolstered me. It carried me to the front of the church where a tall, gangly priest stood just behind him with a Bible clutched tightly in his hands. He had a full head of short, gray hair. It looked like a bristly mop on the top of his head.

Dominic held out his hand to me, and I took it, staring at our joined hands while he led me a few steps forward. His hand was bare, but it wouldn't be for much longer. In a few moments, there would be a noose around both our fingers. *Both*. Not just mine. He was just as trapped as me, even if he'd accepted his captivity more gracefully than I had.

I clutched his hand tighter, for the first time feeling like we were both victims in this game. He squeezed back for just a moment then released me and turned his attention to the priest.

The priest spoke. His voice was deep and clear, which surprised me. I'd expected a higher pitched voice for some reason. But though his words came out clearly, I couldn't seem to take them in. It was just noise, and with every passing second, the noise grew blurrier like it was coming to me through a tin can.

The occasional word slipped through. "Sanctity… Marriage… Lifelong commitment…" But they might as well have been gibberish. There was nothing sacred about this union. There was no commitment. Only coercion.

The priest took hold of my hand and placed it in Dominic's.

"Dominic Luca," the priest said.

A knot in my stomach grew tighter, but my hearing cleared. Every sound was suddenly magnified.

"Do you take Fallon Moore to be your lawfully wedded wife…" The priest's voice resonated inside my head. "…to have and to hold, from this day forward, for better, for worse, for richer, for poorer, in sickness and in health, until death do you part?"

"I do," Dominic said without hesitation. There was no quiver in his voice. His words came out just as clear, just as strong as ever.

It hadn't escaped my attention there had been one part of the vow missing. *"To love and to cherish…"* It should have been in there somewhere, but I had a feeling it hadn't been omitted by accident.

"Fallon Moore," the priest said, turning his light brown eyes on me.

In his gaze, I could see the truth reflected back at me. He knew, and yet, here he was, playing his part in binding me to a man against my will.

"Do you take Dominic Luca to be your lawfully wedded husband…"—Every word he spoke slammed into my chest, knocking the air out of my lungs—"…to have and to hold, from this day forward, for better, for worse, for richer, for poorer, in sickness and in health, until death do you part?"

My lungs were empty. I couldn't breathe. I couldn't speak.

Dominic squeezed my hand. It was gentle, not demanding. He was lending me his strength. I grabbed hold of it and clung to it.

"I do," I said. It came out too quiet to carry throughout the church. Would he make me say it again? I wasn't sure I could do it.

But the priest nodded, and two rings appeared in his deeply lined hand. Two nooses. Would they squeeze the life out of Dominic too?

He picked up the smaller one, took my left hand, and slipped it onto my finger. The priest was speaking, but I paid no attention. All that existed was a pale gold band, now wrapped around my ring finger. It didn't look like an ordinary wedding ring. It was made of two different metals that had been molded together in some way that made it look handcrafted. It was… perfect, but that made it worse, not better.

The priest held out the remaining ring to me, a plain gold band nothing like the one that encircled my finger. I picked it up, squeezing it in my hand to hide my trembling.

Dominic held out his hand, and I took hold of it, but I was shaking so much, I was going to drop the ring if I tried to do this.

"It's okay, *limone*," he whispered under his breath.

Though I didn't agree with him—nothing about this was okay—I used his words and the confidence in them to steady myself long enough to slip the ring onto his finger.

And then it was done. It was over.

"You may now kiss the bride," the priest announced.

My breath caught in my throat. Apparently, it wasn't quite done. It really shouldn't have come as a shock. It was the climactic moment of every wedding—the magical first kiss.

Dominic's hands settled on my hips, and he drew me close. I could feel every eye in the chapel on me. It made me want to run, but the only way out was to focus on the hands on my hips and the light press of his firm chest against mine. The touch of his lips, the glide of his tongue along the seam of my lips. The mint and scotch flavor of his mouth when I parted for him. Scotch first thing in the morning? It made me feel a little better to know he'd had a drink, maybe two, before the ceremony like he'd needed fortification to get through this. Just like I did.

Seconds or minutes passed. I wasn't in a hurry. Though we stood in front of a crowd of strangers, I felt sheltered in his kiss.

Too soon, he pulled away, and the sea of strangers applauded our performance. The noise was loud and abrasive. I wanted to cover my ears, but I stood there instead until the priest led us through the chapel to a small room to sign the official papers.

I'd thought this part would have been the most difficult—signing my name as Fallon Moore for the last time—but my hand flowed across the page, signing away my life in a few quick strokes. I'd said the words, I wore the ring. It seemed like nothing more than a formality to sign on the dotted line.

Now the deed was done. Fallon Moore was nothing more than a distant memory, a string of letters lost in time.

I was now Fallon Luca.

Chapter Twenty

Fallon

I sat in the back seat of a long line of black Escalades that transported us from the chapel to a reception hall. Neither Dominic nor I spoke. He seemed caught up in thought, and I had nothing to say.

I was glad it was Leandro driving us to the reception. Though he hadn't said a word, his presence was reassuring, like it had been in the chapel. It seemed like it would have been easier to strike up a conversation with him, my maid of honor, at the moment than with the silent man, my now husband, sitting next to me, but I had no idea if it was even allowed. There'd been no Mafia-101 class. I had no idea what my role entailed. It felt like I'd just stepped foot into a royal household, and now I had to learn all the rules of proper etiquette, but nobody had given me the damn bible.

At least now that it was all done, Dominic had to let me regain some semblance of normalcy in my life. He wasn't going to keep me locked in his apartment forever… was he?

I glanced up at him out of the corner of my eye. He was looking right at me.

"You did well, *limone*," he said.

I scoffed. My heart was still racing, I was still a little light-headed, and my legs hadn't felt like they were completely under my control since I'd stepped inside the chapel, but sure, I did *well*.

"You don't think so?" he pressed.

"I think—" I closed my mouth. What I thought was that this was insane, that it was wrong, but I didn't have it in me to fight with him right now.

He smiled. "You're learning."

"What?" I didn't realize I was in school.

"You're learning to choose your battles," he said. He looked so smug.

"This from a guy who kills people?"

He smiled, unperturbed. "You'll recall that I do choose my battles, *limone*. I fight the battles that need fighting."

He was talking about the man who'd handed me up to Tony, and I couldn't find a voice to argue. It wasn't that I was okay with murder, but I also couldn't get the image of those crushed pieces of metal out of my head or the dark look in Tony's eyes when he'd shown up at my clinic.

The Escalade slowed to a stop in front of a large building. The reception hall, I presumed. I looked at it through the car's dark windows, imagining the throng of strangers inside.

"We have to make an appearance here, but if you'd like to leave early, we don't have to stay long," Dominic said, placing his hand over mine. It was the first time he'd touched me since the kiss in the chapel.

I sighed as a wave of gratitude washed over me, but it was short-lived. After the wedding reception came the wedding night. Was

Dominic expecting me to put out just because we were married now? It irked me that part of me was more than happy with that plan.

This was supposed to be an arranged marriage—a marriage of convenience—but nothing I felt for him was convenient. Not the anger or resentment, not the gratitude or the attraction. But then, no one had been concerned with what was *convenient* for me or else we wouldn't have been here in the first place.

Before I could respond, the door opened, and I could see Maria standing just outside the car. She waited while Dominic and I got out. Then she took my hand and led me off to a small dressing room inside the hall with a garment bag over her arm.

She dropped the bag the moment she closed the door then turned and wrapped her arms around me.

"You did wonderfully, *cara mia*," she whispered against my shoulder, squeezing me tighter. "Welcome to my family."

A tear escaped and slipped down my cheek. I was sad. I was mourning the loss of the life I should have lived. And yet, something sparked to life inside me hearing her words. Whether I wanted it or not, I was part of something now. I was part of Maria's family. I was a Luca.

And then, in what I was coming to see as usual-Maria fashion, she leaned away, picked up the garment bag, and did what needed to be done.

"We have to get you changed in a hurry," she said, maneuvering me around so she could unfasten the long row of tiny pearl buttons down my back.

The woman could have been a quick-change artist. I was out of my gown and into a long, white sheath with a slit all the way up the thigh in two minutes flat.

She stepped back and looked me over.

"*Bellissima*," she exclaimed before returning me to the doors outside the hall where Dominic waited, talking in quiet tones with Vincent.

Following Maria and Vincent, we walked inside the hall to an uproar of applause. Again, I wanted to cover my ears, but I focused on the sage green and light terracotta décor instead. The earthy colors were broken up by a veritable sea of white flowers. Lilies, I realized—the same flowers Dominic had given me after our disastrous date.

I stared at the flowers as Dominic held out a chair, laden in silk, for me at the head table. I wondered what would have happened that day if I'd rejected the flowers and sent him on his way. Would that have been the end of it? Somehow, I doubted it. Still, it made no sense that he'd bothered with all those dates if this was going to be the outcome no matter what.

He was trying to make this easier for you, a voice whispered inside my head, but was that right? It was true he could have just dragged me down the aisle the day we'd met. I had a feeling the priest would have been no more help than he'd been today.

I looked over at him. He sat next to me, conversing in Italian with a middle-aged man and the twenty-something pretty brunette that hung off the man's arm. I tried to wait patiently, fiddling with the ring that was wrapped around my finger. I could feel the weight of it, the strange pressure against my skin, but it didn't feel quite like the noose I'd expected. Constricting, but not strangling.

"Penny for your thoughts?" he said as the couple wandered away, leaning in so that his lips brushed my ear.

A warm shiver rushed through me.

"Why did you wait?" I blurted out.

Dominic leaned back and raised a brow at me, waiting for me to explain.

"If this was going to be the outcome all along, why did you bother with those dates? It doesn't make sense."

He shrugged.

"I thought we'd have more time. There was no reason to rush you if there was any chance it could have gone more smoothly." His words were spoken lightly, but it felt like they'd been chosen carefully.

"Would you like to dance, *limone*?" he asked, standing up and effectively putting an end to the conversation.

He offered his hand, and I took it, pausing to look around. There were already couples dancing on the pale wood dance floor. It seemed there would be no official first dance for husband and wife, for which I was grateful. I'd had enough of strangers staring at me for one day.

"Satisfied?" he asked with a quirk of his brow and a smile playing at the corners of his lips. *Cocky mind reader.*

I let him pull me up, and he kept my hand in his as he led me around the head table and out to the dance floor.

Once there, he kept my hand in his and placed his free hand on the small of my back, leading me into an easy waltz.

We floated across the lacquered dance floor like we were weightless. Around and around we went, as though each movement had been meticulously choreographed.

Fuck. He was good at this.

He pulled me closer until no more than a hair's breadth separated my chest from his. I could feel the heat of his body seeping through the thin fabric of my dress and licking along my skin.

If I closed my eyes, it was so easy to get lost in his warmth. Despite the friction that was ever-present between us, this part seemed to come so naturally. If I just shut off my mind and let my body take over, I had no doubt the result would be cataclysmic. And it was so damn tempting. To turn off the anger, the frustration, and bitterness. To get caught up in the heat and the lust and the sexual energy that was sparking between us.

"Give in, *limone*," he whispered close to my ear so I'd hear him over the music.

So tempting.

"Did I tell you how amazing you look in that dress?" he asked, his words slipping over my skin like a caress.

He twirled me around then pulled me back against him with so much force it left me winded.

He leaned in even closer until I could feel his lips graze the shell of my ear. "Did I tell you how amazing you'll look when I get you out of it?"

Tiny jolts of heat shot through my body, setting a fire burning low in my abdomen. *"Just give in,"* he'd said, and all the hot, sparked up parts of me cried out in agreement.

"I'd like to leave, Dominic," I said.

'Then what are we waiting for?"

He pressed his lips against my neck, just beneath my ear, sending a fresh wave of heat through my body.

Without waiting for the song to finish, we left the dance floor, walking hand-in-hand toward the exit.

Corrupted Heir

I caught sight of Leandro just before we left the hall. He was standing with his back ramrod straight and his hands clasped in front of him, next to one of the exits. He nodded to me as Dominic and I passed by, but I didn't miss the quirk of his lips.

"…you and Dominic may be better suited for one another than you think," he'd said.

I bet my maid of honor was feeling pretty smug now.

Chapter Twenty-One

Dominic

She was looking at me the same way she had on our third date. Fire and lust shone bright, not tainted by the anger and resentment that had clouded her eyes ever since. Whether they were gone or just subdued for now, I didn't care. Fallon was mine.

In a few short minutes, we'd be home, and I couldn't wait to rip the dress right off her body. I wanted her naked. Now.

Once we got into the back of the Escalade with Marco at the helm, she seemed to get smaller, sitting quietly, nearly as still as stone but for the way she was twirling the ring on her finger around and around.

Usually, I wasn't much of a jewelry man, but the thought of her body bare but for the ring around her finger did crazy things to my head and to the blood that was pumping hot and heavy through my veins. It wasn't an ordinary piece of jewelry; it was a symbol of my claim on her.

"Do you like it?" I asked, grazing my finger over the ring.

"It's very… different," she said.

"It's made from the bullet you removed from Bullet."

"It's from the night we first met," she said, looking at it like it was the first time she was seeing it. "I mean, if you think about it too much, it's a little grotesque. And yet, it's…" She trailed off, searching for the word.

"Perfect?" I posited, lifting her hand to my lips and kissing from the ring to the tip of her finger.

She nodded, and I could feel the slight trembling in her hand and in her thigh that was pressed against my own.

I wasn't typically the sentimental guy, but the ring really was perfect. Two metals, light and dark. Smooth, refined gold, and the rough etching created by the bullet's metal. It was just like the sweet and sour that defined the woman next to me. My wife. *Mine.*

And with that thought, I used her hand I still held and tugged her toward me.

I covered her lips with mine, and she let out a breathy sigh. Her lips parted for me as I plied the seam between them. She tasted like champagne, and it went straight to my head.

By the time I came up for air, her breath had grown ragged. With my hands in the hair at the nape of her neck, I tipped her head back and planted a trail of kisses along the soft skin of her jaw, down her neck, down to the upper swells of her breasts where her dress prevented any further descent. Her hands had found my shoulders, and she clung to me, tipping her head back obligingly as I retraced my path from her breasts to her jaw.

The car door swung open. I paused, not realizing we had stopped.

Fallon leaned away, brushing the loose strands of hair over her shoulders like that could somehow hide what we'd been doing. I decided it would be in my best interest not to laugh.

"Sorry, boss, didn't expect rain. I'm afraid I don't have an umbrella," Marco said as rain sluiced down him.

"All good, man. We'll just have to sprint up," I said. "Are you okay with that, Fallon?"

As much as the interruption irritated me, it was about fucking time. Home, finally. As soon as we were inside, I could focus all my attention on getting rid of that damned dress. Burn it, maybe—just to make sure it could never get in the way of what I wanted again.

Fallon nodded while she unfastened the straps on her shoes.

"Don't want to slip in the rain," she said with a wry grin.

Two seconds through our mad dash, the pelting rain had soaked us right through. Fallon let out a squeal and stuttered to a stop halfway to the building's front door. She spun around with her face tipped up to the sky and her dress plastered to her body. Though only the streetlamps shone down on her, I was quite certain in that moment, I'd never seen anything more beautiful in my life.

She grabbed my hand when she'd finished her spin, and we jogged toward the entrance where she stood dripping wet and giggling.

"My dress is soaking wet," she said, patting the white material, which became translucent against her skin. It clung to her body, showing off every one of her curves and the hard peaks of her nipples, sending all the blood in my body south.

She was laughing, but the moment her gaze met mine, the laughter fell away. Heat flared in her eyes, and she stood there with her hands pressed to her stomach where she'd been patting herself down.

I grabbed her hand and pulled her along to the elevator. The moment we stepped inside, I lunged for her, pressing her hard up against the wall as my lips retraced the path they'd taken before, down her jaw, her neck, to the upper swells of her breast.

Reluctantly, I leaned away as the elevator door opened, and Fallon followed me out of it and through my front door. When I locked it behind us, we froze in place.

She was a mess, her wet hair matted to her face. Her mascara ran down her cheeks, a waterfall of black. Her bright blue eyes left me breathless. Fallon was tiny, her form petite in comparison to mine. When she parted her lips, my breath grew ragged.

I crushed her lips beneath mine as the rest of the world melted away. How could someone who I couldn't stand half the time taste so damn good? When I speared my tongue between her lips to deepen the kiss, Fallon let out a whimper that shot straight to my cock.

My hands slithered across her body, settling on her hips. With one push, I pressed her back against the wall, pressing my throbbing cock against her.

I tore my lips away from her and delved for her neck, kissing and nipping her with my teeth. She tasted like rain, and salt, and something sweet that made me want to dig in deeper.

"Dom," she whimpered as I reached the upper swells of her breasts. "Maybe we shouldn't…"

I leaned back just enough to meet her gaze.

"Shouldn't we?" I cocked one eyebrow and kept my eyes on hers as I reached my hand between her legs, trailing my fingers down her mound. The fabric was wet from the rain, but it was warm between her thighs.

"I mean…" she whispered, but there was nothing but fire and certainty glittering in her blue eyes.

Abandoning her warm heat for just a moment, I grabbed hold of the neckline of her dress with both hands and ripped it down the center with a tearing sound that shot through my veins like a lightning bolt. Shoving it off her shoulders, it puddled on the floor at her feet in a wet heap. Now only her panties remained between me and what I was after.

"Open your legs," I instructed.

She whimpered, but complied, making my cock twitch.

"That's perfect," I whispered then slid my fingers over her pussy through the soaked fabric of her panties. Were they wet from the rain, or was it her own juices?

"Take off your panties, Fallon," I told her, removing my hand.

Her gaze shot up to meet mine, her eyes imploring, but I remained still, waiting for her to comply. Fire and just a hint of self-consciousness shone in her eyes—a heady combination—but she hooked her fingers in the sides of her panties and slid them down her legs to pool on the floor with her dress.

Completely naked. And by the look in her eyes, for now at least, she was all mine.

I ran two fingers up and down her delicious slit, coating them in slick juices. And then I plunged my fingers inside, and she let out a yelp.

"You're soaking wet," I growled in her ear.

Staring deep into her eyes, I pressed against her sensitive bundle of nerves. I wanted to be inside of her more than anything. My cock was so hard it felt like it would explode. And if she'd been any other woman, I would have spun her around, pressed her up against the wall, and fucked her hard and fast.

But she wasn't any other woman.

She was Fallon Luca.

I kept my fingers crooked, stroking that spot inside her that I knew would drive her wild. Moans tumbled from her lips as she ground her pussy against my fingers.

I moved faster and faster, sending her into a frenzy. Soft moans that grew louder. The dig of her fingernails into my shoulders as she held on tight. She couldn't keep still under my touch, but her eyes were squeezed shut tight.

She was so close; I could feel it building inside her with every ragged breath, but I wanted to see her. I wanted to see the look in her eyes when she tumbled over the edge.

"Look at me," I instructed, clutching her chin in my free hand and forcing her gaze up to meet mine. "Look at me when you come."

Her hips bucked, and she yanked her face away.

Her moans reached a crescendo, and her pussy convulsed around my fingers. My cock felt like it was about to explode just *looking* at her.

Fallon grabbed my shaft through my pants, fisting along the length and momentarily disrupting the steady rhythm of my fingers stroking her inner walls.

"Mmm," she moaned. "Fuck me, Dom. Please, fuck me."

Don't mind if I do…

Frantically, I unzipped my pants just enough to pull out my cock. Gripping the backs of her thighs, I lifted her to pin her up against the front door behind her.

With her back against the door, her legs wrapped around my waist, she grabbed my shaft and guided it toward her wet slit. With a rough, quick movement, I pushed myself inside of her, and then her tight, slick walls gripped me.

"Fucking hell, you're so goddamned tight," I whispered breathlessly against her ear.

My breath came in quick successions. Her pussy felt so right, so warm, gripping my cock like her life depended on it.

We were rabid animals free of their cages.

I dug my fingernails into her arms, clawing at her rain-slicked flesh. Fallon ran her fingers through my hair, tugging and pulling on the short strands. The tingling at the base of my spine intensified as I plunged into her over and over.

The door rattled as I fucked her. Slow to pull out, and quick to shove my cock back in, seemed like her favorite way to be fucked.

Her nails dug into my back, no doubt leaving marks on my skin. The pain only served to enhance the pleasure.

Her moans grew louder. Her grip grew tighter. She was so close, and I was teetering on the edge.

And just when I wasn't sure I could last a moment longer, she slammed her head back against the wall and screamed. Her pussy convulsed around me. I thrust in once more, deep—so fucking deep—and emptied my cock inside her.

The tension in my core disappeared all at once, and I felt just about ready to collapse down onto my ass. We didn't say anything while we both caught our breath, and I slowly lowered her to the ground.

I kissed the top of her head, breathing in the light floral scent of her hair. She entwined her fingers with mine as I kissed her brow and then each of her closed eyelids.

It was strange, this first moment of tenderness between us after such animalistic sex. Strange, but not unpleasant.

Quite the opposite; it felt more right than I could ever have imagined.

Chapter Twenty-Two

Fallon

It was strange waking up next to Dominic. And not just next to him, but nestled in the crook of his arm with my cheek against his chest. I could hear the steady thump of his heart, and my head rose and fell with his breathing. It was like the soothing motion of a boat on calm water, just the slightest rocking that made me want to close my eyes and let sleep pull me back under. But I forced my eyes open, taking in the warm, cheery glow cast by the morning sun that slipped through the part in the curtains.

Even two days ago, I never would have thought we'd be here, limbs entwined, in some sort of truce that I was hopeful would hold.

I stretched against him, casting off the last vestiges of sleep, and right away, excitement began thrumming through my veins.

The wedding was over. The contract had been signed, and the man who'd handed me up to Tony was dead. There was no more reason for Dominic to keep me locked up in his apartment. I couldn't get out of the deal, and he'd taught me how to protect myself. Corinne, my clinic… I could finally have my life back, or at least some modified version of it.

The urge to drift back to sleep was gone. I shifted against Dominic, too excited to keep still.

"Good morning, *limone*," Dominic said sleepily, pressing me tighter against his chest. "If you squirm any more, I'm going to have to tie you up."

He caught my wrists together in his hand and rolled us until I was trapped beneath him with my hands over my head. I could feel the length of him growing harder against my thigh.

"Then I guess I'm just going to have to keep squirming," I said, wriggling beneath him.

He growled playfully and nipped at my neck.

"Dominic, wait," I said before I lost all thought to the arousal that was coursing through my veins.

He kept his lips against my flesh but stopped moving.

"Would you mind telling me what I'm waiting for, *limone*?" he asked. "Because I'd much rather keep going."

"I just wanted to talk to you about going back to work. I'd like to—"

"No," he said, leaning up just enough to look at me.

"What do you mean 'no'?" I yanked my wrists out of his grasp and wriggled in earnest now, trying to buck him off me.

He relented and rolled off me, propping himself up on one elbow so that his perfectly chiseled chest was right in front of my eyes. I looked away, not wanting his perfection to distract me.

"We're married now. You got what you wanted. Why the hell can't I go back to work?"

"It's not safe, and because I said so, Fallon," he said with a one-shoulder shrug.

I sat up, dragging the sheets with me. It pissed me off that he could be so damn cavalier about it.

"Being a veterinarian is a big part of who I am. And I miss Corinne. You can't keep me locked in your apartment forever." I stood up, taking the sheets with me and leaving his naked body uncovered. He didn't seem the least bit uncomfortable, but with a body like that, who could blame him? I couldn't keep my eyes from grazing over every inch of him, stopping too long on the very prominent part of him protruding proudly between his legs.

I could feel the cocky grin he was wearing without looking, but it changed nothing. He might have been built like a god, but he was acting like an ass.

"I want to go back to work," I said, stating it as plainly as I could.

"What you want is irrelevant. Your job will have to wait."

"My job? It's not just a fucking job, Dominic. It's my career; it's what I spent years of my life working toward and building up and growing every day. You can't just rip that away from me, goddamn it."

For fuck's sake, I was a grown woman in the twenty-first century. There was no way in hell I should have needed to ask my husband for permission to work.

"I can, and I am. You'll remain here until I say otherwise," he said, sitting up and swinging his legs over his side of the bed. I watched the play of muscles across his back as he rolled his shoulders and stretched his neck, completely unperturbed.

"I have a gun now. And you saw that I could shoot. If you don't let me go back to work, then we both know damn well it has nothing to do with my 'safety' and everything to do with you being a controlling bastard," I said, losing what cool I had left.

Dominic sighed. "Call me whatever you want, Fallon. I've made my decision, and you'll live with it." He spoke in that low, clear voice that sent a cold shiver down my spine.

He stood up. It seemed like he was towering over me even though he was on the other side of the bed. My survival instincts were screaming at me to let this go.

"This isn't your call to make. It's mine," I said because I knew I was losing the battle. I hadn't known Dominic long, but long enough to know he didn't vacillate. He wasn't wishy-washy. And he always did what he knew needed to be done.

"It's my call because you haven't lived in my world long enough to know what you're saying, Fallon."

"So, you're saying I'm not competent enough to make decisions for myself? That's just great, Dominic. You know what? Just go to hell," I said then stormed out of the room and down the hall.

It was just like my first day here, slamming the door closed behind me in the pale-colored guest room. Unlike then, though, my mind tried to poke holes in my anger. It tried to call up an image of Tony, the night he'd walked into my clinic, and the way he left me shaking after. It called up the image of the eleven bullets Dominic had retrieved from my apartment. Eleven bullets that could have been lodged in any of the 206 bones in my body.

***

There was a knock at the door in the late afternoon. It was weak, almost timid. Maria had been the only person to visit me here, and she didn't knock.

Confused, I stepped toward the door. Dominic had left hours ago.

There was no peephole, but the ever-present guard dogs outside wouldn't let anyone questionable through. Maybe Dominic had locked the door behind him and forgotten his keys. I smirked at the image of him standing outside the door, forced to knock to get inside his own home.

I debated making him stew a little longer but thought better of it and reluctantly opened the door.

I nearly slammed it shut.

"What the hell are you doing here?" I ground out between gritted teeth instead.

"I came to see you. Please, Fallon," my father pleaded around a giant bouquet of peonies, geraniums, and cosmos—bought with dirty money, no doubt.

"I brought these for you. I thought… Well, I don't know what flowers are your favorite…"

"Lilies," I spat, surprising myself.

"Oh," he said, staring at the bouquet dejectedly.

The guards in the hallway were looking at us. One of them I'd never seen before, but Leandro was there. He shot me a sympathetic smile, and it made me feel little better. His kind eyes bolstered me enough to step back and let my father inside. I smiled at Leandro appreciatively, and he shut the door behind me.

"Fallon," my father said, placing the rejected bouquet of flowers down on the small table by the door.

I stared at him, waiting for him to continue.

"Fallon," my father reiterated. He fidgeted with the cuff of his sports jacket that seemed to be two sizes smaller than him.

"Is that it?" I asked.

"What?"

"Are you just going to keep saying my name, or are you going to get to the point?" I crossed my arms over my chest.

"I'm… I'm sorry. That's why I came. I had to tell you."

It wasn't good enough, not this time.

"You sold me off like a thing, and then didn't even have the decency to show up to see the transaction take place."

"You're angry I didn't come to the wedding? I couldn't be there, baby—"

"No! Don't call me that. You don't get to call me your 'baby girl' anymore."

A father took care of his "baby girl". He loved her and cherished her. He did not treat her like an object that could be bartered and sold. The back of my throat stung, and I could feel the tears creeping across my eyes, blurring my vision.

"Please, Fallon. Let me explain." He looked at me with wide beseeching eyes.

A tiny spark lit inside me. My mind salivated for an explanation, for some reason for what he'd done. Words that would somehow make this all right.

I nodded and sat down in one of the big armchairs so he wouldn't sit down next to me.

He stared at the arm of the chair for a long moment then plopped down in the chair next to mine. He reached out to take my hand, but I drew it back, placing it in my lap to hide the slight tremble.

He dropped his hand and nodded. "It was never my intention to hurt you. I never thought they'd go through with it, Fallon. Twenty-eight years and no talk of the marriage. The Moores have been loyal to the Lucas for decades, so I thought it wouldn't be necessary for us to join… families. I've done everything they've asked of me."

I shook my head.

"You should have fought it. You should have moved away. You should have grabbed mom's hand and run to the other side of the earth to keep me safe. To keep her safe from the goddamned mob." I was almost shouting by the time I was done, and hot tears burned my cheeks.

"Your mother wasn't killed by the mob. Those people that started coming over, the ones you've always asked me about, were the Lucas. They and their men were there to protect us," he said. "They were there to keep us safe after what happened to your mother."

Something clicked in my brain.

That's why Maria had felt so familiar. I'd completely forgotten about those weeks and months after my mother died, the warm embraces from the kind, pretty woman who'd materialized seemingly out of nowhere.

It was Maria.

But if it hadn't been the mob—the Lucas or the Novas or whatever other mob—then who had killed my mother?

"I was still a rookie, getting my bearings. It was my first big break. A new casino opened up a few months before. There was talk of some shady business, but no one could find the guy behind it, nor could they arrest anyone who worked for him."

"You've told me this before."

"Yes. But only bits and pieces, and I never explained the consequences of my breakthrough job." He stared down at his hand where it laid rejected on the arm of his chair. "After three months of pretending to be a drunk with a serious gambling addiction, I finally found something. I spent thousands—even blew through your entire college fund." He let out a soft chuckle. I didn't see what was funny about it. "Anyway, I was such a big spender that I got close with one of the shady patrons. He led me right into the hornet's nest.

"It all snowballed into me finding the ringleader responsible for money laundering, fraud, and weapons deals. The person behind it was so powerful that he only got a year in prison. And boy, was he angry that some low-level cop had caught him. It was a thrill, you know? Like I was finally living up to the family name."

He looked up at me, and I could see the young man he'd once been reflected in his eyes. The ambition. The thrill of the chase.

He continued. "The second he got out… It would have been easier if he came after me… but killing me would have put me out of my misery, you know? So he came after your mother…" He cleared his throat. "I know he still operates to this day, without resistance because honestly, I couldn't bear the thought of what he'd do if I tried to put him behind bars again."

I looked away, closing my eyes. He'd practically painted a bull's-eye on my mother's chest. My stomach roiled, and my hands felt cold and clammy despite the warmth of the apartment.

All I could see was my mother's lifeless eyes. All I could hear was her scream. It reverberated inside my head so loud I wanted to squeeze the sides of my head to keep it from coming apart.

"His name was Harry," he continued. "Harry Belemonte." He spat the name like it was something vile in his mouth, but I could barely hear him over my mother's scream "I just hope that this can bring you some peace. I've never been able to tell you the truth because there were answers I couldn't give you. I never wanted to expose you to this life."

He slumped in his chair. I averted my gaze. I couldn't look at the man who was responsible for my mother's murder. He was the reason her scream was the last sound I ever heard from her. He was the reason I'd cried myself to sleep more nights than I could count, begging God and fate and the night sky to give her back to me.

"Get out," I forced out past the boulder stuck in my throat.

"Fallon, please." He reached out and touched my shoulder, but I swatted his hand away and sprung to my feet.

"Get out now," I shouted, pointing one shaking finger at the door.

He stood up. "I…"

If he didn't leave now, I had no idea what I would do. I'd never felt like this, so twisted up inside my whole body ached and shook. I wanted to cry and scream and hit something so badly.

I stared at the ground as he crossed the room and left.

As the door closed behind him, the quiet click let loose the floodgates. I dropped to my knees and smothered my screams into the sofa, hitting it over and over again. I screamed until my throat was sore. I punched the sofa again and again until my muscles shrieked in pain.

Corrupted Heir

It was like my mother had died all over again, here, now, and my own father had all but pulled the trigger.

Chapter Twenty-Three

Dominic

We were back at square one. Separate bedrooms, separate lives. Fallon hadn't spoken to me once in the four days since I'd told her going back to work was out of the question.

Worse than that, I'd spent four days wondering if I'd made the wrong call. During the rare times she was out of *her* room, I'd watched the way the light in her eyes had begun to dull. Even when she'd stormed past me, it wasn't anger that radiated from her, it was sadness, loneliness.

I wanted to keep her safe, but I was killing the life inside her, snuffing out her light, in my efforts to keep her heart beating. There had to be another way. But whatever way that was, it would have to wait.

Like every day for far too many days, I had a job to do. And today's job reached a whole new level of unsavory.

I watched as he appeared from the room in the back and strode toward me. I was the first Luca in a decade to see this man's face. I didn't feel honored in the least. Repulsed was a better descriptor. But we needed all the support we could get as Tony's forces grew stronger by the minute.

"Dominic Luca," the man exclaimed as he stopped in front of the barstool next to mine and took a seat. He motioned to the bartender, and a drink appeared in front of him seconds later.

Despite his graying hair and brows, and the deep-set wrinkles around his eyes and mouth, he was still in good shape. I had no doubt he could go a few rounds of hand-to-hand combat without breaking a sweat.

"Belemonte, it's good to see you" I lied, clenching my jaw.

I shook his hand. It was just an ordinary hand, but it seemed slimy. Or maybe it was just that giving him this ounce of respect left a bitter taste in the back of my mouth. But desperate times called for desperate measures. I just hoped this artificial partnership wouldn't come back to bite us in the ass in the future.

Belemonte's eyes narrowed at me. "You come to stab me in the back?" he said, his voice low and rough from years of whiskey and cigarettes. "I heard about Johnny approving your plans. If you build that casino, I'll burn it to the fucking ground."

I laughed. Sure he would—the day hell froze over.

He laughed and patted me on the shoulder while I resisted the urge to break his fucking arm. "I was just messing with you."

"That's good to know." I could feel a headache coming on.

"Hey, I've heard good things about you, boy. Making such great strides, and still so young," he said.

If he called me "boy" again, I was going to do more than rip off his fucking arm.

He squinted his beady brown eyes like he was trying to see into my mind. Could he see the hatred lurking behind my eyes? Part of me hoped so, even if it did nothing to further my cause here. But it was time to play the game.

"I've seen the good work you've been doing in Queens," I said. A lie, of course, but smooth-talking was part of the game.

"All right." He laughed. "Enough beating around the bush. I accepted this meeting because it takes balls of steel to do something like that after I screwed you out of money."

I nodded in agreement. Inane chitchat wasn't really my thing.

"I've decided I'm a gambling man today, Belemonte."

I glanced left and right, taking stock of the five men in cheap suits who had moved closer to Belemonte in the past three minutes.

"I'd hoped that we could put our *differences* aside and form a partnership."

"Honestly, that whole warehouse burning down? Water under the bridge," he said. "The production line wasn't to my tastes, anyway. Really, you saved me from having to do it myself."

Yeah, right. He could brush it off all he wanted. That fire put a big kink in Belemonte's profits. But I could play along if it got me what I wanted.

"So, you're not against a partnership?"

His crow's feet grew deeper, and he smiled like the Cheshire cat. His teeth were unnaturally straight and white. It reminded me of Jonah Hill in Wolf of Wall Street. It was uncanny; he didn't look quite human.

"Did you think I was an idiot? When you asked for a meeting, I knew what you wanted," he said. "Why else would you be here? I don't care if you want to build those casinos. You do you. The mob and the cartel are like foxes and wolves. We exist in harmony, until there's a food shortage. Right now, things are flush, and I'm willing to see where this could take us—out of curiosity more than anything else."

I hadn't calculated that it would be this easy, but maybe that was just because I was used to challenges and roadblocks around every corner. Still, it never hurt to anticipate the worst. It sure as hell beat underestimating some asshole and winding up six feet under for the error.

"Build whatever you need, as long as it's not on my territory within Queens," he said. "You know I have to ask, though. What's in it for me?"

Although we owned Queens, the cartel had small sections of land within the state where they could operate freely within certain bounds. It was a complicated agreement that my grandfather had established. The Free Birds grew out of control over the years, though, so the Lucas couldn't keep full control of them. Belemonte was a slinky, successful man. If nothing else, he was good at his job.

"Partnership. That's what's in it for you. Fifteen percent of the profits at every casino, barring the laundering. And the dockside warehouse operation, it's all yours," I said.

The last part was only to sweeten the deal—our drug production was at full capacity. We produced far more than we could ever sell.

"That's millions a year. You're willing to give that all away just to build your casinos? What's really going on here?" Belemonte leaned in closer, eyeing me closely. "Is there some kind of trouble afoot? The Novas, perhaps."

It didn't faze me that he knew; Belemonte had many ears to the ground.

"That is correct. Do we have a deal?" I asked.

"I don't see why not. Here," he said, handing me a card. "I've got a couple tricks up my sleeve if you run into any trouble with permits and licenses. It's easy when you've done it for decades."

"Thank you, Belemonte," I said, but the words scraped and clawed their way up my throat. It was physically painful to ask this asshole for help. But it needed to be done I just hoped like hell it would be worth it.

***

I stared at the tumbler of whiskey in front of me. One deal with a slimy asshole was taken care of. Next, was one angry wife to placate.

"So, what are you going to do?" Leo asked me from where he sat across the table.

I'd reported the outcome of my meeting with Belemonte to my father then ran into Leo in the hallway and unloaded on him about Fallon.

"The smart thing to do would be absolutely nothing," I said, reigniting the battle in my head between logic and something else. Something that only seemed to peek its ugly, irrational head up when Fallon was involved.

"But you're not going to do that?" It came out like a question, but there was no question in Leo's eyes. He knew damn well Fallon had me second-guessing myself. And I bet the smug asshole was getting a real laugh out of it.

"I've got to talk to Marco," I said, picking up the tumbler and downing the rest of the whiskey.

"You're not going to make Marco follow Fallon around all day, are you? The poor guy would go stir-crazy with no need to use his baseball bat." Leo swirled his whiskey around his glass.

"Oh, so what is it you propose? Have you ever tried keeping a hellcat locked up in an apartment?"

I liked Marco. I even sympathized with him. Standing guard over Fallon all day at the clinic was going to drive the man up the wall. But when it came down to it, he'd do what he was fucking told.

"I'll watch her," Leo said with a shrug.

I shot my head up. "Found a new calling?"

If my brother wanted to stand around, bored shitless in an office building all day, certainly there were easier ways to accomplish his goal. Besides, Leo had never struck me as the office-type.

"Nah, man. I just know the girl's important to you."

The offer was genuine. I could see it in his eyes. But there was something off in the tone of his voice.

I stayed quiet, waiting for him to elaborate, but he didn't. I could have pressed the issue, but I trusted my brother. If there was something that needed to be said, he'd say it. And in truth, if I couldn't be there to keep her safe, my brother was the next best thing. He'd defend what was important to me with his life.

"*Grazie, fratello.* Fallon will be relieved to hear she can get out of her cage."

Leo laughed. "*She'll* be relieved, huh? I have a feeling she's got your balls in her purse, and you're just hoping she'll give them back if you play real nice."

"*Stronzo*" I cursed at him, loathing that there might have been an ounce of truth to his words. Not that I was ever going to admit it. "You just worry about your own balls."

"Will do."

And with that, I was anxious to leave, to get back to the woman who currently wasn't speaking to me but who would be smiling as bright as the sun soon.

At least, that's what I'd been expecting until I stood in front of her a half hour later, and she was staring up at me with a blank look on her face. I'd shared the good news. She could go back to work. Wasn't that what she'd wanted?

"Fallon?" I smiled, hoping it would start the ball rolling.

"You arranged for a babysitter for me? Are we going to have snack time and nap time too?"

It was something other than the monotonous silence that had filled my apartment the past several days, but it wasn't the reaction I'd been hoping for.

"I arranged to have someone there to keep you safe. My brother, Leo."

She crossed her arms over her chest, drawing my attention to breasts I hadn't seen in too many days. She looked ready to let loose a tirade, but then her expression changed.

"You don't like this very much, do you? Arranging for me to go back to work, I mean."

I shook my head. It went against the grain to let her out of my sight or out of my home when there were dangers nearby.

"But you're doing it anyway." It seemed more like she was talking to herself.

"You're doing this… for me," she said softly.

No shit, I thought, but I said nothing.

The look on her face shifted. She smiled, but it wasn't the smile that caught me. It was the look in her eyes. I couldn't put a name to it, maybe because I'd never seen it before. It was something soft and warm and it seemed to come from somewhere deep inside her.

"Thank you, Dominic. Not just because you're doing this, but because I matter enough to you to let me choose, to let me have my life."

And then she kissed me. It was a soft, featherlight touch, but whatever had been shining in her eyes reverberated in her lips and filled me with a warmth that was just as foreign as the look in her eyes. Whatever it was, though, it was like a drug. The ultimate fix. And at least for the time being, I was hooked.

Chapter Twenty-Four

Fallon

The morning of my first day back at work was nerve-wracking. At the same time, I was giddy to get back to work. To see Snowball, to hold a paw in my hand, to sweep down all the fur in my clothes.

I couldn't wait to see Corinne. Time had lost all its meaning since the morning Dominic and I set off running from my apartment. I couldn't tell how long it had been since I'd last seen her. My emotions were all over the place.

The second I finished getting ready, my hair tied back into a neat bun, Dominic's brother arrived at the apartment. He was the near splitting image of Dominic, although he was younger. His hair was slightly lighter, a dark brown instead of a black, that was slicked back. He wasn't at our impromptu wedding—for some reason.

He seemed a little more... full of life than his brother. He smiled more, and he had this energy about him that reminded me of a Golden Retriever.

"Leo," he said, giving me a small salute. "My brother wanted me to keep you safe while you're at work. I'll be with you throughout the day, drive you there and back. You know? All the usual stuff that will drive you up the wall."

He was right—a freaking bodyguard at work was the last thing I wanted—but the goofy, charming smile he flashed me made it impossible to scowl at him.

He pulled on the collar of his coat, a black trench, as we made the trip to the car. He had a muscle car that looked an awful lot like the McLaren to me, but not an exact replica. It hit me as he opened the passenger door for me that he probably wasn't thrilled about this babysitting detail either.

"Thanks for making the time to do this," I said. "I've been going a little crazy holed up in the apartment."

Was I allowed to say things like that to Dominic's brother? I kind of wanted to take the words back the moment they were out.

"Hey, you're all good," he said, sliding behind the steering wheel. "I get it. I got stuck at a safe house for a while once. Wasn't fun. Only me and some beauty magazines to keep me company." He turned to me, his eyes comically wide. "It changed me."

I couldn't help but laugh. Why weren't all the Luca brothers like him? Leo made me feel comfortable. Don't get me wrong, Leo was still a beast among men—I knew he would be able to protect me if things went south. A chill shivered down my spine, remembering what "things going south" could entail, but I pushed it away. I wouldn't cower for the rest of my life.

"I hope you like puppies and kittens," I said as we pulled up in front of the clinic. It was strange to see the sign with my maiden name out on the front. My eyes glazed over it as an itchy sensation climbed up my throat.

"I'll try to stay out of your way," Leo said. "You won't even know I'm here," he added—a lie, if ever I heard one.

When Dominic said he'd have a bodyguard keep me safe, I assumed that he meant they'd be stationed at the front door. That was definitely not the case. Leo followed me everywhere I went, hovering only a few feet away at all times. I wondered what would happen if I told him I had to use the washroom… then decided I wasn't in a hurry to find out.

Corinne wasn't in yet while I set things up for the day. Granted, I was early, but I wanted to get the ball rolling as soon as possible. Ten minutes before opening, Corinne arrived.

When she walked into the operating room and saw both me and Leo, her eyes widened, instantly bright with tears, but she pressed her lips together, casting surreptitious glances at Leo. (Like I said, Leo seemed nice, but he was still a beast among men.) And the looks continued, glancing back over her shoulder as she went to put her things away in the staff room without a word. By the time she returned, there were clients filtering in the front door, and we had no choice but to get to work.

I didn't see her much all morning, though every time she passed by, I could feel her gaze, darting back and forth between Leo and I. What was she thinking? Was she angry? Hurt?

By lunch time, the uncertainty was killing me. As soon as I spied Corinne entering the break room, I shot after her.

"Leo," I said softly just outside the door. "I need to speak to my friend. Do you mind giving me a few feet of space and pretending you're not listening in?"

"I actually have a filter in my head. Tunes out all girl-talk, so you're safe," Leo said with a grin.

Still, I walked past Corinne—who eyed me the whole time—to the fridge, where I had packed an extra sandwich. I handed it to him, and he looked up at me like I had just gifted him life.

"Here's some lunch. Maybe the chewing will help drown out anything your girl-talk filter doesn't catch."

"Good thinking," he said, remaining in the doorway while I took a deep breath and marched to my doom—or my best friend… it all depended on how the conversation went.

But before I could open my mouth, Corinne lunged to her feet. "I tried to call you so many times! I was so scared, Fallon. What happened? Are you okay? Where have you been? What's going on? And what the hell is with Stalky McSexy over there?"

I took a deep breath. "I'm fine, Corinne. I'm sorry you were so worried. I couldn't call… I mean, I can explain…"

It seemed now that I finally had the opportunity to explain, I was having difficulty finding words.

Her eyes darted back and forth between me and Leo again. My poor friend was going to give herself a headache!

"That's Leo. You can stop looking at him like that. He's a good guy." Wait. Did I just call a guy who was part of a crime family a "good guy"? Oh well, I'd deal with that later. "I—"

"What is that?" Corinne gasped as her eyes spotted my wedding ring. She grabbed my hand, pulling my arm over the table to inspect it, nearly dislocating my shoulder.

"It's…"

"You got married? All this time, I've been worried sick about you, and you were… you were, what? On your honeymoon?" she said incredulously.

There was no way even Leo's girl-talk filter could block out Corinne's voice. I was pretty sure anyone sitting in the reception area could hear her—maybe anyone sitting in the reception area two buildings over.

"I wasn't on my honeymoon," I hissed in little more than a whisper.

"What's going on, Fallon? I don't understand. Your dad said you moved out of town for better opportunities. I tried to call you. Your voicemail is full. I knew something was up. You like your routine, you don't like change. You wouldn't just leave town like that. You wouldn't leave *me*... would you?"

I quickly stood up, crouched next to her, and wrapped myself around her waist. She looked on the verge of tears.

"And now you're back, and you're married, and I don't know what the heck is going on. I'm so confused."

When Corinne calmed down, I looked up at her, hoping to convey some small piece of how much I cared about her in my eyes.

She put her hand on my cheek. "You didn't leave town, did you?"

I shook my head.

"And you weren't ignoring me?"

"I wasn't. I haven't had my phone." I sighed, glancing over my shoulder at Leo while trying to figure out just how much I could tell Corinne.

Leo was staring straight ahead, just over the top of my head, but he smiled when he saw me looking at him.

"If you ladies want to kiss and make up... all I'm saying is I'm okay with that," he joked, and even Corinne let out a tiny laugh.

And just because I felt like flustering Leo after he'd flustered me all morning by staying close on my heels, I leaned up toward Corinne and parted my lips.

Corinne smiled devilishly and played along, leaning down ever so slowly. I could almost hear Leo holding his breath.

And just as our lips were about to meet, I leaned back and sprung to my feet.

"Have some potato salad, and I'll explain everything," I said, sliding the container on the table toward her and shooting a triumphant grin at Leo.

"I'm telling you, Fallon," he pressed on with his goofy grin, "it would make you both feel better."

I stuck out my tongue at him and pointedly turned away, exchanging a wicked smile with Corinne. So quickly, it seemed like she'd forgiven me, reminding me just how grateful I was for her friendship. But what to tell her? Could I tell her the truth? Then again, Leo would step in if I tried divulging more than I should. Maybe he was useful, after all.

"I need you to swear on your life that you won't tell another soul," I explained to Corinne, which also would have signaled to Leo that an info dump was coming. Any secrets the Lucas wanted kept were about to be spilled.

"Okay…?" Corinne replied, confused.

When Leo made no move to interfere, I plowed on. "It's sort of… life and death. They wouldn't take kindly to someone knowing all of this without being part of the *family*."

"Family?" Corinne tilted her head, and I gave her a stern look so that she knew I was serious. "Okay. Okay. My lips are sealed." Corinne gestured zipping her mouth shut.

And then her eyes went wider and wider while I spilled all the beans. I told her about my father, and who the Lucas were, and where I had been. I told her about the wedding and felt myself tearing up because Corinne couldn't be there.

She shoved a cube of potato in her mouth when she was finally able to close her jaw.

"So, yeah, things might get a little hairy, but I've convinced Dom to let me get back to work in the meantime. I missed you, honey. I'm sorry that I couldn't talk to you. I wanted to, but my hands were tied."

"I had no idea. All I kept thinking was that you had to come back... eventually."

"And now I'm back," I said with a soft smile and placed my hand on top of hers.

Leo cleared his throat, and when we glanced up at him, he waggled his brows.

Corinne leaned in close. "And who is that sexy as hell hunk following you everywhere you go? Because wow, does he pull off that monochrome fit. All he needs are some leather gloves, and I'm all his."

I laughed. Maybe Corinne and Leo would be a good fit. They both seemed to have their minds permanently stuck in the gutter.

"That's my brother-in-law, you horny creep."

We laughed, but then I turned serious one last time. I had to make sure. "Are you still mad at me, hon?"

She shook her head. "I don't even know what to say, but I'm sorry, Fallon. I'm sorry you got caught up in all of this."

She polished off the potato salad. "Have you guys... you know... done *it* yet?"

My cheeks went scarlet red.

"Yes," I admitted, but that was the only detail she was getting.

"He was packing, wasn't he?" She winked.

"You betcha." I bit my lip as flash floods of his naked body filled my mind.

"I mean, at least he's good in the sack. I know that look on your face."

"What look?"

She laughed. "Tell me you're not turned on just thinking about him."

I crossed my arms over my chest. "No, I am not."

Corinne shook her head, chuckling. "So, I know there's no way out. And that sucks. But maybe it won't be so bad. You might just… start enjoying each other's company if you give it some time. It sounds like you've got plenty of heat in the sack," she said, waggling her brows.

"I don't know. It's confusing. I have no idea what I feel for him. I'm all over the place."

"I'll be here for you, honey," she said, pulling my hand into hers. "We'll get through this together."

Our break was over, and we got back to work. Telling Corinne the truth lifted the weight of the world off my shoulders. My mind felt clearer, and after just one day spent with her, I didn't feel so alone anymore.

***

Dominic cleared his throat from the threshold of the bedroom door.

"Pack your things," he said, throwing a few suitcases on the bed. "We're moving in with the family."

I paused, holding the makeup brush inches from my face. "Why the sudden change?"

I turned on the small round stool to face him.

"Things are getting a little crazy. Don't freak out—no danger yet. We're just working on some plans. It's best we're all together in case the shit hits the fan," he said. "If you forget anything, Marco will come pick up the rest."

"Oh… okay."

That seemed troublesome. I wasn't sure what the implications of "shit hitting the fan" were, and I wasn't sure I wanted to know. How bad could things get for a family like this, after all? Their *bad* had to be a thousand times worse than mine.

Within the hour, we were packed and ready to move in with the Lucas.

When we got there, I was surprised by the sheer size of the place. The property was enormous, a massive estate with greenery, healthy pruned grass, and even a hedge maze. The forecourt had a fountain at the front of the mansion, with a naked woman draped in a marble cloth that barely covered her lady parts. This was far from what I had imagined. For some reason, I'd pictured floor-to-ceiling windows, sleek stainless steel panels… something modern; not this amazing stone structure that could have been a small historical palace.

When we stepped out of the car, I stared up at the house. Old architecture, of course, but I wasn't sure from what period, considering I wasn't clued up on that stuff entirely. Maybe Colonial Revival? I wasn't sure, but it looked familiar, with its symmetrical, boxy build. The front door had pillars that held up a small balcony that overlooked the front of the property. I counted ten windows overlooking the yard, and it made me curious, wondering how many rooms the house had.

The entryway was grand with a central staircase leading up to the second floor. From the base of those stairs, I could see another set that led up to the third floor. This was my first experience being fully inside their world. The house made me feel small the second I stepped inside. Definitely different from what I was used to—cramped tiny NY apartments with a nice view of a dumpster-filled brick-lain alleyway.

There were constant streams of people coming in and out, all looking battle-hardened, some even scarred. It looked like they were preparing for war. Most of them spoke among themselves or shouted at one another in Italian. Was it always like this, or were they so frantic because of the Novas?

I felt like a foreign object, and at any moment, would be cast out because I didn't belong here. Dominic disappeared without me realizing, probably to speak to someone, so I was left to wander the halls.

Several associates, soldiers, and drug runners filled countless rooms in the house, sitting together, plotting their next move. They would glare at me, and stop speaking, until I was far enough to not understand what they were saying.

I went past a room with thick doors that reached the ceiling. The wood had ornate carvings on it, of plants and flowers and women. Inside the room, Vincent stood with several men his age, talking in hushed tones. It seemed something had just happened, something big, insurmountable.

Vincent greeted me with a stiff nod, but I was distracted by a familiar excited pitter-patter on the hardwood floors. Bullet stormed me from beneath the table, where he had been resting at Vincent's feet. Bullet jumped up, whimpering, his tail swinging from left to right. I crouched to meet his level and gave him some scratches. The little pup recognized me as the lady who saved his life. I couldn't stop myself from inspecting his wounds. He seemed to be healing up nicely. The hair around his wound was slowly growing back. Good. He didn't look good with a bald spot.

I couldn't help but giggle when Bullet jumped up into my arms, and I hugged him as tightly as I could without hurting him.

When I looked up, Vincent was standing in the doorway.

"Hello, Fallon. You are looking well." He looked down at his dog. "It seems he likes you," he mused. "Bullet is picky, an astute judge of character."

Was that a compliment? By the unreadable expression on his face, it was hard to tell.

"It's good to see that he's doing better," I said, standing up.

The expressionless mask slipped for just a moment, just long enough for me to see a glimpse of gratitude beneath it.

"You took good care of him," he said gruffly.

"Thank you. I'm glad I could help."

Having a conversation with Vincent Luca was strange. Not entirely unpleasant, I supposed, but weird.

"I'm sorry for intruding. Dominic disappeared, and I'm a little lost."

Vincent chuckled. "Yes, it's easy to get turned around in this big, old house." He looked past me, searching for something. "Leo," he called. "Will you see that Fallon finds her way to your mother? She's probably in the kitchen."

Leo nodded, coming up behind me.

"Of course. Follow me, my fair lady." He motioned grandly, and I nodded to Vincent, then turned to follow Leo with an internal sigh.

I was definitely more comfortable around Leo, and in all this chaos, I was most certainly looking forward to some quiet time with Maria.

Chapter Twenty-Five

Fallon

Following Leo to the kitchen took a while. The house seemed like a maze to a person who had never stepped foot in it before.

When I entered, I cleared my throat to let her know I was there. She looked up at me with a smile. Maria looked angelic, with the light streaming through the lace kitchen curtains. She wore a white dress tight around the bust that flowed down to her ankles. She looked like a model, with her dark and silvery hair clipped up into a messy bun. She stood at the sink, peeling some fruit, setting them aside in a large bowl. Maria had peeled perhaps a dozen apples already.

"Ah, *nuora*." She pulled the gloves off of her hands and threw them down on the table.

"*Nuora?*" I said. "What does that mean?"

She gave me a smile. "Daughter-in-law."

I leaned against the counter. "Things are crazy here. Are Dominic and Vincent planning something dangerous?"

"Don't you know?" She tilted her head at me.

"Dominic doesn't tell me much."

"Hmm. Strange." She gave me another warm smile. "Yes. Of course, they are. Danger is a prerequisite of our lifestyle. If you ever want to ask that question, assume the answer is always yes."

"How can you…"

"Go ahead," she said, nodding for me to continue.

"How can you live a normal life doing normal things, like peeling apples at the kitchen sink, knowing your husband and sons are doing dangerous things?" I fiddled with the hem of my shirt. "I mean, Dom and I aren't that close, but it still makes me so nervous knowing he's going into the fray."

Maria peeled the last apple, setting it in the bowl, filled it with water, and added salt to it. "To keep the apples fresh," she answered without me asking. "You soak them in salt and water. I'm making apple pie for later."

Maria untied her apron and hung it on a hook. "Come with me, *cara mia*. Let me show you what I do when I'm not making pie."

She took me to a stairwell landing, and we descended the stairs. The basement was bright, not like a typical cellar or the dungeon-like basement I'd pictured beneath this house. The floor coverings and the furniture was just as elegant as the stuff upstairs, but when I got closer to the bottom, I froze. If it had been anyone other than Maria leading me down here, I would have been quaking in my boots.

At least a dozen antique-looking swords hung on the wall opposite the stairs, each one of them with decorative hilts, inlaid with gemstones. Ornate knives and daggers, some small and almost dainty looking, while others were long and curved with jagged teeth. And in the middle of the large room was an elaborate workout center. Mats all over the floor, hand weights of all different sizes, punching dummies—many of them with holes through their heads and chests.

"Don't look so shocked, *cara mia*," Maria said with a smile. "The Luca women are more than just pretty faces."

Well, that certainly explained why the woman looked as fit as any twenty-year-old.

She crossed the room to the wall with all the weapons, selected one of the knives, and carried it back with one hand beneath the hilt and the other beneath the tip. It wasn't until she held it out to me that I saw the delicate etching along the handle and blade. A bird in flight. A flower letting loose its seeds in the breeze. And by the proud light in Maria's eyes, it was clear she'd done the etching personally.

"It's beautiful," I breathed, for the first time in my life, truly fascinated with a weapon.

"All of our weapons are etched in a similar manner—my way of sending a small piece of me with my husband and my sons wherever they go."

"That's…" I trailed off. "Beautiful" seemed redundant, but what other word was there for it?

"I do this because I love my family. And I put up with worrying that they won't come home, because I love them. I trust my boys, I trust my husband will do everything in their power to come home alive. If I didn't put that faith in them, they wouldn't be where they are today. I give them the support and the love they need in order to keep going. We're just like any other family, really." She paused. "Barring all the crime, of course," she added with a sly smile.

"I don't know how you do it."

"Because we're loyal to one another to the very end. We will always be there for each other. I love my lifestyle, and honestly, a little bit of danger here and there is healthy for the mind."

"My father told me everything. He reminded me of something," I said lightly. "I remember you."

"I was wondering when all the puzzle pieces would fall into place." She set down the container.

"I remember spending time with a boy a little older than me when you guys started showing up at the house. Was that Dominic?" I asked.

"Yes."

I found it amusing that Dominic and I had known each other all along. We weren't only connected by the engagement.

I also remembered the time Maria helped bury Cheshire, when I was sixteen years old, after my father had thrown him in the trash instead of helping me bury him. Even after all those years, the memory of Cheshire left me with a stinging in my chest. It would always sting. But Maria had been there for me when I had no one else.

"You have no idea how much your kindness meant to me," I admitted. "You're the reason I became a veterinarian. Your empathy. You taught me the importance of life."

"I was only doing what was right. You were in pain, and I helped you. That's nothing to commend." Maria put her hand on my shoulder, in that affectionate, maternal way. "As you know, Vincent and I were forced to marry, as well. I was just like you, until we started loving each other. And now my love for him is paramount to anything else. You're a strong woman, Fallon. You've got a lot of fight in you. And I know you will grow accustomed to this life."

***

I retired to the bedroom in the late afternoon after Maria and I finished making enough apple pies to feed a small army—because we apparently were feeding a small army.

Dominic's bedroom looked like it hadn't been touched in years other than the occasional dusting. Frozen in time, like a time capsule. Posters on the wall, shelves filled with comic books, and two books, both heavily creased, laid on the bedside table. *A Canticle for Leibowitz* by Walter M. Miller Jr. and *Childhood's End* by Arthur C. Clarke. So, my husband had been a sci-fi fan in his younger years.

It almost felt like I was intruding, snooping in something extremely personal by looking through his things. But hey, we were married, right?

I changed into a tank top and a pair of shorts, picked up *Childhood's End* from the bedside table, and began reading.

"I've been looking for you," Dominic said. He looked around the room and laughed. "I still can't believe she kept it like this all these years."

I looked up, startled. When I glanced out the window, orange hues had started to blend with the purple night sky.

"I hear mothers are sentimental," I said.

His gaze settled on the book in my lap.

"It seems you were a bit of a sci-fi nerd in your younger years,' I teased.

Dominic approached me, nudging my legs apart to position himself between my knees. I stared up at him, feeling the familiar heat begin to pool in my lower abdomen.

"Are you trying to provoke me, *limone*?" He pulled off his overcoat and dropped it on the bed. "Because that's not going to work on me."

"Isn't it?" I purred. I lifted my leg, slowly bringing my foot up to graze against his crotch. "Because I'm sure I could think of one or two ways you could punish me…"

"Is that so? Do you want me to punish you, Fallon?" he asked, meeting my eyes like he was trying to look beyond them.

I nodded, though I wasn't entirely sure it was the answer I meant.

I could feel his cock lengthening fast beneath my toes as something hot and dangerous flashed in his eyes. I'd seen hints of this side of him, enough to know it was there, but I'd yet to feel the scorching heat of it. Until now.

"I like this side of you, *limone*," he said, taking a step back so that my foot dropped to the floor. "Stand up and take off your clothes."

I got to my feet as butterflies fluttered in my stomach.

With hands that shook just a little, I grabbed the hem of my shirt and yanked it off over my head, revealing my bare breasts beneath.

"No bra?" he said as his eyes grazed over me, making my insides tremble. He palmed my breasts, catching my nipples between his fingers and tugging.

The friction shot through my body, making me squeeze my thighs together at the same time I pressed my breasts more firmly into his hands.

He shook his head and drew his hands back.

"You're not finished yet," he said, eyeing my shorts pointedly.

"Yes, Dominic," I said, and a sizzle of electricity shot through my veins at my own words.

I pulled off my shorts, revealing nothing underneath them either. And then I stood there, feeling his hot gaze travel over my naked body. I waited for him to touch me, to kiss me, but he didn't move.

When his eyes finally met mine, there was so much heat in them, it was a wonder I didn't combust.

"Get on your knees, *limone*."

I hesitated.

He put his hands on my shoulders and pushed me to the ground, forcing me down onto my knees.

He unzipped his pants and pulled out his massive erection. Dear god, it was even bigger than I remembered. My mouth watered, and my pussy throbbed needily.

"Suck my cock, Fallon," he said.

I wrapped my fingers around the base of his erection, stretching to make my fingers meet, and then I grazed my tongue along the underside of him, from the base to the very tip. I flicked my tongue along the ultra-sensitive ridge, and he let out a low, deep groan.

He thrust forward, and I opened my mouth wide to take him in, inch after inch until I could go no further, then worked my way back to the tip of him. Again and again, I took his hard, heated flesh into my mouth. He kept his hands at his sides, though I could see the way they were fisted, so tight his knuckles had turned white.

I picked up my pace and worked my hand in tandem with my lips until he grabbed a fistful of my hair and held me still. His hips thrust, driving his cock further, deeper. I willed my throat muscles to relax, to let him in, even if only for a few brief seconds.

"Good girl," Dominic ground out between gritted teeth. "You're doing so well."

He only pulled his cock out long enough for me to take in a deep breath before shoving it back inside my mouth all over again.

"Put your finger in your pussy," he said while he continued to fuck my mouth.

I obeyed, slipping a finger into my soaking wet slit. My walls contracted around me, and I could feel my own wetness dripping onto my inner thighs.

"Are you wet for me, Fallon?" he asked, gripping my hair tighter.

I mumbled a yes as best as I could, considering my mouth was a little busy.

"Good," he said as he pulled himself from my mouth and spun me around. He pressed down between my shoulder blades until I was on my hands and knees, faced away from him with my ass high up in the air.

And then the thick head of his cock pressed against my slick opening. He teased me for just a moment, running his cock up and down my slit. Then all of a sudden, he rammed in. One hard thrust, and he filled me up as he groaned out a sound so feral it sent a shiver down my spine.

He withdrew until only the tip of him remained inside me, and I whimpered at the loss before he drove back in, filling me up and rubbing hard against the bundle of nerves inside me that had me moaning and writhing against him.

His fingers dug into my hips as he picked up his pace, fucking me in earnest, pulling me back against him to meet his every thrust.

I dug my teeth into my arm, trying to stifle the moans that tumbled out, one on top of the other.

There was a knock on the door. Three quick taps that jolted through me. Dominic held onto my hips, keeping me impaled on his cock.

"Who is it?" he called out.

It was amazing how his voice sounded almost normal.

"Mamma says it's time for dinner," Leo called back through the door. "I hope you two crazy kids aren't doing anything in there I wouldn't do."

My cheeks flamed red even though he couldn't see us.

"Go fuck yourself," Dominic ground out, though I could hear the humor in his tone.

"Now, Dominic, maybe I'll just have to ask Mamma to come check on you herself," Leo taunted.

Dominic growled. "We'll be there shortly, *fratello*. Now, go away."

I had absolutely no idea how I was going to face Leo after what had just transpired, but as Dominic withdrew, then thrust back into my pussy, I really didn't care.

Chapter Twenty-Six

Dominic

I stood outside the closed door at the end of the upstairs hallway. It was always closed, though I knew my mother went inside sometimes. Not often, just once in a while when I'd lived here, I'd heard the quiet click of the door late at night.

I'd avoided the room at first, like I could pretend she was still here so long as I saw no proof she was gone.

I turned the handle and pushed the door open. I reached for the lighter in my pocket by habit, fiddling with it as I stepped inside and closed the door behind me.

The walls and floors had been repaired, but the room had been otherwise left bare aside from a small table in the corner where my mother had placed the things that hadn't been burned—a decade ago. There weren't many. A few books, two stuffed bears, and a small stack of hand-drawn pictures. I'd looked through them so many times that even though it had been years since I'd been in here, I remembered every detail on every page. Rainbows, birds, my mother, the park my father had taken us often. A picture of me, though if my name wasn't scrawled across the bottom, no one would have known it. Sofia had been a terrible artist.

I breathed deep, pushing away the familiar ache in my chest. I wasn't in here for a trip down memory lane, but because I needed some place quiet, and every other room in the house was anything but quiet.

We were one signature shy in the first stage of getting our casino underway, but that signature was proving difficult. And difficult was the last thing I needed when we were preparing to go to war.

There was one person who could help get the signature on the page, but it made my skin crawl to even think about it.

I stared down at Belemonte's business card. He was a financier by trade according to the card. The letters were printed in bloodred. Each number I punched into my cellphone burned a hole through my fingers.

"Mr. Belemonte's office, how can I help you?" A sweet feminine voice came from the other end.

"Mr. Belemonte, please."

"May I ask who's calling?"

"Dominic Luca," I said.

"One moment, please."

"Dominic!" The man's excited voice came from the depths of hell. It left a sick feeling in the pit of my stomach. "I knew you'd call."

"Belemonte," I said. "I've been having some trouble with getting the last signature on the license."

"Ah, it's always something, isn't it? Don't you worry about it, Dominic. I've got connections. I could have it sorted out in a few days," he said. "You do understand, though, that I'm going to have to ask you for a favor if I'm to go above and beyond for you."

"Of course. What is it you want?"

I'd been in this business far too long to expect something for nothing. There was always a cost.

"Don't worry about it. I'll put this favor in my pocket for now. But Dominic, when the day comes, there will be blood on your hands."

When wasn't there?

The click of a closing door made me turn around, but there was no one here. I listened for a moment, but there were no sounds of footsteps in the hallway.

"It's a deal, Belemonte," I said then hung up the phone.

It was a necessary evil, perhaps, but I was so fucking tired of all the blood on my hands.

Chapter Twenty-Seven

Fallon

"You've been acting strange, you know that?" Corinne said as she, Leo, and I delved into a plate of fries in the center of the table in the diner a few blocks away from the clinic.

I'd had to get permission from Leo for this little lunch away from the office. No doubt, he'd had to run it by his fucking brother first—a brother I hadn't seen in several days.

I'd left for work early each morning and stayed at the clinic as late as I could ever since the day I'd overheard Dominic's phone conversation. When Leo brought me back to the Luca estate, I made a beeline for my room and locked the door behind me.

I felt bad that the long hours were probably taxing on Leo, but he never complained.

Corinne and I had grown accustomed to having him around, so much that we didn't bother censoring our conversations. It was possible he was reporting every word we said back to Dominic, but I had a feeling he wasn't doing that. Leo just didn't strike me as a gossip.

It was comical today, the way he looked in the diner's small seats, like a grown adult sitting on children's furniture. He should have been uncomfortable, but with his long legs stretched out, he looked right at home.

"I know I've been acting weird," I said to Corinne, poking at my cheeseburger.

"Are you going to talk to me about it? Or maybe you'd like to hear every juicy detail from my date last night?" She waggled her perfectly shaped eyebrow at me, knowing perfectly well I did not want the details.

"I could stand listening to a detail or two," Leo piped in with "the grin"—that's just what we'd resorted to calling it.

I rolled my eyes and ignored him. "I don't know if I'm ready to talk about it, Corinne." I wanted to, but it felt like the moment I spoke the words aloud, there'd be no taking them back, no pretending I'd heard Dominic wrong on that phone call.

"Okay, well, I think you should probably give it a go because, in truth, the only hot date I had last night was dinner with Mr. Napoleon."

Leo tried to stifle a chuckle, but he failed miserably. He'd been hanging around us long enough to know that Mr. Napoleon was Corinne's ten-year-old cat.

I opened my mouth to try to force the words out, but they wouldn't come.

"Boy troubles?" Corinne teased. "I need to find myself a convoluted love life like yours." She sighed, but I didn't miss the "come hither" look she flashed at Leo.

"Let's switch, then," I teased, chuckling. "Bleach your hair, and I'll dye mine red. Then, you can have him."

I let out a sigh. Corinne was trying to crack jokes to make me feel better. I tried, I really did, but I just couldn't forget about it.

The rest of our lunch passed in silence. I was eager to get back to work. It had served as a much-needed distraction lately.

My phone rang. It wasn't a number I recognized.

"Hello?" I said.

"Miss Moore?" a man replied.

Well, it's Luca now, I thought. "That's correct."

My heart sped up as I hung up the phone. My mouth was dry. It took a monumental effort to force words out.

"We have to go," I said then shot to my feet.

"Wait a minute," Leo said, standing up and blocking my path.

"Leo. I need to be at the clinic. Now."

He stared at me for a moment. I wanted to plow right through him, but there was no way I could make him budge an inch even if I put all my effort into it.

But just when I was ready to scream in frustration, he nodded. He threw some money down on the table then strode toward the door without a word.

Corinne and I followed him, and I had to hand it to him. The guy could drive. He drove at double the speed limit, taking corners like they were nothing.

"What did the man say?" he asked when we were still two blocks away.

I repeated the man's words verbatim, and Leo nodded.

"You let me handle this, Fallon. Understand?" he said as we turned onto my clinic's street.

My heart sank.

Flames and smoke. A half dozen emergency vehicles.

As we approached, I could see one of my techs covered in soot, sitting on the sidewalk.

The animals! my mind screamed.

The moment the car stopped, I threw open the door and dashed out. I almost dropped to my knees.

The front window and door were blown out. Flames licked up the brick.

An arm wrapped around me from behind, but I pulled against it.

"Fallon, you can't—"

"I can't just let them burn," I cried, spinning around to face him.

He looked at the front of the building that was engulfed in flames, then his gaze traveled around the side of the building.

He nodded. "There's no way they're letting you in the front door. Follow me, and don't breathe a word of this to Dom."

He led me around the side of the building. I couldn't believe none of the emergency personnel tried to stop us. Looking up at Leo, though, I wouldn't want to be the one getting in his way either.

The service door at the side of the building seemed unaffected. It hadn't been blown off its hinges, at least. He tested the handle then threw open the door.

We both coughed as thick smoke billowed toward us, but I covered my mouth and nose with my scarf and followed Leo inside.

The narrow passageway that led to the treatment rooms was relatively clear, but flames licked out from the doors of each room. My stomach turned. My knees threatened to buckle, but I forced one foot in front of the other.

At the end of the passageway, we turned right. Flames had begun to lick along the walls, but the kennel was unscathed at the moment. Not for much longer though.

Animals yelped and barked and cried. *Oh god*, there wasn't enough time.

"Work fast," Leo barked, moving to open the first cage. "Unlock the cages and move on. The animals will find their way out."

I nodded, unlatching one cage after another. Dogs and cats and my very first ferret patient leaped from their cages and followed the narrow passageway back the way we'd come.

My eyes stung. I had to squeeze them shut over and over again, making a steady stream of tears cascade down my cheeks. My whole body was covered in sweat from the heat, but I didn't stop, not for a second.

When all the cages were open, Leo reached in and started gathering up the animals that were too young. I followed suit, filling my arms with as many kittens and puppies as I could.

"That's it, let's go," Leo said when his arms were full. He moved behind me and prodded me forward.

I cast one last glance over the open cages. We'd done it. All of them were empty.

We staggered down the narrow passageway, now having to lean this way and that way to avoid the flames that had crept out further. There was so much smoke, I couldn't see until we stepped outside.

I tried to sit down right there on the walk, but Leo grabbed my arm and tugged me back the way we'd come. My legs felt like jelly, and the moment he stopped, I collapsed on the ground and released my armful of animals. They scurried in all directions. My heart ached thinking that some of them would disappear forever, but at least they would still be alive.

The tears came without any sobbing. They flowed without effort.

I looked up at my flaming building. All my hard work, down the drain. The Novas were behind this, no doubt, but in the pit of me, I blamed *him*. This was all Dom's fault. He forced me into this life. He made me marry him. If I never went on a date with him, this never would have happened. Tony would have never even spared me a single glance.

I sat across the street, empty, defeated. It felt like a part of me had died.

"I came as soon as I could," Dom said from behind me. "I'm so sorry, Fallon." He sat next to me and tried to put his arm around me, but I recoiled from him.

"Don't touch me," I spat. "Don't you dare."

"I'm sorry, Fallon," he said, surprising me, but it wasn't enough. He worked with the man who murdered my mother. No amount of words would ever be enough.

"Go away, Dominic. I never want you to touch me again," I bellowed.

He was silent as I stared at the smoke and flames. The animals I'd tended with my own two hands. The fire. Everything I'd worked for up in flames. It was too much. Too goddamn much.

My head spun as tears streamed down my cheeks. I couldn't breathe. No matter how hard I tried to gasp for air, it wasn't enough.

Dominic's arms wrapped around me.

"Stop," I croaked, but he only held me tighter.

"Let me go," I cried, but he didn't let go. I'd already learned there was no way I could overpower him. All I could do was fall apart in his arms while he tried in vain to hold me together.

"I'm going to fucking kill him for this," he seethed against my ear.

Kiana Hettinger

Strange that they were the most beautiful words he'd ever said to me.

Chapter Twenty-Eight

Dominic

Emergency services, police, and animal control filled the narrow street. Slowly but surely, the animals were being caught and taken to a safer place. The fire had died down. Now what poured from the building was thick, black smoke. It plumed out of the shattered door and windows and floated up toward the sky. The acrid stench clung to my clothes, weaving itself into the fabric so it would never come out.

"I'll make this right, Fallon," I said.

Fallon looked at me, her face tear stained and red. "How?"

She looked at me with so much sadness in her eyes, it tugged at something inside me. But there was more there, something harder.

"I don't know," I answered honestly. "But I'll find a way."

I kissed the top of her smoky head like I was sealing the deal with a kiss. I didn't miss the way she flinched away from me when I did.

When Leo had called to say there'd been a fire, the wretched images that had flashed through my mind nearly made me lose my shit. Fallon screaming. Fallon engulfed in flames. Fallon… dead. Gone.

I'd almost had myself convinced I wanted nothing to do with her. I'd barely seen her the past few days. She left early and came home late. But seeing her like this, a tumbleweed of emotions twisted in my chest.

I'd been brought to my knees by a woman who barely came up to my chin.

As Fallon wiped her face with her sleeves, my cellphone rang, and I closed my eyes. Whatever it was, it would be something that took me away from her, something that meant I couldn't watch over her like a hawk.

I pulled out my phone and looked at the number.

It was Dante. It kept ringing as I stared at it, trying to guess what he was calling about. After a few more rings, I finally answered the call.

"Dante," I said. "Everything all right?"

"No." He scoffed. "It sure as hell isn't."

"What is it?" I asked, pinching the bridge of my nose.

"Fire, *fratello*. A lot of fucking fire."

I looked up at the black smoke that still poured from Fallon's clinic. *Fuck*. It had been a goddamn distraction.

Tony, you motherfucker. He'd burned down Fallon's clinic to keep me distracted.

"What did he do?"

"It's a long list, Dom. Just…" I could picture him pinching the bridge of his nose. "We need you, *fratello*."

"Of course. I'll be right there."

Fallon had her arms wrapped around herself in a sort of self-soothing hug. I willed to cement my feet on the ground. Her lemon waves had been stained with soot. I closed my eyes and dug my hands in my pockets, fiddling with my lighter.

I slipped my arm back around her. She didn't fight me this time.

"I have to go," I said, gritting my teeth. "Are you going to be okay, *limone*?"

She shook her head, then nodded, then shook it again.

"You're strong, Fallon. This didn't break you. Nothing ever will."

Maybe I said it as much for me as for her.

I looked around for Leo, who was standing nearby. He approached once I caught his attention.

"Take care of her, Leo. Take her home and make sure she gets cleaned up and comfortable, then call me. We have a bit of a situation in our hands."

"*Si, fratello,*" Leo said. His face was covered in soot. "Good luck."

"Vivere."

I squared my shoulders and walked away. I was doing what needed to be done. That's what I did. That's what I would always do.

I let the McLaren stretch her legs, speeding toward the address Dante had texted me. But it was Fallon in my head the whole time. I couldn't get her out no matter how hard I tried. She was always there, pissing me off or making me laugh or driving me fucking crazy. I didn't want to care for her, but I couldn't help it. It seemed she'd written herself onto my soul and there was no erasing the mark she'd made.

I squealed to a stop next to the address Dante had given me. I'd been so caught up in my thoughts, the flames seemed to come out of nowhere. They leaped from the building, and even inside the car, I could hear the crackling and the occasional *crash* as another window shattered.

Burying everything inside me down where it belonged, I got out of the car. Dante waited near the curb, a handkerchief covering his mouth and nose.

The scene was similar to Fallon's clinic, a building on fire, this one was roaring, and still very much alive. Dante didn't waste any time briefing me on what was going on.

"I've gotten reports from our men and associates that any and all businesses that are pertinent to the operation of our family are being taken out. They started with the Laundromats." Dante pointed at the building behind him.

"Fucking Nova," I cursed, imagining exactly what I would do to him when I got my hands on him.

"This is a fucking disaster, brother. Everyone on our payroll is being hit—hard—and they're going to want compensation." Dante moved the handkerchief out of the way and lit his cigarette. "The Laundromats being destroyed means we have lost millions. According to my sources... Brother, they're hitting businesses all across Queens. This is a coordinated attack to weaken us for the final blow."

"Why aren't you telling our father this?" I leaned against the vehicle and looked up at the sky. My ears honed in on the sounds of the city. People screamed, and cars raced across the streets. A few shots were fired here and there, and the occasional window exploded from the heat. The city was playing an orchestra of absolute chaos.

"You know Dad's sort of... rusty these days. You're basically running things while he sits at the head of the table. It's been like this for years, Dominic. You're the first person I'd come to for this," Dante said.

"Considering what Nova's up to, we've got hundreds of weak points across the city. We need to start moving our assets to secure places so we don't lose everything. Weapons first. Money second," I said.

"I'll make a few calls. Send it along the grapevine. Where should we store everything?"

I sucked through my teeth, trying to figure things out.

"The house is big enough. We'll have to make space. The bedrooms are all filled up, but we have a few offices that our soldiers use as meeting rooms and sleeping quarters. I'm sure we'll find space. We also have the pool house and the additional maid's quarters at the back of the property. We'll worry about cleaning cash when things get back to normal. Call Douglas to send in reinforcements where he can."

"Right," Dante said. "I'll get some trucks ready and start—"

Something exploded. The sound was so loud it nearly knocked me off my feet as I stumbled to the side. Dante grabbed onto the car to steady himself. The ringing in my ears became deafening. I could see his lips moving, but I couldn't hear what he was saying.

"What?" I practically shouted. "I can't hear you."

Slowly, my hearing came back as the ringing died down.

"Fucking bomb at the Italian place down the street," Dante said. He looked past me to inspect it. "Fuck, man, they made the *best* meatballs."

"Every Italian place makes the best meatballs." I scoffed.

"Yeah, but every time I bring a girl there, I get laid. That place had sentimental value," Dante said. He threw his cigarette on the ground and stomped on it. "I'll see you around."

"Of course," I said. "Before you go." I grabbed his shoulder and squeezed. "Be safe."

"Jesus, Dom. You getting all soft on me?"

"Maybe."

"Good." Dante patted my hand. "It's about time you're no longer a husk of a man."

I spent the rest of the day orchestrating the biggest shift in asset storage in Luca history while simultaneously organizing searches of every one of our remaining buildings and business interests. From a brief investigation, it seemed some of the fires had been caused by small-scale demolition explosives, and others were set on fire with a couple of Molotovs.

I had men stationed outside of buildings that hadn't been destroyed yet. I instructed them to report anything to me—even the smallest fucking bird that flew by.

By the time the moon was high in the sky and the city was asleep, it looked like the attacks were over.

But the Lucas never slept.

Chapter Twenty-Nine

Fallon

I glanced at the clock.

2:26 AM.

I paced back and forth across my bedroom in the dressing gown Maria had dressed me in. She'd taken care of me when Leo brought me back here. She'd helped me bathe and dress, and then sat on the bed with me and let me cry against her shoulder.

She'd left hours ago, long after the sun had set, but minute by minute, my chest tightened.

Dominic had been gone all day, and all Maria could—or would—tell me was that he was "sorting out business". But I'd heard the explosions. The staccato bangs that had sounded like gunfire.

What if he'd walked into a situation he wasn't prepared for? What if he'd been too close to one of those explosions? What if he'd been shot? Every question was like a tendril of fear that had snaked its way through my body and wrapped itself around my heart. And then the worst, the most terrifying tendril of all; it squeezed so hard it left me gasping for breath: What if Tony had won?

I shouldn't have cared. I didn't want to care. I didn't want to feel the sharp stab of pain in my chest every time I thought about him lying lifeless somewhere. This man worked with the monster who'd killed my mother. I could picture the two of them plotting moves in some dark corner, shaking hands and smiling like the devils they were.

I grabbed one of Dom's sci-fi novels from the nightstand and chucked it across the room.

"I don't care about you, damn it!" I shouted at the book.

If he was dead, I'd be free. Freedom was what I wanted… wasn't it?

I stared at the stupid book, trying to muster up the certainty that wouldn't come.

The door opened behind me, and I spun around. It was Dominic.

Safe.

Unharmed.

No blood.

I rushed at him with my hands in fists and slammed one into his shoulder. *Goddamn it, that hurt.* He was as solid as a freaking rock.

But now that my fears had been proven unfounded, I was pissed. I was pissed at him for working with Belemonte. For dragging me into this life. For making me worry about him so much I felt sick.

I punched him again, and this time, his shoulder jutted backward. I did it again and again. He became more like a rag doll, taking every blow and letting it push him backward.

Tears cascaded down my cheeks. My arms ached, but I couldn't stop.

"Where the hell have you been?" I yelled at him as I kept up my onslaught. "I didn't know if you were alive or dead, goddamn it."

Slowly, my punches weakened. I dropped my arms to my sides, exhausted, letting out a deep sigh.

"Feel better, *limone*?" he asked, cupping my face between his hands. They were warm and just a little rough. He tipped my face up to meet his gaze.

"Why didn't you stop me?" I asked, staring at the proof he was unharmed. Other than the day's stubble along his jaw, he looked no different than any other day.

"Because it looked like you needed to do that. Now, what's wrong?"

"I didn't know where you were, what was going on, or if anything happened to you?"

"I'm sorry," he said, swiping at one of my tears with his thumb. "I didn't think my absence would worry you."

It shouldn't have, but it did, so much more than I wanted to admit.

"I *hate* that I was so worried," I confessed. "I just want to hate you."

Maybe it was the relief coursing through my veins that made the words slip out so easily.

He backed me toward the bed until the backs of my knees bumped the mattress. I sat mechanically, and he knelt down in front of me.

"Why do you want to hate me, *limone*?" He put his hands on my knees and looked up at me. He wore no mask, and there was no storm brewing in his eyes.

"You work with the man who killed my mother," I said as his fingers drew lazy circles up my thighs.

His brows arched before they turned into a frown. "Who?"

"Harry Belemonte is the man who killed my mother. And you work with him. How can you work with a monster?" Anger boiled up again. I wanted to hit him. I wanted to hurt him as much as he'd hurt me, but then he took my hand in his and pressed his lips to the flesh of my palm.

"I can't stand the guy, Fallon," he said against my skin. "If there were any other way, I'd shoot him rather than look at him. But with the Novas on the attack, I had no choice."

"You're so loyal… to your family." I looked away, to the moon that shone outside.

Even though I understood it, it felt like another blow. Another chance for Dominic to put his loyalty to his family above me.

He nodded. "Yes, to my family, but also to you, Fallon. You are my family, don't you understand? I'll do whatever I have to do to keep you safe. I realized that today." He kissed my palm again, then again, forging a path to my wedding ring and then along my finger. A tingling sensation traveled up my arm.

"You did?"

He nodded, kissing back down my finger, across my palm to my wrist. The tingling transformed into tiny jolts that shot through my body and started a fire burning low in my abdomen.

"So, am I forgiven, Fallon?" Dominic continued his path up the underside of my forearm. "Because I've worked up quite the appetite."

"Appetite? For what?" I arched a brow at him.

"You," he said at the same time he tugged on my hips until my ass hung off the bed.

The force made me fall back, bouncing the back of my head against the mattress.

"What are you doing?" I asked. I sounded breathless to my own ears.

He didn't answer, but instead he grabbed the sides of my shorts along with my panties and yanked them off so fast they probably left a rug burn. He pushed my thighs wide open and buried his face between my legs. His tongue lapped at my slick folds like I had the fountain of youth between my legs. When he dragged his flattened tongue up to my clit, he let out a deep, guttural groan. He was *enjoying* this almost as much as I was.

He circled my clit over and over again, making me throb while my hips writhed beneath him.

His fingers dug into my thighs, pushing them open until they'd go no further, and he held me there, wide open for him as his tongue continued driving me higher. And then he suckled the sensitive bundle of nerves into his mouth.

Dear god, I saw stars. I dug my fingers into the mattress beneath me as the coil inside me wound up tighter and tighter. Moans slipped from my lips. I couldn't hold them back.

Dominic worked his magic tongue, flicking at my clit gently while he applied suction. It drove me wild. I tried to wriggle free when the sensation was too much to handle, but he held me in place so easily that it seemed like no effort for him at all.

The tension grew heavier in my stomach. Bolts of electricity traveled through my body, all honing in on my pussy.

"Oh, fuck," I moaned. Dominic had turned me into a babbling mess. "Please, Dominic. Don't stop. Just like that."

I propped myself up on my elbows to watch. I wanted to see him. He was terrifying and magnificent, and a fucking expert with his mouth.

The sight did me in. The coil inside me sprung loose and my back arched clear off the bed as wave upon wave of pleasure coursed through my body. I covered my mouth with my arm, trying desperately to shut myself up. I rode it out, biting the flesh of my arm to stifle the screams that begged to escape. I could hardly breathe, and I felt like I was on the verge of losing consciousness.

But Dominic didn't stop. His tongue glided lower, parting my lips until he reached my throbbing hole and shoved his tongue inside of me. He lapped everything up, all that my body could offer him.

He stood up, and I tried not to whimper at the loss. I started to scoot backward on the bed, but he shook his head.

"Don't move, Fallon," he said, keeping his eyes locked on my pussy while he slipped off his jacket and unbuttoned his shirt.

His gaze didn't waver as he stripped off his shirt and unfastened his pants. He kicked off his shoes and tugged off his pants. He stood there in all his naked glory. He was a perfectly sculpted creature, and the massive erection that jutted between his legs was so perfect it made my mouth water.

"Maybe later, *limone*," he said with a cocky grin that said he knew exactly what my mouth had been thinking. "Right now, I'm going to bury my cock so deep inside you, you won't know where I end and you begin."

He took a step forward, settling himself between my thighs. I could feel the thick head of him press against my slit, but he lingered there. Seconds passed, and I writhed against him.

"Please," I whispered desperately, and his eyes flared with heat.

He drove forward in one smooth thrust, filling me up, stretching my walls until I wasn't sure I could take any more. And yet, I couldn't fight the need to pull him closer, to wrap my legs around him and draw him in deeper.

And then, when all of his thick throbbing cock was buried inside of me, he wasted no time using my pussy like he owned it. He buried his face between my breasts, kissing, nibbling, and biting his way from one peak to the other. When he flicked at my erect, puffy nipples, I let out a mewl. It made him chuckle, and my cheeks flushed bright red.

Dominic ran his hands up and down my torso, my waist, and my hips, until they settled on the latter. He gripped them tightly, pulling me into each one of his vicious thrusts. His grunts were fierce and animalistic, accompanying each pump inside me.

When he leaned up, I was trembling. And when he reached between us to thumb at my sensitive nub, the stimulation sent me over the edge. I thrashed from side to side, overstimulated, but he didn't stop.

He fucked me without mercy.

Dominic slowed himself. I could feel his thighs trembling against my body, and they eased up once he came to a stop. I didn't want this to be over. Not so soon. He pulled himself out of me, grazing over every inch of my body with his eyes, his gaze so intense it seemed to scorch my skin. I didn't feel embarrassed by his intense perusal. In fact, Dominic made me feel sexier than ever before in my life.

His body was sculpted in muscle, and every single groove and plane was the most beautiful thing I had ever seen.

"Get on your knees," Dominic said.

Covering my mouth, I let out a soft chuckle. "An ass man, are you?"

"Maybe," he said, licking his lips, "I'm an everything man when it comes to you."

I turned around and got on my hands and knees for him. Like a good girl, my ass was raised and my torso was nearly flat against the mattress. He gripped the meatiest part of my hips with both hands and guided himself inside of me. My walls immediately tensed up around his thick cock, and Dominic let out a grunt.

Dominic fucked me harder than he had before. My legs shook so violently I couldn't feel them anymore. Only pleasure.

My legs collapsed beneath me, and I fell onto my side, still giving him access to my aching pussy. He gripped me so tight his fingers left grooves in my skin. Part of me wanted it to bruise, so he could mark me, claim me as his.

I grabbed his wrist and held tight, because all I wanted to do was touch him.

He was getting close. His pace quickened, becoming erratic. Frantic. He put his hands on either side of my head, bending over me further, allowing for deeper penetration. A hapless whimper escaped my lips as he hit every single one of my sweet spots with each thrust.

I lost control with him, and it wasn't something I was used to. Dominic collapsed on top of me, leaving our faces inches apart. With his cock buried deep inside me, I looked into his gray eyes, feeling as if they were my universe. I didn't look away, and neither did he. Dominic's furious thrusts slowed down to a gentle, soothing pace. Slowly, deeply, he slid in and out of me. His eyes were wide, those gray eyes, I could get lost in the storm for hours.

Dominic's stare was inescapable, all consuming. Something in the air shifted.

We both looked at each other, holding each other's gaze. The blue and gray mingling in this unclaimed moment. He closed the empty space between us, touching his lips with mine.

As he did, I felt his heart pounding in his chest, strangely in time with mine.

Chapter Thirty

Dominic

"Everyone doing okay?" I asked while I stared down at an egg I hadn't touched. I pierced the yolk, and it oozed out. "Because I'm going to need you on top of your game today."

"*Sì*," Leo huffed, rubbing the back of his head. "Had a bit too much to drink yesterday."

I shot my head up, eyeing Leo. Drinking after what had happened yesterday? What the hell had they been thinking? But Leo cocked an eyebrow, and I shut my mouth.

Leo knew I would have been tossing back shots right alongside him not so long ago. I nodded in acknowledgement and took a sip of my espresso.

"What Tony did was an attempt to weaken us," I said. My jaw clenched hard, and I was forced to pause. "And he was successful, not because of the money or the product we lost, but because of the message it sent. We looked weak, vulnerable."

The words tasted like bile in my mouth.

Dante sighed. "It's bad."

"It's not the end of the world." I tried to reassure him, but it sure as hell felt like the sky was falling. "Our family has been hit by worse. The only difference is this enemy has vengeance fueling him. We've got to hit him hard in hopes of evening the playing field."

"You sure?" Leo asked. He had lost some of the color in his face, and I couldn't blame him. He'd suffered plenty at the hand of enemies in search of vengeance.

"We need to hit hard to show we're still strong. We need to send the message that nothing can shake the Lucas. Not ever," I said. "Now, I'm going to need both of you to get your shit together. No more binge-drinking for now, *sì?*"

I downed the rest of my coffee. It was nine in the morning, and I already needed a drink. Maybe Dante and Leo had the right idea.

"Marco had some of our rats lurk in the shadows last night. The Novas are receiving a few weapon drops along the coast of his territory. Marco's got some old friends who can help. Ah, speak of the devil."

Marco stepped into the room and took a free seat beside me. He greeted the others with a nod before unrolling a map on the table.

"It's too dangerous to set foot inside Brooklyn," Marco began. "It's his territory, and he has men everywhere." Marco looked each of us in the eye. "It's risky enough that I got them in there to get this info, so we have to make this worth it." That was the longest sentence I had heard him say in years. He cared about this as much as we did. I clapped him on the back.

Marco showed us the routes we would take to get to our destination, pointing at the map with the tip of a pen. "It's about a twenty-minute boat ride to Coney Island, where he's receiving his package. We'll have to take the long way around to Jamaica Bay, where we'll set off from Breezy Point. Make sense?"

We all nodded.

"Thank you, Marco," I said. "Now, for the fun part: We're going to wreak as much havoc as possible. There are five boats coming in and out, and our sources say that he likes to have all the shipments put together before sending them off deeper into Brooklyn. So, we have to be patient, and take it all out at once. There's no doubt he's receiving his armaments to be prepared for when he tries to take us down. We pull this off, and we're on equal footing. We fuck this up…" I left the thought unspoken.

We all knew what was at stake.

"Understood," Dante said.

"Boss," Marco said quietly. "We could hit them even harder. There's a warehouse just off the shore…"

"Absolutely. Yes," I agreed before he even needed to continue. "Anything we can do to fuck that bastard's day up."

***

The surface of the water was blanketed in a layer of liquid silver. The moon was full and low tonight, like a spotlight shining down on us. It was a good thing, though, because without it, we'd have been going into this blind. Five speedboats bounced up and down on the gentle nighttime waves, awaiting our entry.

This was like any other job, but I couldn't shed the sensation that there were bars closing around us with every passing second. It was an unfamiliar and unwelcome feeling to want to turn this boat around. If something went wrong, how quickly would he retaliate? Would Fallon be caught in the crossfire?

We had been waiting here for an hour already, and the mini army behind me, standing at the ready, was growing restless. Some of our most trusted and skilled men were joining us tonight, but they didn't have much patience. They wanted to shoot some people and blow shit up, not wait out in the cold for hours. And if we were doing this, I sure as fuck wanted to get a move on too.

Chapter Thirty-One

Fallon

Dominic had kissed my lips and promised to come back to me, and then he'd left with at least half a dozen weapons on him; in holsters across his back, around his chest, and at his ankle. Just like Dante and Leo, just like Leandro and all the other men who'd gone with him.

He'd left twelve hours and seventeen minutes ago. 737 minutes ago. I wondered if this was what the wives of soldiers had felt when they'd sent their husbands off to war. Had they hugged them tight, hoping for the best while knowing another hug may never come? Had they committed every second of that moment to memory, knowing it might have to last them a lifetime?

He'd been honest with me, but now I almost wished he hadn't been. I almost wished I was blissfully unaware of the danger he faced this very moment. Almost. But we'd forged something together that had no room for lies, no matter how well-intentioned they might have been.

I padded down the stairs to the kitchen, not really hungry, but the four walls of our bedroom were starting to close in on me. There was no point in me trying to sleep. There was a vise around my heart, and I knew it wouldn't ease until Dominic was safe at home.

When I got to the kitchen and turned on the light, I nearly screamed. Vincent stood by the kettle, stirring something in a cup. I didn't want to bother him, and quite frankly, he intimidated me, so I turned around to leave.

"Fallon," he said. "Don't run away. Are you hungry? Thirsty? I just made some tea."

"Sorry… I don't want to get in your way," I said, standing there awkwardly.

He was wearing pajama pants, the kind that grandpas wore. No shirt. Beneath the light sprinkling of graying hair across his chest, his muscles were toned. The man was in incredible shape, just like Maria.

"You're not in the way, Fallon. Would you like a cup of tea?" Vincent offered.

I opened my mouth, but no words came out.

He tilted his head at me. "Are you okay?"

It was almost surreal—this terrifying man offering me tea and asking if I was okay.

I shrugged. "I'm just worried about Dominic."

He chuckled, not unkindly, and set his teacup down. "Come with me."

I followed Vincent like a lost puppy. He led me to what they called the war room, which felt uncanny because it was so empty. Usually, it was teeming with people. In their absence, the room felt empty. Lonely.

"Sit," Vincent said. He pointed at a seat next to the head of the table.

He went for a shelf up against the wall and reached up high to grab a bottle of whiskey from the top. He brought it back, wiped off the dust, and set it down on the table along with two crystal whiskey tumblers.

"This whiskey's fifty years old. I've been saving this for a special occasion," he said. "I never did get to congratulate you on the wedding."

He filled each glass halfway with the golden liquid.

"Oh, Mr. Luca, you shouldn't have wasted this on me."

He waved away my concern. "I have an eighty-year-old whiskey; that one's for a great tragedy. And whiskies I bought each day my children were born, too. It's nothing, really," Vincent said.

He took a sip, savoring the flavor before swallowing. I followed soon after, and we savored the smooth, warm taste in silence.

"I never told you why I didn't walk you down the aisle," he said after a moment.

I shook my head as I took another sip, and my arms and legs began to tingle pleasantly.

"I wanted to, Fallon. No young woman should ever have to walk down the aisle alone. But I couldn't do it. All I could picture was walking my Sofia down the aisle—a privilege I will never have. I will never walk my little girl down the aisle."

"I'm so sorry, Mr. Luca," I said, though the words felt too small. Dominic had mentioned a little sister in passing once.

"Please, call me Vincent," he said.

This was the longest we had spent alone together. It felt weird, but not nearly as uncomfortable as I would have expected. He smiled when I finished the first two fingers of whiskey and immediately topped me up.

"He'll come back triumphant, Fallon. He's my son, and I can tell that my boy cares for you. He loves you. He wouldn't lose this battle because he wouldn't want to leave you."

I smiled, wishing I had his kind of confidence that everything would be okay and wondering at the same time how he managed it.

"Well." He patted my hand. "Maria will be waiting up for me." He rose to his feet. "She never could sleep all those nights I was gone either," he said, smiling with a knowing look in his eyes. "My son is a lucky man, Fallon. Don't think I'm not grateful for that."

And then he was gone, and I was alone in the war room. I tried to draw Vincent's confidence into myself, but my fingers still trembled as the minutes since Dominic left stretched on. I had a feeling it was going to be a long night.

***

"Fallon," a deep voice whispered in my ear.

It felt like I'd only just drifted off.

"Fallon," the voice whispered again, and this time, warm fingers ghosted across my jaw.

I could remember curling up in the big armchair in our bedroom sometime just before dawn, but even with my eyes closed, I could feel the bright light of morning against my eyelids.

I struggled against sleep and forced them open, and Dominic was there, right in front of me. He was alive. Safe. The vise that had been squeezing my heart let go, and I flew out of the chair, making him stumble back.

"You're safe," I breathed, throwing my arms around him.

He grunted but wrapped his arms around my waist. "Of course, I am."

His voice sounded strained. I leaned away to look at him and gasped.

"Jesus, you look like shit."

"Grazie, *limone*," he said with a wry grin. "I didn't think I'd be coming home to your sour side."

Gently, I held his chin to move his face as I inspected it. Someone had *tried* to beat the shit out of him. His left cheekbone, once a glorious defined work of art, was swollen and cut. An angry black and blue contusion marred his perfect jaw, and a long cut down his temple had already begun trying to scab over. It was still new enough that I could clean him up to make sure it didn't get infected.

"You know I didn't mean it like that. Do you have a first aid kit somewhere?" I asked.

"In the bathroom." He pointed toward the ensuite, wincing as he lifted his arm. He was in worse shape than I thought.

When I got back, I zipped the red bag open and laid out the tools. Dominic's left eye had swollen even more in the last few minutes. It was nearly swollen shut. I'd get a cold compress on it soon, but first, I disinfected the wounds with antiseptic.

"Putting those veterinarian skills to use, huh?" Dominic chuckled but stopped quickly. He must have taken a beating to the ribs as well.

"Now that I think of it, I guess so." I dabbed around a wound with a warm, damp cloth to clean off the dried blood. "This isn't much different, is it?"

Once his face was ready to be patched up, I took out a bandage.

He scoffed. "You're not putting a damn Band-Aid on my face. Absolutely not."

"You have no choice in the matter," I said, staring him down.

He laughed then grimaced at the movement.

"Like hell I don't," he said then rummaged through the kit with one hand and came up with a bottle of liquid bandage. He smiled triumphantly, though the bruising all over his face kind of mocked his victory.

I stuck out my tongue at him but took the tube and applied it along the shallow four-inch cut. "Satisfied?"

His eyes grazed over me, sparking with heat. "Not really, but I suppose it'll do for now." He laughed, but then his expression grew serious. "Thank you."

He took my hand in his and pressed it against his less-swollen cheek.

I shrugged, trying to ignore the shiver of electricity that rippled through my veins. "A girl's got to be useful, right?"

He shook his head, still holding my hand against him. "You're useful just by being you, Fallon. Always remember that." His voice was low and deep, and his words seemed to rumble pleasantly through my chest. "But you shouldn't have waited up."

"I couldn't sleep. I didn't know what was happening, if you were okay…"

"And I couldn't stop worrying about you," he said.

I'd been safe in his family's home the whole time.

"But, *limone,* you shouldn't wait up for me anymore. I'm going to have late nights often until this Nova mess is sorted out."

I nodded, though we both knew I didn't mean it.

He unbuttoned his shirt, and I helped him pull it down his shoulders and off his arms. The right side of his torso was heavily bruised. Right—I needed to get cold compresses… a lot of cold compresses, it seemed.

"I… I don't like sleeping alone," I confessed. "I'm so used to having you with me when I fall asleep, that when you're not there, it's nearly impossible for me to fall asleep, you know?"

Dominic pouted, which looked like an attempt to hide his smile. "That's so fucking adorable, *limone*, you know that?"

I bit my lip, thinking about what Vincent said earlier. "You know what's adorable? Your dad said something interesting. He thinks you love me."

Dominic raised his brow, and I worried it would rip the cut at the arch, but it didn't. "That's just ridiculous. I don't know what he's talking about."

My heart dropped, and if it could, it would have hit the floor and shattered into a million pieces. "Oh."

"Don't we hate each other?" He narrowed his eyes at me. "Or have you fallen madly in love with me? I wouldn't be surprised. It happens *all* the time."

"I… I don't… I just…"

Dominic erupted in thunderous laughter, grabbing his side because of the pain.

"Jesus, Fallon," Dominic said. He grabbed my wrist and pulled me into him. "Don't look so heartbroken. I was *kidding*."

"Oh…" I bit the inside of my cheek. "That was a shitty joke."

"Of course, I love your silly, stubborn ass," Dominic said. It came so easy that I knew he meant every word he said. My heart swelled, and I wanted to pull him in my arms, and never let him go, so I did. I tackled him, and he fell over on the bed, and I held him tighter than I ever did before.

"I love you too, Dominic. Don't ever scare me like that again."

Chapter Thirty-Two

Dominic

It was already dark out, we had full bellies, and we were naked in bed together.

Absolute bliss.

Fallon made me feel like I could finally breathe again. Realizing that I loved her, and that she loves me, awakened something in me. Something I hadn't felt ever since the world broke me.

Things finally felt like they were going to be okay. Fallon and I were in a good place at the moment. I never thought admitting that I was head over heels in love with her would feel so liberating.

The past few days, even when working, I felt strange, in a good way, like life was finally worth it. God, Fallon was changing me into one soppy little fucker.

It was like a huge weight had been lifted off of my shoulders, and it allowed me to understand myself a little bit more. I *did* have the capacity for love, and compassion, and happiness. I just hadn't allowed it all these years.

I had been staring at Fallon in complete awe of her for what felt like hours. She stared back, only blinking when she absolutely had to. She was hauntingly beautiful to me, in mind, body, and soul. The kind of feeling only a man who was madly in love with a woman could appreciate. I swore I could see her eyes sparkling, as though she were staring at a constellation instead of me.

Fallon scooted closer and closer, her naked body finally pressed against mine. Everything felt so… new with her. The way her fingertips traced the grooves of my abdomen, edging closer to my crotch.

"Can I ask you something?" Fallon said.

"Of course. As long as it's not about that one thing. Or that other…" I joked.

"Shh. I'm being serious." Fallon put her fingers on my lips to shut me up. "So, considering you've been in this whole… career criminal thing your entire life…"

"Well, technically, you have been too." I nudged her.

"You know what I mean, Dom. Stop being a pain in the ass. I'm trying to ask you something here," Fallon said. "If you weren't born into this life, what do you think you would have been like? What would you have done for a living?"

Her question was sweet, but I couldn't come up with an answer straight away. "You mean what did I want to be when I grew up?"

"Yeah, kinda," Fallon said. She ran the back of her palm along my cheek.

"I probably would have been a salesman, or stuck in a dreary cubicle from nine to five. I'd hate my life and look forward to the weekends, because that would be my only joy in life," I said.

Fallon scoffed. "Seriously? A salesman or an office job was your big aspiration as a kid? What do you think you would enjoy doing if you quit right now?"

I let out a lung full of air. "Honestly? I probably would have become a lawyer because they make a lot of money. Or a homesteader. Who knows? If I wasn't born in this life, I'd be a completely different person with different dreams."

Fallon pursed her lips. "I like the idea of you wearing flannel, chopping down trees, and hunting your own meat. Sounds cool. Oh god, and you gardening shirtless? Ooh-wee, I'm getting hot just thinking about it."

"You only love me for my body," I lamented.

Fallon came closer, brushing her lips against mine, barely touching them. Just as I was about to kiss her, I heard it.

The staccato beat of gunfire. One shot fired, then a second, then a third. It wasn't in the distance, either, it sounded like it was on our property.

Acting on pure instincts, I took her in my arms and rolled the both of us off the bed. We hit the floor, hidden next to the bed, out of the way of any possible stray bullets.

Fallon let out a little yelp.

"Just breathe," I said softly. "Don't panic."

"How am I supposed to—" she started but I covered her mouth. The commotion outside only escalated.

There was a loud knock on the door.

"Dominic," Leo's voice bellowed. "They're here. Let's go, *fratello*."

It wasn't often Leo sound anything but laid-back. This was definitely not laid-back.

Fuck. It was Nova.

I shot out of bed and pulled clothes on as quickly as I could.

The door flew open a second later. Leo stood there armed like he was going to war.

There'd been no word on the street that Tony was anywhere near ready to attack and certainly not in our goddamned home. I stood up, squared my shoulders, and walked toward the doorway.

"Guns ablazing," Leo said. He toyed with the assault rifle hanging on his shoulder. "The war's right on our doorstep, so I guess that means I'm glad you're here. We need you."

"Of course." I put my hand on the back of his neck, pulling his forehead against mine. "We take them down tonight, *fratello*."

Leo nodded. "I need to make sure Mamma's safe and hidden. I'll see you in a bit."

Leo left, and I turned to Fallon.

"Stay in here. Don't open the door for anything," I told her. I wished I had more time to reassure her everything would be okay, but I didn't.

"Wait," she said, her voice thick with emotion as she darted toward me.

Her body collided with mine, and she held on tight as she kissed me with what felt like every fiber of her being. Time stood still, and the world disappeared.

"Don't you die on me, okay?" she said when she pulled away. "Don't you dare."

"I'm too stubborn to die, *limone*," I said. "Just… don't leave this room. No matter what happens."

I closed the door, tugged on the doorknob to make sure it was locked, and shoved the key in my pocket. The sound of gunfire and battle cries filled my ears.

They were close. They'd already breached the property's edge. I clenched my fists, thinking of all the different ways I was going to make the Novas pay for this.

Chapter Thirty-Three

Fallon

It was happening. This was it. It was all over, and we were all going to die.

Shut up, Fallon. Stop being so dramatic.

Dominic had locked the door behind him to keep me safe, and I frantically looked around the room for a place to hide.

My heart beat so hard in my chest, I swear I could feel it pounding against my ribs. It felt like it was going to explode.

Another shot cracked through the air, just below the bedroom window. It was loud, and it nearly made me jump out of my own skin.

My eyes darted frantically around, though I had no idea for what I was searching. I spied my cellphone sitting on my dressing table next to my purse, and suddenly, my father's image appeared in my mind.

More shots rang out, so loud I covered my ears to try to escape the sound. I dropped to my knees beside the dressing table, my back against the wall, hugging my knees to my chest as I dialed his number.

I hated that I couldn't do anything to help. I hated feeling so scared—it made me feel weak. And I felt like that little girl again—helpless, afraid, vulnerable.

I remembered the day my mother died.. The quiet click of the trigger. The roaring bang that followed. My mother's scream. I could still see her face. I still remembered exactly what her eyes had looked like the moment life had left them.

The phone rang, but no one picked up. It rang again. And again. *Please, Daddy,* I silently begged. And then I heard his voice.

"Hello?" he said over voices and classic rock playing in the background.

"Daddy?" I whimpered. The last time I called him that, I'd been a child. But right now, I needed him. I needed my daddy.

"Baby girl? What's going on?" Dad said. He stopped breathing. He was suddenly the attentive father he'd been before my mother died.

"Do you have some time to talk? I need… I need you," I said. Once I finished speaking, the music and chatter became quieter. He must have been making his way out of the bar.

"I always have time for you. Well, almost always," Dad chuckled.

A stream of automatic shots fired out, and I squeezed my eyes shut.

"What's that sound?" he asked.

Yes, my mind cried, but I swallowed it back.

"Just some fireworks, Daddy." I don't know what came over me. He was a cop, for Christ's sake.

"That didn't sound like fireworks, Fallon. What's going on? It's the Novas, isn't it?"

"No, I..." I squeezed my eyes shut tighter. "Do you remember when we went to Central Park? I was young. I don't think you knew what to do with me after Mom died. So, you took me on walks. And this one day, we stumbled on a really quiet part of the park, surrounded by trees. There was a small lake. Do you remember?"

The back of my throat ached as tears stung my eyes.

"I do. There was an entire army of ducks hiding from the people that flooded the park," Dad said. His voice cracked. "They all crammed together in this twenty-foot space. And you were obsessed. We spent hours there. We had to fetch a few bags of frozen peas because you wanted to feed each and every one of them before we left. I actually remember that I missed work that day because of you. I didn't have the heart to put a stop to your fun."

"I love that," I told him. "I think of it every time some weirdo brings in their pet duck."

"People have pet ducks?"

"Oh, yeah." I chuckled and wiped a tear off of my cheek.

I couldn't imagine what it was like to be smack-dab in the middle of the fight outside. Even from my bedroom, the sound of every shot jolted through my body. An explosion went off somewhere on the property, and it spooked me so much that I crawled into the corner of the room.

"You remind me so much of your mother," my father said suddenly. "That's why it's so hard..."

His voice cracked again.

"She was a real fighter. She fought for the people who were important to her, and she loved with all her heart. She loved giving gifts... I wasn't always the best husband," he said, his voice had grown thicker like it was clogged with tears. "Your mother gave so much. I never understood how she did it and never seemed to run out."

"That's beautiful." I chewed on my bottom lip, trying to focus on my father's voice, not the crack of gunshots beyond the bedroom door. Not the screaming and shouting.

"That's you, Fallon. You're just like her."

"I'm sorry I've always been so hard on you. I should have—"

"No, don't you apologize, baby girl. I'm the one who should be apologizing. You deserved so much better. I fell hard when your mother died. I got so caught up in my own grief."

"It's okay, Daddy," I choked out.

I didn't want him to apologize, that wasn't why I'd called.

"Your mother was one hell of a fine cook," he said.

I smiled through my tears. For the first time in so long, I felt like he understood what I needed. No apologies, just his voice.

"Her lasagna, woah, boy," he said. "Now that was a work of perfection."

I could hear a car horn behind my father's voice, but it was muffled. He was no longer outside.

"Daddy? What are you doing?"

"I'm proud of you baby girl. Everything's going to be okay. You just hold on, you understand me?"

Oh no. He wasn't outside because he was in his car.

"Daddy, don't. You can't."

"There was that time you, me, and your mom went to the lake up north. Do you remember that? The first time I showed you how to fish?"

I did remember that, just vaguely.

"I knew right then you were going to work with animals when you grew up."

"Because I wouldn't let you kill the fish," I whispered.

Another explosion sounded, closer than the last. Too close. I could hear the heavy thud of footsteps on the stairs. Luca men? Nova men? I huddled in the corner, pressing my back against the wall, wishing it could swallow me up.

"Dad… I…" I started, but I didn't even know what to say. Tears streamed down my face.

"Just a little longer, baby girl."

But I feared it was already too late.

Chapter Thirty-Four

Dominic

"What the fuck is going on?" I roared over the gunfire. "Can someone tell me what we're dealing with?"

"Dozens of Tony's men have broken through the property line. They're scaling the walls," Leo said as we rushed to the armory. It was difficult not bumping into people along the way as everyone frantically moved around the house to prepare for the hell that was coming at us.

"Sir, we're getting pushed back into the house," Leandro reported. "They just blew up the front gate. Fleets of vehicles are coming onto the property. Time to make our stand here from inside."

I nodded, patting Leandro on the back.

"Listen up," I called to the room full of men. "Board up the windows. Barricade the doorways. Flip all the tables so we have cover. We need to prepare, and fast. Fire only when you need to. We don't have unlimited ammo. Give 'em hell, boys. Don't let any of them walk out of here alive."

We were outnumbered, outgunned, but any one of the fifty men here was smarter and more cunning than Tony's army.

"Leo, Dante, we need to keep eyes on the back of the house. Most of them are coming through the front gate, but they're going to come at us from all angles." A window exploded open near the back door, and I rolled my eyes. "Yeah. Like that."

My brothers and I fired haplessly into the darkness of the night, to keep the attackers at bay.

I shouted louder, over the ringing in my ears, "There's a stash of bulletproof vests in the living room, in a chest near the fireplace. Take some for yourselves and hand them out to as many people as you can."

"*Si, fratello*," Dante said. He had a look of determination on his face, knowing immediate danger was afoot.

Marco rushed over to the back door, and with his sheer strength, he pulled the sofa over to the door and flipped it over to block people from entering.

"*Vivere*, brothers. If you don't come out of this alive, I'll beat the shit out of you," I shouted.

"*Vivere!*" they said in unison, but as the men veered off to their tasks, I grabbed Leandro's arm.

"Watch the stairs," I told him. "Fallon's up there. Don't let anyone get through. Got it?"

"Yes, sir." He nodded, checked his gun, and strode out of the room.

I pulled my phone out of my pocket and dialed Brute's number. It wasn't long before he picked up. Leo tossed me one of the bulletproof vests, and I tried my best to put it on with one hand.

"Dominic, my buddy!" Brute said. "You only call when there's trouble. Is there trouble?"

"You know me so well." I chuckled sardonically. "Tony's decided it's a good idea to attack the family home. Is there any chance you have a few men to spare? We could use the extra hands."

"Oh, man. Tony's such a dickhead," Brute said. He let out a groan. "I'm more than happy to help, but I'm on the north side with most of my men at the moment. It'll take a while to get there—so you'll have to hold them off until then. Can you do that?"

"Of course. Piece of cake," I lied.

Someone burst through a window that was still being boarded up. I aimed my SIG Sauer toward him and fired two shots.

"Yeah, man. I'll bring the big guns. Sounds like you need it," Brute said. "Stay alive, man."

"Stay alive."

Our men stationed themselves in small groups at all the entrances. I made my way to the front door, where a table was flipped over, overlooking the front yard. The front door was open so we could attempt to pick them off as the armada stormed toward us. My father was beside me, firing his trusty automatic into the fray.

These high-stakes gambles of life and death were nothing new to me and my family, but the rush was just as intense as the first time I risked my life. I had already taken five men down, but I hadn't felt a thing. Thrilled by the battle, but no remorse for the ones who hit the ground.

My father ducked behind the table to reload his weapon.

"This is the most alive I've felt in years!" he shouted over the racket.

"You're crazy." I laughed.

"So are you, my son," my father said. "You inherited all of my best traits."

Multiple explosions went off one after the other. Our men retreated back into the building, and someone screamed about the front gates being blown down. The Novas' men were coming through in fleets of vehicles.

The enemies were steadily moving toward us, too close for comfort. There were too many to stop them, and we were forced to retreat further into the house. Fucking Tony. He was going to pay for this.

Slowly but surely, we were running out of ammunition. I had only a few clips left when we got pushed back further. Swarms erupted through every single entrance possible. They spread through the house like a swarm and scattered like rats. I lead my brothers to the back door, where another horde came through.

We emptied a shower of bullets into a wall of bodies, then I looked around the room in search of more intruders. But damn, my mother was going to throw a fit. The house was being destroyed. Bullets flew everywhere, prized vases, sculptures, and paintings were torn to shreds. One of our soldiers dropped to the ground, dead before his head touched the tile.

Our home had turned into a war zone.

We continued our dance of death, the home our stage, the reverberation of gunfire off of the walls our song.

Chapter Thirty-Five

Fallon

A thud in the hallway shook the bedroom door. It was almost as if—

Bang. The door shook again. *Oh god.* My whole body shook as silent sobs wracked my chest. Someone was trying to kick down the door.

"Dad, I love you. You know that, right? I love you," I said, but before he could reply, I hung up.

I shot to my feet, but my legs nearly gave out. I had to press my back up against the wall to keep me upright. I stared at the door like a deer caught in headlights as it shook with another heavy thud.

One more thud, and the door flew open, slamming into the wall behind it.

The devil stood in the doorway to my bedroom. The same man who'd walked into my clinic. The man who'd tried to have me shot. The man who'd burned down my clinic.

I couldn't move. All I could do was stare as he stepped across the threshold. He had a pistol in his right hand and blood spatter on the left side of his face. But whose blood? *Oh god.* Whose blood was that?

He bore no other signs of fighting. No bruises or cuts. No bullet holes. It was like he'd walked right through the war zone downstairs with a force field all around him.

"Fallon Moore," he said lazily.

"I'm a Luca now," I snapped. Immediately, I regretted it. What was I thinking?

He reminded me of a fuse, ready to blow. One wrong word, one wrong step could set him off.

"You're feisty," he said with a grotesque grin. "I like that."

I wanted to scream for help, to call out for Dominic, but I had a feeling that if I screamed, I'd be dead long before anyone could get here.

"Well, since you're a *Luca* now," Tony said, trailing off in thought. He strode toward me, but I took a step sideways for every step he took forward. "This little family's run is over. The battle still churns, but I've won, *signorina*. The Luca's reign is over. I'll have Queens and Brooklyn eating out of the palm of my hand. It belongs to me now." He swept his arms out like his "reign" encompassed the whole damn world.

"We didn't do anything to you or your family. Dominic told me about your father, but I swear he didn't—"

Tony laughed. "I know he didn't. Your precious Dominic didn't have the metal for that kind of move. I did, though."

What? "You… you killed your own father?" The temperature in the room seemed to plunge. This wasn't a man out for revenge, no matter how misplaced it may have been. This man was a monster. A freaking psychopath.

"The old man and I had different visions for the Novas. These cities should have been mine a long time ago. And now, they will be." He shrugged and took another menacing step toward me.

There was nowhere to run, nowhere to hide.

Another gunshot sounded beyond the door, and my body jolted. My heart pounded so loud in my chest it was a wonder I'd heard anything over it.

Tony laughed. "You're very cute, aren't you? As skittish as a mouse."

A man I'd never seen before ran past the bedroom door, but on his heels were two men I recognized: Marco and Leandro. Leandro slammed to a stop when he saw me.

Help me, my eyes screamed, but I'd made a mistake. I'd brought him to Tony's attention. Tony spun and fired, and I could do nothing but watch in horror as the bullet tore through Leandro's chest. My friend. *My maid of honor.*

I couldn't tell if I screamed as he fell to the ground. Sound seemed to have been sucked into a vacuum. Everything disappeared. There was only Leandro, crumpled on the floor with blood pouring out from a neat, round hole in the left side of his chest.

He was dead. Gone, just like that.

"Such a pretty little thing, though," Tony said, making the vacuum spew out all the sounds around me, all at once.

My own rapid breathing, which contrasted sharply with the slow and steady rise and fall of Tony's chest. The gunfire, staccato beats that volleyed back and forth across the house. The constant barrage of shouting, peppered by the occasional wretched scream.

Tony closed the distance between us. I wasn't sure if I would have been able to make my legs run from him, but it didn't matter.

There was nowhere to go. I was trapped, wedged between the wall and my dressing table.

He raised his gun to my cheek, the metal cold against my skin, and followed the path of my tears down to my jawbone. "It's a pity I'm going to have to kill you."

Chapter Thirty-Six

Dominic

"Dominic!" Marco's voice came from close behind me.

I could hear his quiet footsteps as he crept closer, keeping low to the ground until he was right beside me. I'd taken up position just inside the dining room, picking off Tony's men as they hurried past. At least a dozen bodies littered the floor, but they just kept coming.

"Boss, they got in the living room window. We got overrun on the stairs. Tony's up there. He's got Fallon."

My heart skipped one beat, and then the red haze slammed down on my vision. Pure rage replaced the blood in my veins and pumped through my body. If that motherfucker had laid one finger on her, he was going to die the most horrifying death any man had ever seen.

I surged to my feet and stepped out into the dining room, daring any one of Tony's minions to try to fuck with me now.

The first one shot around the corner. He hadn't been expecting me to be so close, so I had plenty of time to take aim and shoot the fucker in his throat. He went down in a spray of blood.

The two men who followed after him went down just the same.

Outside the dining room, I bolted down the hallway that led to the foyer, a gun in each hand, but they were just about empty. Not that it mattered. Nothing would stop me from getting to her. Absolutely fucking nothing.

Eight more of Tony's soldiers stood spread out on the stairs, from the first step to the second-floor landing. All of them had weapons, and they stumbled down the stairs to get to me. Tony probably wanted me taken alive.

I took aim, only shooting at torsos and down. I couldn't risk missing by aiming for the small surface area of their heads. A knee here, a stomach there, a thigh there. By the time there was one person left, I had no bullets left. But Fallon needed me.

If Tony had gotten to her, I wasn't sure what I would become. A ghost. A shell.

The last obstacle in my way raised his gun. He was twice my size. He would have been so fucking easy to hit with a bullet.

Instead, I grabbed a candelabra and charged.

His gun went off. The loud crack reverberated in my ears as fire shot through my calf, but it didn't slow me down.

It was easy to kill a man with nothing to lose. I was that man a mere month ago. But Fallon had given my life new meaning. I cared again. About others, about my own life. I didn't want to be alone anymore.

I couldn't have another loss like this behind me. Not again.

Chapter Thirty-Seven

Fallon

"You are a beauty, *signorina*," Tony said as he grazed the gun down my neck, pressing hard enough it dug into my flesh as I swallowed.

I tried not to move. I didn't want to give this monster the satisfaction of seeing me cower, but I couldn't help it. I couldn't keep my body from shaking or tears from streaming down my cheeks. I couldn't stop my breathing from coming so frantically, I feared I was going to pass out.

"I have a particular fondness for feisty women, you know? So much more fun to break," he said, grazing his gun down over my left clavicle. He was just inches from my heart.

My gaze shot toward the door, willing Dominic to appear, but no one came.

Tony laughed. "They're dead by now. No one is coming for you."

Dominic dead? It just wasn't possible, no matter the way my heart cried out in anguish. It made me angry. It infuriated me that part of me fell for Tony's ridiculous lies.

"He's going to rip your heart out." I lashed out in the only way I could.

Tony just smiled. "So, you're a beauty with a death wish? I expected more from you, *signorina*."

"Fuck you," I spat.

The smile vanished. Cold steel flashed in his eyes, just as cold as the barrel of the gun that he held over my heart.

"You don't get to speak to me like that, you fucking bitch!" he shouted. Spittle glittered in the air as he lost his temper.

I whimpered, shutting my eyes and looking away. "Please don't."

"Ah, there it is. It's all a farce, isn't it? You're not the tough girl you try to make everyone you think you are." He whipped the pistol back up to my face, pressing it against my cheek. It traveled down my face, to my neck, and to my chest.

I couldn't stop the sobs that wracked my chest, making the barrel bounce against me.

"Hmm. No bra? Maybe… just maybe, I shouldn't kill you. I can see it now. I need a queen by my side, don't I?," Tony mused, smiling. "I'll wipe out the Lucas, and take you as my bride."

Tony's pistol traversed my body, moving lower, inch by inch. Down my ribs, my abdomen.

I was shaking so much, the back of my head thudded against the wall behind me. "No…"

"It'll be glorious. You could be my little pet," he whispered. "Have you ever been a man's pet, *signorina*?"

I couldn't bring myself to respond.

He leaned in close until his lips pressed against my ear, making my stomach roil in disgust. "All that's left is to consummate the marriage."

The Hellcat!

I inched my hand to the side ever so slowly. My purse was right there on the dressing table. Inside it sat the gun Dominic had given me. It seemed ridiculous at the time, but his words came back to me now.

"I guarantee that the day you've got a gun pressed to your skull, you won't have any qualms about killing the motherfucker."

This man wanted to kill me or turn me into his whore. I had to fight back. I didn't have a choice. But the moment I pulled the trigger, I'd be a killer. A murderer.

I'd rather be a murderer than his plaything, but as I slipped my hand into my purse and wrapped my fingers around the Hellcat's handle, my joints locked. I couldn't move. And even if I could, he'd pull the trigger before I could fire.

My cellphone rang, drawing Tony's attention for just a second, but the noise shot down my spine, loosening my joints, and I pulled out the gun.

I pointed the gun right at him. It was heavier than I remembered. My hands trembled so much, I would have dropped the gun had I not been holding it with both hands.

Instead of fear, something dark flashed in Tony's eyes and then he smiled. And every bit of comfort the cool metal in my grip had given me evaporated.

He took a step back, but it did nothing to slow my trembling. He raised his gun; I could see right down the barrel.

"You shoot, I shoot," he said with a confident shrug. "I'd suggest you put that gun down and start begging for my forgiveness, *signorina*."

Chapter Thirty-Eight

Dominic

The candelabra dripped with blood. I hadn't stopped hitting him until his eyes had rolled back in his head and his chest stopped moving.

I grabbed the dead fucker's gun and checked the ammo—half a clip.

Dozens of footsteps sounded in the foyer behind me. But I was so hopped up on rage, I was ready to tear any number of Nova men apart piece by piece. Whatever I had to do to get *her*. I spun around.

"Honey, I'm home," Brute roared with a giant grin on his face.

I sighed. "You're just in time, *amico*, *Grazie*. Will you clean up the rest of this for me? I've got to get to my wife."

I was already climbing the stairs two at a time.

"Go get her, my friend," Brute called out behind me, and I could hear the Old Dogs' footsteps spreading out.

I slipped on the stair, three steps from the top. So much blood dripped down my leg, it had soaked the bottom of my shoe. *Damn it*. I yanked off my shirt and tied it like a tourniquet around my leg.

There was nothing to conceal the bulletproof vest I wore, but Tony was more of a headshot kind of man anyway.

As I climbed the last three stairs, three more of Tony's men crawled out of the woodwork. They were easy pickings, arrogant in their abilities to protect their master.

The last obstacle was finally out of my way. Every vein in my body felt like it was going to explode. I had to be in time. She had to be alive.

My heart clenched in my chest. She couldn't be dead. I couldn't have her blood on my hands. Not Fallon's. *Dio, per favore,* I pleaded silently.

And then I heard a gunshot. It came from the bedroom.

My bedroom.

Our bedroom.

Time froze.

Every step was like trudging through quick sand. I was sinking. I was falling.

Outside the bedroom door, all the pain hit me at once, and I had to grab onto the frame to keep my balance. I nearly buckled over.

And then I saw Fallon.

Not lying on the floor; she was standing with her arms out in front of her, pistol in hand. She was shaking like a leaf, but it was Tony on the floor, on his knees in front of her, clutching his stomach.

Chapter Thirty-Nine

Dominic

Holy shit. She'd shot him. She'd fucking shot him. I wanted to *whoop* like a teenager. I wanted to throw her up on my shoulders and parade her around like she'd just scored the winning touchdown.

That's my limone, my heart cried proudly.

And then she looked at me. Her eyes were an ocean of terror, leaking a constant steam of tears. Her jaw was clamped shut, but it trembled violently.

"Dominic, help me," she cried as the gun in her hands shook so hard it bounced precariously in her grasp.

She was breathing so fast I could see her chest heaving from across the room.

"Dominic, help me. I shot him. I killed him," Fallon said between breaths.

"I'm not dead yet," Tony croaked.

"Shut the fuck up, Tony," I barked, limping forward and kicking his fallen gun out of his reach. "You shut your fucking mouth."

Tony cried out in pain but then let out a bitter laugh. A bitter laugh filled with defeat. He knew he was done.

Fallon dropped the pistol, and thank fuck it didn't misfire.

"Oh my god," Fallon cried. "I can't breathe. I can't. I shot him."

She panted. She wasn't getting enough oxygen.

I limped the few steps left between us, ignoring the piece of shit on the floor. "Fallon, you're having a panic attack. I need you to try to take in slow, deep breaths."

When I put my hand on her shoulder, she jolted.

"It's going to be okay, Fallon. Close your eyes. Just close your eyes, and don't look at him," I said, rubbing her arms up and down.

I was so proud of her, but I wished to hell I'd been the one to shoot the motherfucker on the floor. I pulled her toward me, forcing her face into my chest. I wrapped my arm around her head, blocking any noise and all the death and destruction around us.

"I'd put a bullet between your eyes and put you out of your misery," I said to Tony, "but that's too easy. She shot you in the gut, didn't she? Right in the stomach?"

Tony had lost all color in his face and swayed from left to right.

"Good. A shot to the stomach is one of the most gruesome, slow ways to die. I'd rather you suffered and died alone. Have fun in hell," I spat.

"I'll... I'll get you for this."

"Sure thing. Fuck off," I said.

I led Fallon out of the room, picking the Hellcat up on our way out. I closed the door behind us. Her breathing had steadied, and she came up for fresh air.

"Is it too soon to say this?" I looked down at her, more in love than I had ever been. "I fought my way up here to save you, but it looks like you saved yourself. So… I'm proud of you."

She managed to give me a weak smile.

"I had a good teacher," she said in a shaky whisper.

"Looks like things have died down. Let's go check on my mother," I said. "And hide out while the place gets cleaned up."

Fallon averted her eyes from the bodies on the floor, some of which were being dragged to a big pile near the front door.

We had no spoils of war to celebrate with, only dead men. Men who had followed their leader into a battle they could never have won.

Chapter Forty

Dominic

The basement door was open, just a crack. It should have been closed, locked tight. But maybe Leo or Dante had gotten here first. Slowly, I pushed the door open, my muscles taut, ready, just in case.

The stairwell landing was empty. No sounds coming from down below. So, why was the back of my neck prickling?

The old wooden stairs creaked as we descended but I could barely hear it over the ringing in my ears. Tinnitus? Maybe. It grew so loud I couldn't even hear my own thoughts.

"*Mamma?*" I called out halfway down.

No answer.

When we reached the base of the stairs, I froze.

My mother laid on the ground, not ten feet from me—but flat on her back. She was wearing one of her favorite white dresses, but it wasn't white anymore. It was red. Her chest, her abdomen, all the way up to her neck. It was like someone had taken a careless paintbrush to her beautiful dress.

A body laid prostrate on the ground next to her, one hand wrapped loosely around a pistol while the other clutched the knife that protruded from his chest. My mother's knife. Even from here, I could make out the intricate etching on the handle. A decorative *L* embellished with whorls that made the initial look imperial.

Bullet whimpered on the ground next to her, nudging my mother with his nose while he scampered around her.

"*Mamma*," I cried out as I dropped to my knees beside her. As I fell, the world seemed to crash down with me, crumbling into pieces I'd never be able to put back together. "No. No. No."

My mother's eyes fluttered open and closed while her chest rose and fell slowly.

"No, no, no, don't you die on me."

I brushed her hand aside and found the wound; a hole in the middle of my mother's chest, spewing blood. Too much blood. I pressed down on it, trying to stem the flow, but it was too late. In the back of my mind, I knew. I'd seen death so many times. Blood seeped between my fingers and spilled over.

Her arms shook as she raised her hands to cup my cheeks, and I nuzzled into her touch. These were the hands that had carried me when I was young; the hands that had hugged me, and guided me, and chastised me when I'd needed it.

I couldn't remember the last time I'd cried. But this… this threatened to rip the heart right out of my chest. I knew this pain; I'd lived through it once before, and I wasn't at all certain I could do it again.

"My boy," she croaked. The color had drained from her face. She was too pale. My mother had never been so pale in all my life. "My beautiful, beautiful boy. I'm so glad you're here."

"I don't know what to do. What do I do?" I looked at Fallon. "Call an ambulance."

It was futile, but I had to do something. *Anything.*

"No, my boy. They won't get here in time. *La morte* is near," my mother said. "Just be with me."

I sniffled. "Okay. Anything you need, *Mamma.*"

Carefully, I lifted her into my arms, resting her head in the crook of my elbow.

"I love you, and your brothers. And your father. You tell them that, all right? You tell them I love each and every one, and no matter where I am, I will never stop loving them."

"I will." I nodded. "I will. I love you too, *Mamma.*"

Fallon crouched beside me, gently placing her hand on my back. I sat in a pool of my mother's blood, knowing the memory would be burned into my mind for all time. The heavy, coppery scent. The labored sound of my mother's breathing. The warm, sticky wetness beneath my fingers.

"I need you… to do something for me." Her body spasmed as she coughed, coating her pale lips with tiny droplets of blood. "You have to promise me something. Dominic. Find your sister."

"What do you mean? Sofia's…" I couldn't say the word. I couldn't force it past my lips while my mother struggled for breath.

"She is alive, Dominic. You must find her. You must reunite this family. Bring her home."

"She's…" I wanted to argue, but I couldn't do that, not now. "Okay, *Mamma.* Where do I find her?"

"I don't know. But you must find her. You must bring my baby back home, and you must tell her I never stopped loving her." A single tear ran down her cheek, and I caught it with my thumb, cradling her cheek as she'd cradled mine. "Promise me, my son. Promise me you will find her."

"I promise," I said. I had no idea how I could possibly fulfill that promise, but I meant it. I meant it with every fiber of my being. "Everything's going to be okay, *Mamma*."

My mother nodded. "I know. Look after this family, my boy."

I nodded back, shaking tears from my chin. They landed on her furrowed brow.

"Vito..." she whispered, "Costa…"

The words came out as little more than a breath. The last words my mother would ever say. Words that made no sense. Words that didn't matter as I watched her chest rise and fall for the last time. I held my breath as the light left her loving eyes.

My mother was gone.

EPILOGUE

Fallon

Three months later

Dominic and I had just come back from a late lunch at La Grande Madeleine. I thought the day was over, but we didn't take our usual route home. We were cozied up with one another, and I lazily stroked my hand through his silky, dark hair as he drove. It had been a difficult few months. We had a lot of mourning to do. Many men had fallen that day, and we all had an angel leave our lives.

I hadn't known Leandro for long, but I missed him. And Maria…

My throat still clogged with tears every time I thought of her. I *had* known Maria, maybe not for long, but in a way that perhaps no one else did. We'd shared a common beginning, a rocky initiation into this family. My heart mourned for my kindred spirit.

I could understand Dominic's sorrow as well; I knew what it was to lose the woman who had given me life.

But we had shared such a wonderful day together, and I wasn't about to ruin it by dwelling on the tragedies we'd endured.

"So, where are you taking me?" I asked, turning to look at him.

He had a giant smile on his face.

"If I wanted to tell you that, I would have already," he said. "We're actually a few minutes away."

He slowed to a stop at a stoplight then pulled out a long bit of fabric from the glove compartment. "Turn around."

"Why?" I asked.

"Always with the questions, hmm? Come on."

I twisted in my seat, grinning. He brought the silky fabric to my eyes. "You know I don't like surprises. You don't have to blindfold me."

"Everyone who says they don't like surprises is lying. They just never had a good enough surprise," Dominic said. He pulled the sash tight, so that I was completely blinded. I felt silly, but he kissed the back of my head.

"Are you ready?" he asked a few moments later.

"I don't know if I am, you know? Since I don't know where we're going."

"Shh. It's not like I'm taking you to some dark alley or a field in the middle of nowhere," he said.

I heard him step out of the car. Then he grabbed my hand to help me out.

"Then again, maybe I am."

"Still trying to be all mysterious, huh?" I teased.

"Of course."

Dominic grabbed my shoulders from behind and guided my every step. I'd said I didn't like surprises, but maybe I lied—just a little. Every now and then, Dominic snickered. This had to be good because he seemed more excited than I was.

"Okay. We're here. Don't cry, okay?" he said, "I know you're going to cry."

He took off the blindfold—so slowly he must have been trying to drive me insane.

When the blindfold was gone, all I could do was stare.

"You've got to be kidding me, right?" I said.

"Have I ever struck you as the jokester type?" Dominic stood by my side, looking up at the building, his hands rested on his hips.

"It looks so different," I said.

The storefront had changed. The sign was nicer—much nicer. I remembered the day I had the sign commissioned. I'd had to choose between kick-ass graphics and quality medical supplies. It had kind of been a no-brainer.

Instead of a boring red brick wall front with a single door, the wall had been replaced with glass. It allowed a peek into the reception area, which looked wonderfully sleek and modern.

"I hope you don't mind that I gave the architect a few ideas." Dominic scratched the back of his head. "I wouldn't want to ruin something so special for you."

I flew into Dominic's arms, making him stumble backward.

"So you like it, huh?" he said with a lopsided grin.

"I love it. And I love you. Holy shit, this is amazing."

And damn it, he was right. I was crying.

Dominic gave me a tour of my new clinic. Rooms were moved around and shifted to allow for more spacious treatment areas. The operating room had the latest and greatest equipment that I had been dying to purchase for years, and every shelf and cupboard was fully stocked.

"How did you do all of this? I mean, you don't know much about vet stuff," I said.

"Corinne and I collaborated. She was there almost every step of the way," Dominic said. "This is just as much her doing as mine."

"Thank you, Dominic. This means so much to me."

"I'm glad. I know how passionate you are. I don't want you sitting around not chasing your dreams, you know?" he said.

I pulled him in for another hug, and he twirled me around until my legs lifted off of the floor. My heart swelled.

Things really did turn out okay in the end. Just as Maria had said it would. *Thank you, Maria… wherever you are.*

***

"What's going on with you, honey?" I asked Dominic, who had that thousand-mile stare.

It was different than the look he had when he thought about his mother. That pain wouldn't ever go away, not really—I knew that firsthand—but he seemed to be coming to terms with things. I tried my best to be his rock in his time of need, but I was flying blind. I'd never had the kind of support I wanted Dominic to have, but I was damn well determined to give it to him.

Dominic raised an eyebrow at me. "We doing cute little pet names now? Want me to call you pumpkin? I bet you prefer *limone*, hmm?"

"You know I love whatever silly little nickname you throw my way. Especially the mean ones." I laughed, but I wasn't willing to accept his attempt to divert my attention. "But I'm concerned about you. There's something up, and you're not talking to me about it."

Dominic ran his hand up and down his face. "Do you trust me?"

"You've asked me this before. I don't trust you further than I can throw you," I teased but then smiled genuinely. "All joking aside, of course I do. With my life. I'll stand by you until the day I die."

"Then get dressed. I'll explain on the way."

I started pulling on a dress, but Dominic interrupted me. "Nah. Something old. And thick jeans."

"O-kay," I said, confused. "This seems awfully suspicious."

"I need to get my thoughts together. I'm not sure if it's a little too insane, even for me. If we don't leave soon, I might talk myself out of it again."

Dominic pulled on a sweater and a pair of jeans. And then, like he was about to do something shady, he pulled his hood up. "And sneakers."

"Okay." Although he wasn't giving me much to work with, it had to be important to him if he was acting like this.

In the car, Dominic's arms were locked straight ahead of him, both hands gripping the steering wheel tightly. We had been driving for a while now, and he still hadn't said anything. He would open his mouth, make an unintelligible sound, then close it again.

"Do you think you could tell me where we're going now?" I asked.

He ignored my question, but with his bearings gathered, it seemed he was finally able to speak. "You don't think my mother was crazy, do you?"

"She was the sanest family member in that house," I said confidently.

"Okay. All right." He sighed heavily. "But do you think she was delirious? Do you think that's possible?" Dominic looked at me with a pained expression when we came to a stoplight. "She sounded so certain that my sister was alive. She made me *promise* to find Sofia. But it doesn't make sense. I was at the funeral. I-I… was there when they lowered her coffin into the ground…"

"So, you think she was telling the truth?" I asked.

We pulled up into the parking lot.

"Well, I spoke to my father—bad idea, I know. He dismissed me entirely, like I was stupid for even asking. But I guess something about the way she said it. I just couldn't get it out of my mind. I haven't been able to stop thinking about it since that night. And now I'm having dreams about Sofia and…" Dominic trailed off.

I put my hand on his thigh. "It's okay, Dominic. Breathe. I heard what your mother said. She sounded so sure. Could it really have been anything but the truth?"

"I don't know. I just know I'll never be at ease until I know for sure."

I followed him to the back of the car, and he popped the trunk.

"I've had this in my trunk for two months. I kept trying to work up the courage to do this, but it seems so far out. And messed up. And… and I don't know what I'm doing, but I need answers. I have to be sure she's in that grave."

Two shovels and two pitchforks waited in the back of his trunk. I took one of each and followed him. Sofia's grave had a simple headstone with her name, her date of birth, and the day she died. There was an engraved rose on the top left corner.

Dominic crouched near the grave, running his thumb across his lips. "She loved roses. Absolutely obsessed with *Beauty and the Beast*. She even had a preserved rose underneath a glass jar, just like in the movie."

"It's those funny little quirks we remember about our loved ones," I said wistfully.

He sighed heavily, staring at the headstone. "All right, let's do this."

I didn't think grave-digging would be easy work, but wow, it was a whole lot harder than I'd thought it would be. The tightly packed ground gave way inch by slow inch. I tried my best to contribute as much as possible, but Dominic was stronger than me, plowing through four times as much dirt as I did. Hey, it wasn't my fault he was built like a Greek god.

I tried to distracted him, chattering on about my second ferret patient and Corinne's unrequited infatuation with Leo—that one raised Dom's eyebrows.

He stuck the shovel in the dirt and looked at me with his lips pressed tight together and one eyebrow cocked. "There is no way in hell I'm going on some double date with my younger brother."

"Don't worry. It seems Corinne hasn't had any luck snagging Leo's attention," I said, thinking it would have been kind of cool if she had.

He resumed digging, but a minute later, his shovel thumped against something solid.

We'd done it.

With renewed vigor, we cleared away the rest of the dirt, revealing the black lacquered coffin beneath. We actually did it. But with our success, reality settled back in, and Dom's expression turned somber.

He leaned down and searched for the coffin lid's edge, but unfortunately, the coffin had been buried so long that it wouldn't budge.

He grew frustrated with every attempt, and in his manic state, he lost his temper and slammed his palm against it.

"Do you want me to do it, Dom?" I asked, placing my hand on his back to bring him back down.

"No. I have to do this."

I understood what he meant, so I left it.

Dominic had to bludgeon it open with the shovel. The scene was macabre as the lacquered wood flew into the air with each hit. In time, a hole formed and made the rest of the job easier.

I held a flashlight for him, and when there was enough give to pry it open, I closed my eyes. I couldn't look. What if his mother wasn't delirious?

What if?

I peeled one eye open at a time and looked down at the hole. Dominic had already climbed out of it. He collapsed to his knees, holding the flashlight in one hand and shining it down into the coffin.

"Holy shit," I breathed.

Dominic was silent, like he couldn't quite process what he was seeing.

"Fallon," he whispered eventually. "Her death broke me. It molded me into the man I am today. I was… I've punished myself for it damn near every day since she's been gone. I should have been there… I should have smelled the smoke…" He looked up at me. "What am I going to do now?"

I'd never seen Dominic like this.

"You're not alone in this," I said. I dropped down to my knees beside him. "We'll figure this out. We'll…"

We would… what? I couldn't even begin to imagine where to go from here without Maria.

Dominic was silent again, this time for so long, I thought he might have gone into shock. But when I placed my hand on his shoulder, he turned to look at me. His eyes were a little wild, but there was resolution in the hard-set of his jaw.

"My sister's alive, Fallon, and I'm going to do whatever it takes to find her," he said in a voice filled with conviction.

I nodded, taking hold of his hand, and he squeezed my hand tight.

"Of course," I said, like it was as easy as breathing. Because it was. I'd walk through hellfire with Dominic Luca.

"We'll find her," I promised him, just like he'd promised Maria.

* * *

EXCLUSIVE FREE BONUS CHAPTER

His lips pressed against mine, but before I could try to deepen the kiss, he moved lower, kissing a soft trail along my jaw.

I tilted my head back, granting him easier access to continue lower, which he did, sucking and nipping his way down my neck to my clavicle. Deprived of sight, I was painfully aware of the light scrape of his stubble along my flesh, and it sent tiny shivers down my spine.

A breath later, the whole plane shook gently as the wheels touched down. Vibrations tremored through my body as the plane skidded down the runway, slowing a little more with each passing second.

"We're here," he said just as the plane came to a stop.

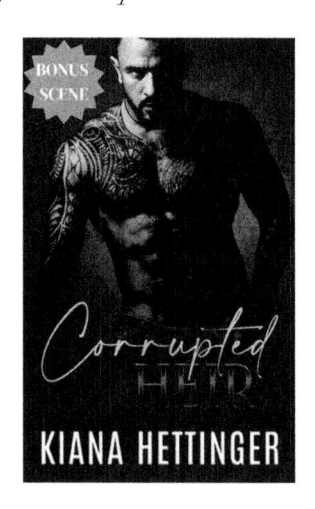

Can't get enough of Fallon and Dominic?
Download the FREE bonus scene for one more spicy chapter here:
https://BookHip.com/ZLDZLCF

What's Next?

Wow, I hope you enjoyed *Corrupted Heir!* Your support means the world to me.

The next book in the Mafia Kings: Corrupted Series is Corrupted Temptation.

Calling all Kittens! Come join the fun:

If you're thirsty for more discussions with other readers of the series, join my readers' group on Facebook, Kiana's Kittens! – facebook.com/groups/KianasKittens

CAN YOU DO ME A HUGE FAVOR?

Would you be willing to leave me a review?

I'd be over the moon because just one positive review on Amazon is like buying the book a hundred times! Reader support is the lifeblood for Indie authors. It provides us the feedback we need to give readers what they want in future stories!

Your positive review would mean the world to me. You can post your review on Amazon or Goodreads. I'd be forever grateful, thank you from the bottom of my heart!

Printed in Great Britain
by Amazon